A Prophecy

Awakens

A Prophecy Awakens

The Prophecy Series
Book 1

Tara & Jessie Johnson

First edition: April 2022

ISBN 9798401000569 (paperback)
ISBN 9798401390646 (hardcover)

Prologue

War has come. For years, war is all we have known. My people were a proud race, brought low by the devastation caused by this conflict. We now cower in whatever shelter we find and hope we escape the enemy for another day. War is all our children know. Born to violence and bloodshed, they spend their lives fighting only to die a brutal premature death. Pain, sadness, loss, and struggle are all we know now. War has shaped the world which will remain this way, unless I ensure us a miracle.

We all remember the day the mountain awoke. As fire and brimstone spewed into the air, the sky turned black with smoke. The earth rumbled as the peak burst open and a monstrous beast took wing. Fearful the end had come for our world, many fled. Others wept for the future we had lost. That day occurred 112 years ago. I remember thinking it was my last day as I watched fire and ash rain down upon our village and the small dwelling my family called home. The memories are still clear in my mind.

However, it was not the fire or the beast that decimated our people. The slaughter came from an unforeseen enemy. We never feared them or thought there was reason to. They were meek and primitive. We never imagined the beast from the mountain would raise them up. Not even the eldest of us fathomed these lesser beings could raze our entire society. The elders hoped we could form a bond with them. They hoped the gifts the beast had given them would allow us to become allies, but this would not be. We learned the brutes worshipped the beast and watched them enslave countless other species in their bid to gain power, proving destruction was upon us as well.

The mountain sleeps again; the beast vanished from existence, but the brutes still seek our destruction. My people are the last to resist and so they doom us to extermination. We persevere and at last there is hope for an end to the conflict. A prophecy made years ago may now come to fruition, thus ending our genocide. It told of a child secreted away to one day return, bringing peace and freedom to the world. How do I know you ask? I'll tell you. I am the courier. My sole responsibility is to ensure we can fulfill the prophecy, so I run ever onward.

As the sweat drips down my face, I look at my precious cargo and smile, unable to believe my people's fate rests on these small shoulders. An innocent, round face peers back at me and for one fleeting second, I believe she will save us. I only hope I am still alive to see it. A twig snaps nearby, reminding me of my crucial task. Fearful they have found me, I quicken my pace. Growing closer to my target, I feel the tinge of magic fill the surrounding air, telling me the others have accomplished their task. Everything seems to have fallen into place when my enemy crashes through the trees and onto the path behind me, crushing the joy welling up inside me. Fearsome red eyes pierce me to the core, while cracked dry lips curl into a crooked smile as he leers at me. The terrifying visage coupled with the fact the creature before me is larger than I am charges me with the fear that, should I fail, my people will be lost. Our continued existence rests on me, so I turn and strike out for my destination.

As I enter the expanse, I am bathed in an eerie blue glow, and I can taste the magic emanating from the center of the clearing. Three elders occupy the expanse. They look exhausted, telling me this impressive feat has taken all they had, but they will not die in vain. I approach the swirling blue doorway. The electricity in the air causes my hair to stand at attention and fills my ears with a tremendous whooshing sound. I cannot believe the elders have conjured the portal. Everyone said it was impossible. Many laughed at the notion, but those who believed knew they must do it. Joy fills my soul as I take the little angel into my hands and stretch my arms out towards the portal. In a flash, the baby disappears, leaving me alone in the clearing.

My mission accomplished, I have provided the people of the world the hope we may one day be free of oppression and subjugation. Not knowing when freedom will come, I can only continue to fight. I turn to face my enemy, who is furious he could not stop me. I unsheathe my swords; faint blue light dancing over the cold steel as the portal closes behind me. Where the portal leads, I do not know. I only hope the child returns someday to free us from persecution. These thoughts run through my mind as I lunge at my opponent.

Chapter 1

Hours spent sitting here have made me restless, so I tap my pencil on my notebook. In fact, all of us are growing impatient. The waiting gets harder as we get closer, and anticipation is palpable in the air. Every one of us stopped concentrating some time ago. A loud, shrill bell rings, setting us free to enjoy our weekend. But, it's more than a weekend. We are now free to enjoy our Christmas break, which overjoys us since we don't have to return to school for the next few weeks. I gather my belongings and shove them into my backpack, making sure I have everything. I prefer not interacting with the others, so I hang back and watch my peers file out of the room.

Paisley looks in my direction, so I turn away from her, hoping she leaves, but she heads in my direction, a smile spreading across her face and long, curly hair swaying with her movements. My body fills with dread, because I suspect what Paisley wants and have no desire to deal with it. I sigh and offer her a weak smile as she approaches.

"Hey Valessa, why don't you come hang out with us tonight?" she asks.

Paisley approaches me with this question frequently, so I smile and give her the same answer I supply every time. "I can't, because I have plans tonight."

"Well, if tonight isn't free, then you could join us tomorrow. We're going shopping tonight and tomorrow we plan to have some fun on River Street. You know where to find us if you change your mind."

"I'll think about it." I know I won't be joining Paisley and her friends for any festivities this weekend.

"Okay, Valessa. We'd love to hang out and get to know you better," she says, walking away.

I breathe a sigh of relief. I don't care to hang out with Paisley and her friends. Everyone considers them the "pretty" girls, which is not where I fit in. I often feel as though I don't fit in anywhere. I look different from the others and because of this, few of them have taken the time to get to know me. They have always considered me 'the strange girl in class', and so I often think of myself as strange. My long, thin face and skin as fair as the full moon are enough to make me stand out, and my tall stature and rail thin physique make others gawk at me, while my long, straight pale rose-colored hair and striking large golden eyes set me apart from everyone I know. Children are often cruel and have bullied me most of my life, labeling me an outcast. Having no genuine friends means it's always been just me and that's all I've ever needed.

I stand, lift my backpack onto my back, and walk out into the hall. The others have cleared out on their way home to celebrate the holidays. I glide through the exit and out into the cool winter air, taking a deep breath as the brisk breeze washes over me. The day is beautiful and clear, so I decide to walk home instead of taking the bus. I need time for myself so I can think. It's time I ask my mother the questions I've had on my mind of late.

I arrive home in time to cross paths with my older brother, who is on his way out. Wade is tall, dark and handsome; at least that's how all the girls at school describe him. He's two years older than me and my polar opposite with a square jaw, pronounced cheekbones and cute dimples, all topped off with the darkest black hair. All the girls want to date him and he knows it.

I scan him up and down, taking in his appearance. "You going somewhere?"

"Just out to see what trouble I can get into."

"Cool. Are mom and dad home yet?"

"Dad isn't, but mom's in the study." He bounds out the door and disappears into the evening. Good. I will have her undivided attention. I find my mother sitting on the sofa in the study, reading a book. She glances up and smiles at me. "Hey there, sweetie." She lowers her book to her lap. "How was your day?"

"Long, but okay. I'm glad it's over. Paisley asked me to hang out with her again."

"You should. It would be good for you to spend time with girls your age. Sixteen is such a hard, confusing time for a young girl. Things are changing and having the support of your peers may make it easier."

"I know, but I don't feel like I belong with those girls."

"Everything will be better once you finish high school and head out to forge your own path." She pats the sofa next to her. "Come, sit with me."

I sit down and take a deep breath to prepare myself for asking the tough questions. "Mom, why don't I fit in? Why am I so different from everyone else?"

My mother sighs and stares at me. "I knew this day would come, and I have dreaded it, but you are old enough to hear the truth. You don't fit in because you're different, but that makes you special. Your father and I adopted you sixteen years ago. Someone found you one cold night, alone on the street when you were but a babe with nothing but a note stating your name was Valessa and asking that someone take care of you."

I look at her, mouth agape. Everything makes sense now. "But where did I come from? Who left me in the street?"

"We don't know, my dear," she says, shaking her head. "No one was around when they found you. We took you in and raised you as our own because we always wanted a daughter, and you have been a blessing. Your father and I love you very much, as does your brother."

What's wrong with me that someone would throw me away as an infant? What if no one had found me or loved me enough to raise me? My mother embraces me and I return her hug. This revelation is overwhelming. I look at this woman who gave me a life, simply because she chose to. I appreciate her so much. "Thank you for telling me the truth, mom, and thank you for choosing to love me when you didn't have to. I love you." I choke back tears.

"Of course, sweetheart, and I love you, too. I know it's a lot, but it was time you knew the truth."

"I appreciate the honesty," I say, rising to leave. "I'm going to go walk and clear my head, since I have a lot to think about."

"Of course, dear."

As I turn to leave, she grabs my hand and pulls me back, wrapping her arms around me in an enormous hug. At that moment, I feel as though I belong. I wasn't born to this woman, but she is my mother none the less. After what feels like a lifetime, she releases me.

"Don't stay out too long, Valessa. I'm making your favorite for dinner," she calls after me.

"I'll be back before you know it." I throw my jacket on and head out into the crisp evening air, making my way into the ever darkening night. My clouded mind races with thoughts triggered by the previous conversation. *Maybe I don't belong because fate did not mean me to be a part of this family. How would I have turned out if my birth parents had not abandoned me? What if their abandonment gave me a life?*

Holiday decor adorns the city. Savannah's squares and parks are alight with bright, colorful lights, and music emanates from houses and businesses alike. Occasionally, carolers make their way through the neighborhoods, spreading cheer. It's my favorite time of the year. Everything is so merry and beautiful and I cherish the time spent with family.

Maybe I should step outside my comfort zone and try hanging out with Paisley and the other girls from school. Perhaps they want to be friends. I remember she said they were going to the mall, so I turn towards the nearest bus stop, thinking I will meet them there, since she asked me to hang out. *Maybe I don't have to be an outcast. Could I have a normal teenage life?* As I near the bus stop, an irresistible feeling strikes me. It's like nothing I have felt before, and for a brief second, I'm overpowered by feelings of nausea and fear, and then it fades just as fast. I stand motionless, thinking how strange it felt, but also how natural. As I move again, I'm struck by the same feeling, causing the hair on my body to prick up and my ears to ring, which alarms me but a sense of wonder washes over me, causing me to question what this incredible sensation could be. I study the people in the vicinity, but no one seems affected by whatever this is. No one seems to notice anything out of the ordinary.

I shrug my shoulders and take another step forward. The same feeling washes over me, stronger than before. I see nothing out of the ordinary, so I proceed a few steps before being hit with another wave of mysterious energy. It hits me harder from one direction as it flows over me, so I turn toward it to find a dimly lit alley. Anxiety fills me, but the desire to know what is causing the sensation pushes me forward as I make my way down the alley, not knowing what might wait for me there. The pulses of energy grow stronger as I advance and engulf my entire body, and although I am fearful, I also feel peace.

I look around and see the strangest thing I've ever seen near the back of the alley, something one would expect to find only in a story. All I can think is how impossible it is. A large, swirling doorway resembling a whirlpool stands before me. The sound of rushing water fills my ears as I am bathed in faint blue light. This must be the source of the strange power I felt on the street. It seems to call to me.

I scan the alley, hoping someone else is witnessing this, but the alley is empty. It seems no one else has noticed anything out of the ordinary. I raise a trembling hand as I turn back toward the mysterious blue circle, and a spark of electricity arcs from the swirling mass to my fingertips, causing me to yank my hand back. I reach out toward the object once again, braver this time, inching ever closer to its surface. As my hand draws near it, I feel a firm tug on my arm, pulling me closer. A fleeting sense of wonder and dread runs through my body, and then there is nothing. I am pulled forward by a current of unknown origin, and the strange sensation I felt before washes over me yet again, permeating to my very core. My thoughts turn to my family, then to terror before blackness sweeps over me.

Chapter 2

An electric energy courses through my body as I sit up. My head is spinning. I remember talking to my mother and deciding to become more open to new experiences and walking through the city, but not much else. I don't know where I am or how I got here, but I'm certain I'm not in Savannah, and feelings of wonder and fear wash over me as I observe my surroundings. A dense, shimmery pale green fog blankets the ground where I sit in the center of a small clearing encircled by tall trees with huge black trunks. I'm in the middle of a vast forest, unlike anything I have ever seen. It's quiet as well, almost too quiet. I gather my legs under me and rise.

It's much warmer than Savannah, so I shrug my jacket off and sling it over my shoulder, then turn in a slow circle and take in my surroundings. A narrow path trails off into the trees, and I decide I can't stay here exposed to who knows what, so I make my way toward the path. I would rather move than sit stationary awaiting rescue that may never come. It's dark. I peer into the sky and see there is no moon or stars shining above. It seems a dreary, overcast night. I strike out down the path, hoping to find some help, or an explanation of how I alighted here.

It feels like I've been walking for hours. My legs ache and my feet hurt. With each passing moment, I grow hungrier and I'm in desperate need of water. I don't know how much farther I can go without it. There are no signs of life except for vegetation. I know it's night, but this forest seems too quiet. It's strange that I've seen no signs of animals, and I've heard little of anything besides my own footsteps. I continue onward, though there seems to be no end to this forest.

More time passes as I walk, and I know I must rest soon or risk passing out again, which is what I fear the most at the moment, because I don't know what lurks unseen in the dense foliage around me. I press on, hoping for a respite as I grow ever more weary.

Just when I think I can go no further, I hear the faintest gurgling sound and at first I believe my ears are playing tricks on me. It sounds like a babbling stream. I make my way toward the sound, hoping I have found a drinkable water source. A break in the trees gives me a glimpse of a stream meandering through the woods. I kneel before it, breathing a sigh of relief. The water smells clean, but it has the slightest tinge of a green glow to it, not unlike radioactive goo I have seen in movies. I'm unsure if I should drink it, but I won't last much longer without it. I cup my hands together and lower them into the rushing stream. The crisp, cool water feels invigorating on my skin. I raise my hands to my mouth and take a small sip of the water. Although it glows green, it tastes refreshing, so I drink more and more as energy returns to my body. This was the very thing I needed to continue my journey.

Once I drink my fill, I stand and gaze around. As my eyes scan the darkness, I become uneasy, and the sense I'm being watched overcomes me, but I don't see or hear anything. I'm filled with anxiety, but believing if I carry on, I will reach the edge of the forest, I gather my resolve and step back onto the path. That's when I see it and think my fatigue has caused an illusion. I rub my hands against my eyes to gain some clarity. When I lower them, I am sure what I'm seeing is no trick of my tired mind. There, within the trees ahead of me, I see five pairs of glowing yellow eyes staring back at me. I'm struck with an overwhelming sense of fear and freeze. *What are these creatures and how long have they been watching me? Will they attack me? Am I in danger?* The forest comes alive with the sound of twigs snapping and dry foliage underfoot, and then the eyes disappear. But I don't feel any safer because I don't know if the creatures have left. They may still be out there.

I feel afraid and alone, but continue my journey, hoping whatever was watching me through the trees has moved on. I'm no longer sure I'm alone here. With each step, I become more frightened. I'm sure I hear footsteps all around me, hidden just out of sight and have a feeling I'm being followed, or perhaps hunted. After all, I did not get the feeling these creatures were harmless, and I'm waiting for the attack. Without warning, there's a heavy foot fall to my right and a twig snaps, and I am overcome with terror as I see a large snarling beast leap out of the trees at me. I scream and am bathed in a bright blue flash as energy pulses through my body. One brief thought that this is the end crosses my mind and then everything goes dark.

When I wake, all I remember is being filled with fear. I'm tied up and unable to move; I'm also slung over the shoulder of a huge, hulking man. Only it's not truly a man. His body is pure muscle, rippling under me as he moves. He is wearing pants and nothing else, and I see something else I can't believe. I blink to remove the fog from my eyes and see a long bushy tail covered in dark gray fur extending from the end of his spine. Below that, his legs are slender and his feet are like a dog's. My exhausted mind is in disbelief. This cannot be real.

I look around and notice he is not alone. His companions are muscle bound, and I see they also sport the same type of tail as my abductor. Thick shaggy hair covers their large, bestial bodies, while their faces, longer than a human's, possess glowing eyes and long mouths lined with sharp teeth. They all share this alarming visage, which is reminiscent of wolves, all save for one, a young boy close to my age, maybe six feet tall, with unkempt raven black hair, who looks strong like the others but lacks the dense fur covering his body, as well as the tail. He has the same glowing eyes and possesses a normal human face, but has long fangs. We lock eyes, and he raises a single finger to his lips for a moment, then lowers it with a fluid movement. I remain silent as I watch him walk toward me.

He leans into my ear and whispers, "For your own safety, remain calm. They haven't noticed you're awake, and it would be best if it stayed that way."

I take his advice and nod as he smiles and drops back. I don't know what these creatures are or where they are taking me, but this one seems to want to help, so I do as he says and try to get some rest as we continue on. After all, I'm supposed to be unconscious, right?

I'm jolted awake when I hit the ground, having reached our destination. I look around and see we are still in the mysterious forest, but have stopped in a large clearing that seems to be where these beasts live. There are small stick and thatch teepees spread around the clearing, as well as multiple camp fires and more of the wolf-like humans scattered around engaged in various activities, such as tending fires or preparing meals. A large cabin, sturdier and more permanent than the other dwellings, lies in the center of the clearing. My captors disappear into it and emerge accompanied by one who is much larger than the others. Jet black fur covers him from head to foot and a wolfish snout extends from his face. He walks with a regal air and I notice all the others bow to him, making my first thought that he must be a leader or something.

They approach me where I lay in the dirt and my breath quickens as I become more frightened. When they reach me, they kneel and the smell of dirt, smoke and nature floods my nostrils as I sit up before them, tied and helpless. I don't know what they want, but if their intentions are malicious, it would mean the end of me because I am powerless to fight back. They smell me, looking for a sign of who I am, where I came from, what I am doing here, and if I mean them harm.

The creature with jet black fur leans into me. "Who are you?"

"My name is Valessa." I notice my voice is shaky.

"Tell me, Valessa, how is it you came to be here in my domain?"

"Really?"

"If I did not mean it, I would not have asked. Now answer."

I only stare at him as my anger grows.

"My patience is wearing thin, girl. Answer me or feel my wrath."

The raven haired boy who advised me on the road approaches and steps between me and my interrogator. *He must possess bravery to stand up to this one.* My interrogator bares his teeth and a deep rumble escapes his throat, but raven hair seems unphased and continues to stare.

"I hardly think that's the way to get the answers you seek, father." He says, his voice soft.

"It is not your place to instruct me on how to handle things, boy. It is my duty to protect the pack. When you are Alpha, you can decide, but until then know your place and stand down."

His father towers over him, but the boy is unafraid.

"True sir. But she is frightened already and scaring her more will not produce answers."

"Go attend to your duties and let me attend to mine."

I lie in the dirt observing the exchange. *Pack? Alpha? Have they arranged their society like a wolf pack?*

Upset with his dismissal, the boy retreats and Alpha turns back to me. "Now, I asked how you ended up in my domain and I am waiting for a response."

"You act as though I came here on my own. I didn't have a choice about coming here because your friends brought me against my will, and believe me, I would rather be anywhere else. Set me free and I will gladly leave."

A chorus of gasps erupts from the surrounding onlookers. Alpha's nostrils flare and saliva foams at his mouth as he bares his teeth at me. He reaches out and strikes me once across the face. I realize I may have been too bold and angered an unknown entity. My face stings, and I'm filled with fear, but I refuse to cower. I sit up straighter, causing a chuckle to escape my assailant's glistening lips.

The boy leaps between Alpha and me again, filled with rage. "You will not strike her."

No one has ever stood up for me before, and I'm at a loss for what to do, so I just sit there and watch.

"How dare you confront me? You have no right to question me, and you will not undermine my authority in front of the pack. Back down now or suffer the consequences. You may be my son, but that does not put you above our laws, boy."

"Father, I only mean to claim this one, granting her my protection. According to our laws, this means none of you can harm her, including you."

"If this is what you want, then so be it, my son. She will come to no harm, but she will answer my questions. With your protection or not, we must know if she is a danger to our people."

"Then if it pleases you, sir, I will get the answers you seek. Only allow me time to do so."

Alpha nods and turns away from us, returning to his cabin accompanied by his entourage. I sit helplessly and watch as they disappear within, before turning my attention to the raven haired boy standing in front of me. "You didn't have to help me."

"Oh, but I did. You don't know the danger you are in. My father is never kind to strangers. You should have answered his questions. Provoking him is not wise."

"I gathered as much, but I'm not sure I can provide satisfactory answers because I don't even know where I am or how I got here."

"We can try to figure that out together, but let's start with the basics. My name is Alkin. Who might you be, my fair lady?"

"Valessa."

"It's a pleasure to meet you, Valessa. You are quite a beauty."

I blush. No one has ever called me a beauty before. "Thank you."

Alkin takes a seat on the ground beside me and

unties my bindings. "Now that we are acquainted, perhaps you can tell me how you got here."

I look at him and see he is quite pleasing on the eyes with his black hair and smooth tan skin. His eyes are a striking deep yellow that reflect the fire light around us in an unnerving manner.

I take a deep breath. "I don't remember much, other than walking through the city in a place much different from this, on my way to the bus stop when a strange feeling washed over me, one that I had never felt before, so I went down an alley and saw the most remarkable thing. It looked like a doorway, swirling and blue. I tried to touch it, then woke up in the forest where I walked for quite a while before your people found me and brought me here. I remember nothing else."

"Well, having taken you under my protection, you are safe now. Would you like something to eat?"

"Yes please. I'm so hungry."

"Okay. I'll be right back."

Alkin walks to a nearby campfire that's surrounded by women and children. He says a few words to one woman, gestures in my direction, and then nods. She gives him a bowl, and he heads back to me.

He hands me the bowl and a spoon. "Stew."

I give it a quick sniff and find it smells good, so I lift some to my mouth and taste it. It tastes good too and I eat it fast. It's the first meal I've had since lunch so long ago.

Alkin leaves and returns with a cup, which I take and gulp the contents. It tastes sweet, like juice. "What is this?"

"That is Moonberry tea."

"It's good."

A smile spreads across his face. "If you'll excuse me, I must report to my father. He'll want to know what I have learned. Wait here."

I nod.

"I'll return as quick as I can."

Alkin walks toward the cabin. He smiles back at me before entering. My face flushes as I watch him disappear inside. I've never had this much attention before and certainly not from a boy.

I take in my surroundings and see the clearing is full of teepee-like structures. Many wolf beings go about their chores of cooking and cleaning, but some watch me. They seem wary. All the eyes on me make me uneasy, so I pull my knees up to my chest and wrap my long arms around my legs. I don't appreciate being left alone among these creatures and hope Alkin will return soon.

What seems like an eternity passes, and I grow tired regardless of the fact that I am so on edge. I yawn, hoping I can get some rest soon. It's been a long day. My eyes are heavy, and I grow tired of waiting for Alkin to return, so I rise and walk toward his father's cabin, aware of all the eyes watching me. I know I should stay put, but I can't wait any longer. As I near the cabin, I can hear the conversation taking place within.

"Did you find out what abilities she may have, if any?" Alpha asks.

"I did not ask yet, father," says Alkin.

"Have you explained about our people and how we came to be this way? Did you explain that she, too, will experience the change and what claiming her means?"

"Not yet. I thought it best to give her time."

"These are important things. She needs to know."

"I know, father. I don't want to overwhelm her."

"I understand, Alkin, but she must know. She will accept these things or I we will dispose her of."

"I know. I will explain and make her understand."

"Very well. Tomorrow, take her into the woods and show her the well. Explain what it does, then tell her about the change and what her life will become now."

"Yes, father."

"And boy?"

"Yes?"

"Make her understand."

I can't believe what I'm hearing. It raises so many questions. *What are these creatures and where did they come from? What is this well and the change they keep talking about? And what does being claimed mean?*

The other occupants of the cabin murmur, but I can't determine what they are saying. I have questions, but all I can think about is how tired I am and how I must sleep soon.

I'm jolted to attention as Alkin bursts through the cabin door. He doesn't look happy, and I know I am not the cause of his troubles. Everything he is going through now is because of me. He looks in my direction, a look of surprise on his face. "I thought you were waiting for me by the fire."

"I was, but you were taking so long, and I couldn't take the eyes watching me anymore."

"We can sleep now. This way." He starts toward one tepee at the edge of the clearing.

I didn't notice it earlier. It's larger than the others and decorated in beautiful murals depicting nature and various animals. As we approach, Alkin moves the flap that serves as a door to the side and holds it so I can enter. The inside is lit by torches and candles and is quite spacious. On one side is a sitting area with piles of pillows and furs and a small round table covered with books and fruit sits in the center of the structure. Opposite the sitting area is a gigantic bed piled high with furs and blankets. It looks very comfortable.

Alkin enters behind me. "It's not extravagant, but I hope this suits you, Valessa."

"It will do just fine. Thank you."

"I hope anything you overheard did not frighten you too much."

"It didn't frighten me, only left me with a lot of questions."

"They can wait until tomorrow. It's time we got some rest."

"Yes. I'm exhausted after today."

"You can take the bed. I'll make a pallet in the sitting area."

I look at him, startled. "You mean we're going to share?"

"We are. Now that you are under my protection, it is

fitting. You have nothing to fear from me. This will make it easier for me to keep an eye on you. "

I'm too tired to argue, so I make my way to the bed, removing my shoes and nothing else. Alkin watches me, making me more uncomfortable than I have been my entire life. I try to shrug off the feeling as I climb into bed. It's much softer than I expected and the furs are so warm. I pull them up to my neck and watch as Alkin removes his shirt, shoes and pants and makes his way across the room to the sitting area where he fashions a makeshift bed out of the pillows and furs there and lowers himself onto it. He pulls out a book and settles in for the night as I drift off to sleep.

Chapter 3

I wake, feeling rested and alert, and cannot believe the events of the past day are real. I take in my surroundings, seeing I am alone and wonder where Alkin has gone as I shudder and remember he promised to protect me. My stomach rumbles and I hope he has gone to fetch us some breakfast.

I swing my long legs over the edge of the bed and rise, looking around the hut. Besides the sitting area, bed, and table, there is a bookshelf filled with books and what appears to be a wash basin. I approach the basin and look at myself in the small mirror above it to see I am a mess, with disheveled hair and dark, puffy eyes. There are also a few abrasions marring the fair skin of my face. I pour some water into the bowl, which I splash on my face. It's invigorating, and I leaves me feeling refreshed. I cross the room to the bookshelf and browse the books, seeing titles I've never seen before. They would be an interesting read and I hope I have time to peruse them.

Bright light fills the room and I spin around, startled, breathing a sigh of relief that it's only Alkin. He enters carrying a bowl and a large mug. "I see you're awake. Good morning, Valessa. I hope you slept well."

"I did. Thank you."

"I brought you some breakfast, bacon, eggs, and bread, along with milk. I hope that will suffice."

"That's perfect. Thank you."

He sets his cargo down on the table and pulls up a chair as I take a seat. The food smells terrific, and I can't contain myself as I shovel it into my mouth. Alkin smiles at me.

"Would you like some?" I ask.

"That's okay. I already ate."

I return to my meal. Once I have eaten my fill, Alkin gathers the dishes and exits the hut, leaving me alone once again. A moment passes and Alkin returns. "Get your shoes. We have a lot to do today."

I put my shoes on, and we exit the hut to be greeted by a bright and beautiful day. The sun is shining and birds sing in the forest, which is not as scary in the daytime. I look around and see many wolf creatures are already up and starting the day's work. It's remarkable to see them get on with their duties. The younger children play while the older children shadow the adults, learning their duties. The females are in various stages of preparing food, cleaning, or caring for the young. I see a few males who seem to be charged with keeping everyone safe, but there's no sign of the Alpha or his friends anywhere.

Alkin takes me by the hand and leads me to a fire near the center of the clearing, which is being tended by a grizzled, elderly female covered in gray and brown mottled fur. She stoops, as if bearing an immense weight on her shoulders, but stretches out her arms as we approach and folds Alkin into an embrace. "So this is the one, is it?"

"It is, Celica."

I hang back a little, not wanting to interfere in their conversation.

Celica beckons to me. "Come child. Let me get a look at you."

I step forward, and she studies me with her clouded eyes, then looks back at Alkin. "Oh, I think she will do, Alkin."

I feel a sense of dread because I don't know what they are talking about, and I'm sure I don't want to.

"Have you seen father this morning, Celica?" Alkin asks.

"I have, young one. He's gone hunting. Said he will be back tonight and that you know what you must do today."

"Aye, I do. We'll head out soon."

"Very well. I packed a few essentials for you, some jerky, fruit and water."

"Thank you, kind Celica."

Celica turns in my direction. "It was very nice to meet you, my dear."

I bow to her. "Likewise."

Alkin takes my hand and leads me toward his

father's cabin. I remain calm knowing his father is out hunting. Two wolf men, who appear not much older than Alkin, greet us as we approach.

Alkin motions in their direction. "These are my friends Jarvald and Rodther. They will accompany us today."

Where we are going, that we need an escort? I shake their hands. "Pleased to meet you both."

"We are more than pleased to meet you," says Jarvald.

Both Jarvald and Rodther appear more human than the other wolf people I have met, except for Alkin. Jarvald is rugged yet handsome, with a long scar running from his left brow to his jaw and reddish brown fur covering most of his body. His human face has the same golden eyes as Alkin, and sharp teeth fill his mouth. Rodther is not handsome. His misshaped face looks human, with the same golden eyes and sharp teeth, and a canine snout protruding from his jaw. Light gray fur covers his body, and his hands twist into claws with long nails at the end of each finger.

Alkin steps forward and the three of them gather some supplies, food and water, like Celica said, but also some crude weapons. The sight of the weapons sends a shiver down my spine. Where are we going and is it so dangerous we need an escort and weapons? I try not to show my fright, but the smirks I get from Jarvald and Rodther tell me I have failed. With packs in hand, the two of them set out. Alkin takes my hand and we follow.

We leave the encampment and head into the woods.

The forest is eery but beautiful in the sunlight, and unlike the previous night, I hear signs of life all around us. There's the rustling of foliage as the critters carry about their day and the sound of birds chirping in the canopy overhead. The sun's rays shine through breaks in the leaves, casting shafts of light throughout the trees.

I look at Alkin. "Where are we going?"

"You will see."

Silence ensues as we follow Jarvald and Rodther down the path through the forest. They talk amongst themselves, but I can't make out what they are saying.

"When are you going to answer the questions I have?" I ask.

"In time, everything will become clear to you."

"Do you know how I can return home?"

"Like you, we don't know how you got here."

Silence falls again. I listen to the songs of the birds and find they are unlike anything I have heard before. They sing in warbled chiming notes, much like wind chimes and nothing like birds. I wonder what they look like, and before long, I'm wondering what all the creatures of the forest look like. If these humans look so much like wolves, then I'm sure the other animals are just as intriguing.

We've walked for hours when Jarvald and Rodther stop and crouch to the ground. Alkin grabs my hand and pulls me to a crouch as well. My heart races and fear rises within me as the four of us crouch there, silent as can be. Something large crashes through the trees in front of us and moves deeper into the forest. I never see what it is.

Once the sound of the beast subsides, Jarvald and Rodther rise and beckon us to follow them. We leave the trail and start off into the forest. Detritus covers the ground and crunches under our feet as we walk, winding our way through the trees and vegetation. I wonder how much farther we will go.

I feel a jolt of energy, not unlike the current I felt from the portal. My skin prickles and I feel chills deep within me. I remember that every time I've felt this sensation; I ended up blacking out, and fear the same thing will happen now. Unconscious in the middle of the woods with these three beings is not where I want to be. Alkin says I'm under his protection, but I haven't seen him fight, which leaves me unsure if he can protect me. I must fight a blackout with all my strength. The tiny hairs on my arms stand up as the electric feeling grows stronger.

Alkin sees the dread written on my face. "It's okay, Valessa. Everything will be fine."

At the sound of his voice, Jarvald and Rodther turn towards us to watch in silence.

"I don't know what's wrong with me. I keep getting these overwhelming jolts of electric current that run through me and then I blackout, and I don't want to black out here with the three of you. Maybe we should just go back."

"We cannot go back, Valessa. We must continue on. There are many things you need to know and you must see the well to understand."

The well? What is he talking about? I remember his father telling him to take me to the well and explain everything, and I must make it there if I am to understand anything, so I grab Alkin's hand and continue onward.

Alkin squeezes my hand. "We are almost there."

We continue onward until we exit into a clearing that is not manmade. It's far more circular than a natural formation should be, and no vegetation grows anywhere within the circle of trees. There's no dead foliage littering the ground, either. Instead, a thick black dirt that has a slight tinge of green, the same shade as the water I drank the night before, covers the ground. As we advance toward the center of the clearing, I notice there is a dense, viscous fog snaking its way across the ground. It, too, is the same green as the water from before. In the center of the clearing, I see a gigantic crater. The fog is thickest directly above it.

I look at Alkin. "What is this place?"

He stretches out a hand, showing that I should continue forward. As I advance, I'm struck yet again with the same overwhelming electric current as before. The sudden jolt tears through my body and I let out a sharp breath as my legs go weak and I fall to the ground. I don't think I can get any closer. Alkin rushes over to me and picks me up in one swift motion. He carries me to the very edge of the crater and I peer into it. The strange fog that floods the forest also fills the crater. It seems to pool within the depths and rush over the sides, much like water would. But this is not water. I've never seen fog behave in this manner.

Alkin lowers me to the ground at the edge of the crater. "Do you see?"

"Yes, but I don't understand. What is it?"

"This is the well, the source of everything that's wrong with this forest. This plagues my people."

"But what is it?"

"It's a font of magic. A powerful font of magic."

I almost laugh. "That's ridiculous. Magic isn't real, Alkin."

He stares at me. "This world is not like the one you are from, Valessa. Magic permeates everything here. This well emits pure magic, which twists everything it touches into horrible beasts. You've seen my people. This well made them what they are. We were once human, but humans cannot withstand the powerful magic seeping from this crater. Over time, it twists us all into these beasts, half man, half wolf."

"This magic from the well turned you into werewolves?"

"It did, Valessa, and it will turn you, too. The magic changes us all. It's twisted even the animals here into fearsome beasts."

"I'm not in my world anymore, am I?"

"No Valessa, I'm afraid you are not."

"How can this be?"

"I don't know. I don't think anyone has ever met someone from another world. You are unique."

I'm close to tears. I don't know what kind of place I have ended up in, and I don't know if I will return to my world or if I will ever see my family again. Alkin senses my distress, takes a seat on the ground beside me, places a hand on my shoulder and pulls me into him. "I know this is a lot to take in, Valessa, but everything will be okay. I assure you of that."

Assurance is something I have not felt since arriving, but I allow myself to relax. I must keep my wits about me. It's the only thing that will help me with my current predicament.

I take a deep breath and exhale. "Where am I, Alkin? What is this place called?"

He looks into my eyes. "We call this place The Chatsraine Forest, which lies in The Enchanted Territory. It's but a small piece of a much greater world we call Sheonaetara."

I let this sink in. "How did I get here, Alkin? Will I ever be able to go home?"

"That I do not know."

I stare at him in disbelief. There are so many thoughts racing through my mind and I don't know where to begin.

"I know you need to process this. Take your time, Valessa. When you're ready, I'm here to answer what questions I can," Alkin says.

I take a few minutes to gather my thoughts. So many questions need answers, but I don't know where to begin. I watch the fog bubble out of the crater and roll across the ground, making its way into the surrounding forest. While Jarvald and Rodther engage in an animated conversation at the edge of the clearing, Alkin watches me, golden eyes focused on my face. I glance away, feeling unsettled by his intense stare and hear a faint chuckle escape his lips.

"This is no time for laughter." I'm upset he thinks anything about my situation is funny.

"I'm sorry, Valessa. You're right. I only found it amusing that you looked away so fast."

"I don't like you staring at me."

"Sorry. I was simply waiting for your questions. I only wish to provide you with what understanding I am able."

I return to my quiet contemplation. A few minutes pass and I look back at Alkin. He's sitting beside me, staring at the ground, and I'm thankful he isn't watching me anymore. "What is this fog that blankets everything?"

"It's raw magic. It seeps out of the well and twists everything it comes across."

"Everything?"

"Yes. Like I said, the well's magic changes my people. We were all human once, but over time, the raw magic from this well changed us into these wolf creatures. Werewolves is what you called us."

"Yes, werewolves. That's what we call half human, half wolf creatures where I came from."

"My people are the Crimsonclaw Nightwalkers. We stalk the Chatsraine Forest doing the one thing we must do above all others: survive. We craft what we need, but what we cannot make, we take, doing what we must in order to ensure our survival. Your word, werewolves, is fitting, since we arranged our society similar to a wolf pack. My father's name is Cronin. He is Alpha, and I will be Alpha after him. My mother was Beta, but she is no longer with us. She passed into the great unknown many moons ago. Her name was Grivina. She would have liked to meet you." He falls silent.

"I would have liked to meet her, too. I'm sorry for your loss, Alkin."

"Thank you."

"So, this change happens to everyone?"

"As far as we can tell, it does. We've met many who have gotten lost in the Chatsraine, and if they survive long enough, they all experience the change in the end. I'm sure you've noticed not all members of the pack have changed yet. We are all in various stages of transformation because the change happens gradually as we are exposed to the well's magic. The longer the exposure, the further the change progresses. And as I'm sure you have seen, the magic permeates every inch of the forest."

I take a second to process what Alkin has said. He sits beside me, awaiting my next question. "So if I remain here, then I too will experience this change? I'll become one of you?"

"Yes, Valessa. With time, you will be the same as us." Alkin takes my hand.

The thought of becoming a werewolf fills me with fear. In my world, I always thought it would be neat, but now that I am facing this harsh reality, I'm not sure it's what I want. "I don't want to become one of you, Alkin. I have to get out of this place. Please show me the way out." My voice breaks from the panic I feel.

"I can't do that, Valessa. Now that you're here, now that I have claimed you, you cannot leave. You will become one of us. You have no choice." Alkin grips my hand tighter.

"What does being claimed mean?"

"It means you will be mine, Valessa. You will be my mate and bear my children, and once I become Alpha, you will be my Beta. We will lead the Crimsonclaw together."

Fire wells up inside me. "What if I don't want this?"

"I claimed you in order to keep you safe. Now, you must become my mate if you want to live. With what you've seen and learned, the pack won't let you leave. My father will not allow you to live if you refuse to join us."

I snatch my hand out of Alkin's. I can't believe what I'm hearing. *How can he make me stay here, knowing I don't want to share the fate of his people?* I stand up and look around, scanning the surroundings for an escape. I don't know where I will go, but I can't stay here. Jarvald and Rodther take a step in my direction. I'm sure they've seen the panic on my face. Out of the corner of my eye, I see Alkin motion to them to back down, and they stop, dropping to their knees.

Alkin stands and grabs me by the shoulders, looking me deep in the eyes. "You must relax, Valessa. You can't run off into the Chatsraine alone and hope to survive."

I stare straight ahead, my mind racing while Alkin

pulls me toward Jarvald and Rodther. "Let's have lunch before heading back."

My stomach growls and I realize I'm hungry. "Yes, that would be nice."

We take a seat on the ground near the treeline. Rodther unpacks the food and Alkin hands me a sandwich made of crude bread with thick slices of meat and cheese, lettuce and tomato. I take a bite of the sandwich and, surprised how good it is; I eat it faster. Once finished, Jarvald tosses me an apple, which I follow with a few gulps of water. I'm the first one to finish eating, so I sit and wait for the others.

After some time, they finish their meal and Jarvald packs up. I watch, so many thoughts racing through my head. At least, I have fewer questions now and I can be thankful for that.

Once Jarvald finishes packing, we make our way into the woods. "We will return to camp now," says Alkin. "We want to get back before it gets dark." I resolve myself to my fate, hang my head, and follow along.

Chapter 4

Time passes. I've been with the Crimsonclaw Nightwalkers for weeks and have learned a lot. When I'm not spending time with Alkin, I'm with the females, who teach me how to cook, tend the fires and the young, mend clothing and structures and how to treat wounds. I've also learned how to hunt and what I can eat and what I should avoid. I have become an avid tracker and archer, often taking down whatever prey is unfortunate enough to find itself in my sights. The pack now trusts and respects me and no longer views me as an outsider, but as a member of their closely knit family, and I do what I can to help us all survive.

I've also seen many things I never thought could exist. The beasts of the Chatsraine are horrible, twisted monsters that stalked my nightmares until now. We must plan and carefully execute each trip into the trees, because every outing could be our last. I've seen a few pack members torn down by huge, twisted creatures that resembled bears, their screams echoing through the brush as the animals tore them apart with their crooked jaws and five-inch razor-sharp claws. Guttural growls and snarls and friend's dying screams will haunt me for the rest of my life. Alkin spoke true when he warned of the dangers lurking in the Chatsraine, and now I have seen how deadly the forest can be.

I've gotten to know Cronin better and understand he was only trying to protect his people when we first met. As an unknown entity, he didn't know if I meant his pack harm or not, and I understand his motivation. I've learned the hunting party that captured me when I first arrived in Sheonaetara was following me for some time without my knowledge. They watched as I made my way through the forest and captured me only when they deemed it necessary. It was when I spotted their eyes glowing in the dark that they decided they must deal with me, for they feared I might cause the pack harm.

I have grown close to Celica, who is the pack mother, a title reserved for the eldest female of the pack. Wise and respected, she is Cronin's most trusted advisor, often joining him in his cabin to discuss what lies ahead for the pack. Celica teaches me lessons on what it means to be a Crimsonclaw Nightwalker and much about the Chatsraine Forest, and even more about Sheonaetara's history and lore. However, she can't teach me the origin of the well, the causes of the change or how it occurs. These are things no one understands.

I have also made a friend, a young she-wolf named Estrilda. Although she's a few years older than me, we have much in common. She's shorter than I am and her body ripples with muscle. Covered in dingy brown fur, she has almost completed her change and has a long snout full of sharp teeth and the most luxurious tail. Estrilda is interested in the land I came from, so we spend our time discussing my world. She was born into the pack, so has never known a life outside it and yearns to experience more, which is what draws her to me. With no close friends before now, it's a most welcome change for me, and I'm thankful to have someone besides Alkin to spend my time with.

I miss my family. *How has my disappearance affected them? I vanished without a trace, something out of character for me, and I'm sure they worry about me. If only I could let them know I'm okay.* The more time I spend in Sheonaetara, the more convinced I am that I will never see my mother, father, or brother again.

There's no reason to return to the well, and I've had no more blackouts since my trip there, but I'm unsure if the visit has anything to do with this. I'm glad I don't have those episodes any more because they scared me and I have no desire to feel that helplessness again. No one knows what caused them and I hope they don't return, at least not soon.

I'm still fated to become Alkin's mate and I try to resist this, but with each day, I know our union grows closer. Alkin seems nice, but I don't want to be forced into a marriage. The only way to escape this fate is to leave, which is a death sentence. I know what lurks in the forest, and I would never survive the Chatsraine alone.

A PROPHECY AWAKENS - 47 -

Besides, if I leave the pack, I'm certain they would hunt me down and capture or kill me. No one has told me this, but I'm sure they won't allow me to leave knowing what I have learned about them, so I've tried to make the best of my situation. Alkin is handsome and always nice to me and I like many members of the pack. They seem to like me as well, so joining them shouldn't be that bad.

There is the matter of the change I keep hearing about, and I'm not sure I want to become a werewolf. Many elder members of the pack say my change should have begun, that after visiting the well and spending weeks in the Chatsraine Forest, I should have already started growing my fur coat and tail, but these things have not happened for me yet. I see the others' puzzled looks and stares and hear them snickering behind my back sometimes. It's just another thing that makes me different. Maybe I won't change after all.

A tap on my shoulder startles me and brings me out of deep thought.

"Sorry. I didn't mean to startle you," Alkin says, chuckling.

"It's okay. I was just lost in thought and didn't hear you come in."

"The hunters have returned. Will you be joining the pack for the feast?"

"Of course. Give me some time to clear my head. I'll be there soon."

He nods and exits the hut. I sit on the bed, reeling from the thoughts running through my mind. Another hunting party has returned unharmed, which means a party is in order. Because the Chatsraine is so dangerous, the pack feasts every time a hunting party returns without casualties to celebrate their safe return. I was never one for parties, but I enjoy the festivities when the hunters return.

I dress and exit the hut. Most pack members have gathered around the bonfire in the center of the clearing. Some of them dance, while others engage in conversation. Several females at the side of the clearing clean the kill, two large deer, their antlers and faces twisted by the magic that runs through the forest. Other females are in various stages of preparing the rest of the meal.

I'm trying to decide if I want to help prepare the food or join the others at the bonfire when Estrilda approaches me. "Hey Valessa. What are you doing?"

"Deciding if I should help with food or scurry over to the fire."

"I think they have the meal prep covered. Besides, Alkin is waiting for you to join him by the fire."

"Thanks. I'll go find him."

"Sure thing." She winks, leaving me to wonder why.

I watch Estrilda hurry off to join the other females preparing our meal before I turn and make my way toward the fire. Alkin sits on a log beside Cronin and Celica. He looks up, and a smile spreads across his face as he stands and walks in my direction. He takes my hand and leads me back toward his father. Alkin wraps his arm around me, which causes me to blush.

"Are you blushing?" he asks.

"I think I might be."

"There's no need to. You know we will be man and wife one day."

"That doesn't mean we have to be affectionate in front of everyone."

I shrug out from under his arm as we reach Cronin, who looks at me and smiles. "He likes you, Valessa. I hope you know that."

"I do, sir."

"Good. I hope you like him as well."

"I enjoy his company."

Cronin laughs. "Very good. It is almost time."

"Time for what?"

"The bonding ceremony, of course. Celica and I have decided the bonding ceremony will take place upon the next full moon."

Knowing the ceremony is almost upon me fills me with panic. I look at the three smiling faces before me and feel myself hyperventilating. I am not ready to be Alkin's mate.

"You don't look so good, my dear. You should sit," Celica says in her caring tone.

I don't want to sit. I want to run far and fast, but I lower myself to the ground in front of Cronin instead. Alkin takes a seat on the ground beside me. Not knowing what to say, I stare at the dirt. I'm awash with fear, panic, and many other feelings. *What does this bonding ceremony entail? I'm not even sure when the next full moon is.*

My stomach does flips inside me. "I no longer feel

like celebrating."

"That's okay. You just got some big news I know you weren't expecting. I'll take you back to the hut if that's what you want."

Alkin stands and I allow him to pull me to my feet. "Please excuse us." He bows before turning and leading me to our hut. "I understand how you feel, Valessa. But it's going to be okay. I hope you know that."

"You can't know how I feel, Alkin. Everyone keeps telling me it's going to be okay, but I don't know that it is."

Fire rises inside me, so I pull away from Alkin to enter the hut. He follows me. "Can you please just leave me be?"

"I don't think you should be alone right now, Valessa."

"I don't care what you think. Just go."

I turn to the bed as he leaves, throwing myself down on the mattress and burying my face in my arms. My face feels hot and I shudder as I sob. *I can't leave the pack because I won't survive in the forest alone, but I don't want to be Alkin's mate, so I can't stay either. If only there was a way to postpone the bonding.*

I don't know how long I've been sleeping when the sound of screams from outside awakens me. I listen, trying to discern what's happening outside. That's when I hear a vicious, frightening roar that reminds me of a lion, only louder and much deeper. Amid the shouting and roaring, I hear screams of terror coming from the women and children. I jump off the bed and hurry to the door to peek outside and see what is happening. Men, women and children are running without purpose, afraid, but I can't see what has caused the camp to erupt into disorder and confusion.

I grab my bow and quiver, then make my way out into the night. I keep low and out of sight. The festivities have descended into chaos. People are running and screaming, fear painted across their faces, and multiple fires burn throughout the clearing. *What has caused this madness?*

Cronin, surrounded by members of the hunting party, is near the center of camp and I breathe a sigh of relief upon seeing Alkin there as well. The cause of this disaster is nowhere to be found, but I know it hasn't gone far, so I make my way across the clearing toward Cronin and the others.

"What's happening?" I ask as I approach.

Cronin nods in greeting. "It's an attack." Surprise washes over me. The campsite has suffered no attacks since I arrived. Neither animal nor human has entered our clearing until now. "What is it? What has attacked us?"

Another loud roar echoes through the forest before anyone answers, and the creature crashes through the trees. A hellish nightmare of a lion stands before us, five feet tall at the shoulder. Sandy brown fur covers its body and a thick shaggy dark brown mane encircles its neck. Eight feet long and close to 600 pounds, his paws are the size of dinner plates, three-inch claws, already bloody, protrude from his toes. Large yellow eyes study us from a terrifying face, and saliva drips from the huge four inch fangs in his mouth.

"Where did that come from?" I ask.

Cronin shakes his head. "No idea, but we must try to kill it. It's our duty to protect the pack."

I nock an arrow, raise my bow and draw the string, taking careful aim at my target. The beast lowers itself to the ground as I line up my shot and fire an arrow. He turns away, and the arrow comes to rest tangled in the thick mane, not even contacting his skin. Cronin looks afraid, a look I've never seen him wear. He's always our stalwart Alpha, no matter what happens.

I grab another arrow and prepare to fire again. As I raise my bow to take aim, the lion lunges forward and charges us. That's when I see her just at the edge of the clearing. Within the trees behind the lion, a woman conceals herself. She's too far away to make out her features, but I can tell she is quite beautiful, and she is smiling, as if she delights in the carnage occurring before her.

The lion draws near and gathers its hind legs under itself in preparation to pounce. At that moment, I'm certain we're going to die and there's nothing I can do to stop it. Frozen by fear, my eyes wide and teeth clenched, I take a deep breath and prepare myself for the end. A shrill scream escapes my throat as the lion leaps toward us and a bright blue light explodes within the clearing, washing over everything. Afterward, there is nothing.

Chapter 5

When I open my eyes, I'm lying on a bed, surrounded by pillows and furs. The small room has three walls made of stone, the fourth is fabric hung on a rod at the ceiling, which is also stone. Opposite the bed, a fire burns in a golden brazier beside a mahogany desk and chair. Books line the remaining wall and an area rug with a beautiful blue and gold floral pattern covers the floor. A small table with a bowl of soup and a glass of water on it sits beside the bed. *Where am I and how did I get here?*

I take a sip of water, which is refreshing and tastes pure. The soup is delicious, and before long, the bowl and glass are both empty. I don't know how long I've been in bed and I feel weak when I stand. Someone has bathed me and changed my clothes. I wonder who did this as I make my way to the desk and search drawers, looking for some sign of where I am or who has cared for me.

The curtain behind me opens and someone enters the

room. I turn around to find a tall boy staring at me with large, periwinkle eyes. He looks young and has pale ivory skin and a dirty round face. His tangled hair is long and silver, disguising his long pointy ears. A knee-length tunic covers his torso and his feet are bare. His not quite human looks give me an uneasy feeling. He does not speak, only stares, so I smile at him, and a look of amazement washes over his face as he exits the room, leaving me puzzled. *Should I follow him?*

Before I can decide whether to follow or stay put, I hear murmuring from another room. I'm unable to make out what is being said and decide I will stay in this room until I figure out who my new captors are and what they want with me. The room is small and makes me feel safe, but I wish I had a weapon. There is little in this room that could serve as one, but if it comes to it, I can use the brazier. My skin prickles and I tense when I hear footsteps approaching. I recede until my back is against the wall furthest from the door and freeze, readying myself for whatever steps into the room. The curtain slides open to reveal the boy from before. For a moment, we stare at each other, then he raises his hand and gestures for me to follow him as he turns to leave. I take a few steps in his direction before stopping again. "Who are you? Where am I?"

Once again, he gestures for me to follow him.

"Where are you taking me?"

He remains silent and gestures for me to follow him yet again, so I take a few steps forward, and he retreats down the hall.

I exit the room and see it's not a room at all, but a small alcove set into the wall of a large cave system. The cave is massive, leaving me in awe. There are more alcoves set into the walls, many cordoned off, creating rooms similar to the one I awoke in. Magnificent area rugs cover the floor of the cave, creating a carpet. Golden braziers line the walls, all of which are ablaze, lighting up the interior of the cave, and stunning works of art, the likes of which I have never seen adorn some alcoves. I wonder who would decorate a cave in such a fashion.

We near the end of the hall, and the boy steps aside, motioning for me to continue. I enter a vast open chamber lit by multiple golden braziers that cast a bright, flickering golden light around the room. Rugs, decorated in lavish floral designs, cover the floor and shelves line the walls, many containing books while others house statuettes and carvings. A large wood-burning stove with a stovepipe that feeds into a hole in the cave's roof sits among them. Beside the stove is a shelf covered with bottles and jars containing unknown ingredients. Strands of baubles and charms crafted from precious gems and metals decorate the ceiling of the chamber, reminding me of the strands of Christmas lights my mother used to decorate. Centered on the wall opposite the stove is a large ornate ebony chair on a platform, the back and arms carved with vines and roses and seated upon the chair is a beautiful woman I recognize.

The sight of her fills me with rage. "It's you!"

She dismisses the boy with a wave of her hand.

"Thank you, Ruven. That will be all."

He nods, then exits the chamber, leaving me alone with the woman.

She seems tall with fair skin and long blonde hair that falls over her shoulders in loose curls. Vibrant green eyes, lined in black with smoky eye shadow, sit above flushed cheeks and ruby red lips. Diamond earrings dangle from her small ears, and rings bedeck her fingers, an enormous diamond on a gold chain hangs from her neck. She's wearing a long, fitted red velvet dress accented in gold, and around her waist lies a chain made of gold.

"I trust your accommodations are to your liking," she says, her voice sweet and silvery.

I glare at her. I don't know what to say.

"It's okay. I'm sure you're still shaken from your ordeal."

"Oh, I'm sure you know much about my ordeal. You were there, after all." She smiles. "I don't have the slightest idea what you are referring to."

"Don't play dumb. I saw you smiling in the trees as that beast attacked us."

"He only attacked those that were holding you against your will."

"I wasn't a captive. They were my friends. I was free to leave if I wanted to."

"I hardly think you were free to leave with your impending bonding ceremony."

"How do you know about that?"

She smiles. "I know many things. The forest

provides."

Curiosity replaces my anger. *How does she know about the bonding ceremony? What does she mean the forest provides?* "Who are you?"

"I can be whoever you want me to be, my child. A friend, a mother, a teacher, a protector. These things I can be for you. All you need to do is ask." A smile stretches across her face.

"All I want are answers. Who are you and how do you know what you know? What were doing at the clearing during the attack?"

"My, my. You are an impertinent one, aren't you?" She raises her hand and snaps her fingers.

A low growl comes from behind me, followed by heavy footsteps. The hair on my body stands at attention and my muscles tense. I turn around to be greeted by the monstrous face of the lion that attacked the Crimsonclaw camp. He looks at me, then joins the woman, laying his enormous head in her lap. She scratches him behind the ear and the lion grunts then lays down at her feet.

I stare at them, mouth agape, frozen by fear. "I... I... I don't understand."

"You will, my dear. It will all become clear in time."

A shiver runs down my spine, and my legs weaken. I rub my face to clear some of the fog from my mind.

"Are you feeling okay?" She asks. "Would you like to sit down?"

"Yes, please."

The woman motions toward a chair nearby. I take a seat and lean forward, placing my head in my hands, taking a moment to process what I have seen and heard since waking. Once I feel settled, I raise my head to find the woman peering at me, smiling.

"I'll forgive your impertinence. This all must be overwhelming," she says.

"Yes, it is."

"My name is Lavina, Lavina Barkridge. What might I call you, dear?"

"Valessa."

"Do you have a last name, Valessa?"

"Yes. Thorley, Valessa Thorley."

"Ah, very good. Now we are getting somewhere." She smiles.

"Where am I?"

"This is Vauxsard Overhang, a cave within the Chatsraine Forest. This is where I live." She gestures around the chamber.

"It's nice for a cave."

"I do my best to make it cozy." She leans forward, studying me. "What were you doing with the wolf people?"

"Surviving. I don't know how I got here. They found me lost in the forest and took me back to their camp, where they watched over me and taught me how to survive. The young one, Alkin, took me under his protection to keep me safe, and so I became part of their pack. I viewed them as friends and family." Tears well up in my eyes.

"They are no one's friends, Valessa. They are horrid beasts that only care about their own. I'm sure they had wonderful plans for you after the bonding."

"How do you know about that? You said the forest speaks to you. What does that even mean?"

She looks at me for an eternity before answering. "As I said, the forest speaks to me. I hear its whispers on the wind. That's how I survive."

"The plants and animals talk to you?" I scoff with disbelief.

"It is quite similar to that, yes. It allows me to know all I need in order to gain the most benefit."

"And how do I benefit you, Lavina?" With every word, I grow more suspicious of this woman's intentions.

Lavina smirks. "That remains to be seen, Valessa."

"The pack is all I've known since I woke up here. I would like to return to them."

"You won't be returning to the Crimsonclaw Nightwalkers."

"Why not?"

"The Crimsonclaw are no more, child. The camp lies in ruins. No one survives."

This cannot be true. She must be lying in order to keep me here. Yes, the lion is large, but the pack has numbers. "I refuse to believe that."

"Oh, you poor, poor thing. You don't know, do you?"

"Know what?"

"You were the one who killed them."

My eyes widen in disbelief. "That's not true. It was the lion, the very lion lying at your feet. You were there." I stand and point a finger at Lavina. "You set the lion upon us. You saw it all."

Lavina laughs. "Yes, girl. I was there, and I saw everything. The hunters returned with their kill and the pack prepared the celebration feast. They danced and had fun. You were told that your bonding ceremony was imminent. I saw the look on your face, the one that said you did not wish to bond with the young wolf. I watched as you returned to your hut and shortly after that is when I sent the lion in."

"I knew you did it. Why are you lying? And why are you blaming it on me? It was the lion. You just admitted you set him upon the pack."

"Oh, yes. A week ago, I sent Reaper," she gestures toward the lion, "into the encampment. But his orders were to insight fear and panic, not to kill. He was only there to cause chaos. Reaper did his job well. The camp descended into the chaos I desired, which drew you back out into the clearing. I watched as you joined the others, and I watched as you tried to bring Reaper down. Of course you failed, as I knew you would. Then, just as he was preparing to pounce, the most remarkable thing happened. The loudest, shrillest scream I had ever heard burst from you. Your body emitted the brightest, most glorious flash of blue light, then everything and everyone fell silent and still. The entire forest died, and I knew I had to bring you here. There is something quite remarkable about you, Valessa."

I am devastated. My face heats and tears run down my cheeks. *How could I go supernova and kill people I loved?*

"You're clearly upset, Valessa, but although you can't see it, they were just beasts. You would waste time grieving for them."

"They may have been mere beasts to you, but to me, they were friends and family. If you don't mind, I would like some time alone to mourn."

Lavina sighs. "Very well. I will allow you to return to your quarters, but you may not leave the overhang. Ruven will bring your supper in a few hours. After you have rested and eaten, we have much more to discuss."

She lifts a small silver bell off the table beside her and rings it. A few seconds later, the boy returns. "Ruven, escort our guest back to her room. Have Dobbohk stand guard. She is not to leave."

Ruven nods, then takes my hand. He leads me back the way we came, only leaving me once I'm back in my room. I lower myself onto the bed and weep for losing so many innocent lives and because I don't know what caused the outburst that destroyed the Crimsonclaw. I feel like a monster.

Lavina said I couldn't leave, but I must get away from this place. There's something about her that doesn't sit right with me. She told Ruven to instruct someone named Dobbohk to guard my room and not let me leave. I pick up the desk chair and make my way to the door as I raise the chair above my head. I slide the curtain open, sure if I catch Dobbohk by surprise, I can incapacitate him. My breath catches when I see him. Dobbohk is no man. I have never seen a creature like the one standing outside my room. It turns and looks at me with beady, bright blue eyes, causing me to gasp, frozen by fear. This creature must be eight feet tall or more and appears to be made of stones held together by some invisible force. It has three fingers and a thumb at the end of its large hands. Dobbohk places one finger in the center of my chest and shoves me back into the room before closing the curtain.

Grief turns to anger, and I throw the chair across the room. It seems leaving is out of the picture. I will need a rather ingenious plan to escape this prison, so I sit on the edge of the bed and think about everything I have been through recently, the family I left behind, Alkin and the rest of the Crimsonclaw Nightwalkers, and my current predicament. How might I get myself out of it? Some time later, the boy, Ruven, arrives with a tray of food. He puts it on the desk, then picks up the chair I threw earlier and returns it to its place in front of the desk. He looks at me, then hurries to the door.

"Wait." I reach out and take him by the arm.

He stops, then looks at my hand on his arm.

"I'm Valessa. Your name is Ruven, right?"

He nods.

I let go of his arm. "Do you think you can help me get out of here?"

His eyes widen, and he shakes his head.

"Please, Ruven. I can't stay here. I have to get away."

Ruven backs away from me.

"If you help me leave, I'll take you with me. I

promise you, Ruven, I will take you away from here. We'll leave together. Please, I'm begging you." I make one last plea.

Ruven shakes his head again, then turns and leaves, closing the curtain behind him.

I throw myself onto the bed and burst into tears. Lavina says I'm a guest, but I feel more like a prisoner, especially with the stone man guarding my door. There's something about Lavina I find unsettling. I can't get a read on what her intentions might be or if she is being truthful. She says there is something remarkable about me, but she's wrong. I'm just an ordinary girl that has gotten lost in an extraordinary place. I wonder what more she wants to discuss with me as I drift into slumber.

Chapter 6

It's been three days since Lavina sequestered me in my room. I only know this because Ruven brings me food twice a day, and I assume this occurs in the morning and evening. Every time Ruven visits my room, I try to convince him to help me gain freedom, but he continues to shake his head and flee, never speaking to me. Dobbohk still stands guard outside my door. I don't communicate with that monstrosity. He frightens me. I spend my time reading, sleeping and thinking and have not devised an escape from this prison yet. I'm getting stir crazy pinned up in this room.

It's the fourth day of my captivity. I awaken, determined to get myself out of my room. With some difficulty, I broke a leg off my chair and spent part of the previous night fashioning it into a crude spear by rubbing a jagged edge on the stone floor. It isn't much of a weapon, but should serve its purpose well. I pull myself out of bed, throw on my clothes, then grab my spear and hide it just under the edge of my mattress before lowering myself onto the bed and folding my hands into my lap to await Ruven, deciding to take him hostage hoping this will spur Lavina to set me free. It's more likely to get me killed, but it's a risk I will take at this point.

I hear Dobbohk grunt and know the moment is upon me, readying myself to spring into action as the curtain at the door slides open.

I take a deep breath. "I'm sorry, Ruven."

"I will let him know," says the silvery sweet voice of Lavina.

"What . . . Why . . . I . . ."

"You are a fool, child. I know what you were planning. I would not endanger poor Ruven in such a way."

"But how did you know? How could you know?" I'm unable to hide the shock in my voice.

"I already told you. The forest, stupid girl. It watches and listens, and I listen to what it has seen and heard. You will never pull a fast one on me."

Anger rises in her voice, and I sink deeper into the bed as feelings of hopelessness and despair wash over me. *If I try anything again, it must be unplanned in order to succeed.*

"Now, if you are willing, I would ask that you join me for breakfast. As I already stated, we have much to discuss." Lavina smiles at me.

I sigh and nod. Breakfast sounds wonderful. I've had only oatmeal and soup to eat since being confined to my room.

Lavina exits the room and makes her way down the hall, her dress bellowing behind her as she hurries away. I skirt past Dobbohk, then follow Lavina to the main chamber.

The first thing I notice upon entering is the most delicious smells filling the air, which makes my stomach growl and my mouth water. A large ebony table decorated in the same carved flowers and vines as Lavina's chair sits in the center of the room. Lavina motions for me to sit as she seats herself at the table. Bacon, scrambled eggs, biscuits, toast, sausage, fruit, coffee, and orange juice cover the table. I take the chair across from Lavina, who smiles at me. She is wearing a dark green velvet dress with a floral pattern stitched in silver thread at the wrist, collar, and hem, and I wonder where she gets such clothing. She looks charming, but I don't trust her.

Lavina waves her hand across the table. "Please help yourself, Valessa."

I place a few spoons of eggs, two slices of toast and a couple slices of bacon on my plate, then pour myself a glass of orange juice. The food tastes much better than the oatmeal she has forced me to eat for breakfast the previous three days. I watch as Lavina pours herself a cup of coffee and note the fact she takes no food. She watches me eat, and I assume she's giving me time to finish my meal. Once I've eaten my fill, she raises her hands and claps them twice. A few seconds later, Ruven enters the chamber and begins clearing the table.

I wait until he finishes, then turn my gaze to Lavina. "You said we had much to discuss, so start talking."

"There's no need to be so rude. I took you in, cared for you while you recovered from your ordeal, clothed you, fed you and kept you safe. You will not sit here in my home and make demands of me."

"You kept me locked up in my room with that thing standing guard for three days. I want to know what is going on here."

"Everything will become clear in time. I'm sure you have many questions. I will try to answer as many as I can. All you need to do is ask."

I do have many questions that require answers, so I decide to move past my anger, at least until I gain a better understanding of my circumstances. I take a few minutes to organize the thoughts running rampant through my mind while Lavina sits across from me, sipping her coffee.

"Who or what are you?" I ask.

Lavina chuckles, a grin spreading across her face. "I am a witch, a highly talented and supremely gifted one, if I do say so myself."

"Witches aren't real."

"In this world, many magical creatures exist. Your precious beasts should have proven that. Believe it or not, I am a witch, a human gifted with the ability to control magic and bend it to my will. It's incredibly rare for humans to wield magic in Sheonaetara, for a human to be gifted in its use is even rarer, and it can make a valuable asset. You are very special, Valessa."

"I'm not sure what you mean."

"Like me, you, too, have the gift. You just don't know it yet."

I laugh. "There's nothing special about me. I can't perform magic and have no gifts. You are mistaken."

Lavina takes a quick sip from her cup, her eyes never leaving mine. "I know what you are thinking, child. I know it's a lot to take in, but it is true. You will see in time. I will help you."

"Help me? How do you plan on helping me?"

"The outbursts, aren't you curious about what causes them? I have this answer and more for you." Lavina walks to a nearby bookshelf. She scans the books lining the shelf, removes one, then returns and lays the book on the table in front of me.

I run my fingers across the cover and gaze down at the title. "The History of Magic and Its Uses in the World. This has the answers in it?"

"It may give you some enlightenment. It's your first lesson. Pay close attention to its words when you read it."

"What do you mean lesson?"

Lavina sighs. "The magic inside you causes the outbursts you have. Being unable to control it leads to a forceful explosion of magic from your body, thus causing the bright blinding light and the blackout that follows. This usually occurs during times of great stress, such as when you're hurt or frightened. The power inside you is what makes you so special. You must learn how to focus and wield it, enabling you to do the most remarkable things. I can teach you all you need to know in order to accomplish this."

Lavina stares at me from across the table, no doubt awaiting a response. I have no words to express the thoughts and feelings inside me. The things she says should make no sense, but they do none the less.

Several minutes of quiet contemplation pass. "I don't know what to say."

"That's okay. I knew it would take time. Just accept my help, read the books, and agree to the lessons. I assure you, you won't regret it."

"Okay, I'll give it a shot."

Lavina smiles. "Very good. I'll give you a few days to read that book, then we will start with some beginner level incantations and potion making. Now, might you have any other pressing questions before we part?"

I nod. "I have a few."

"Ask away. I will answer what I can."

"The boy, Ruven, is he a servant? Does he not speak?"

"Ruven completes minor chores for me. He is not a servant at all. In fact, he is also someone of great importance to me. He is quite wary of strangers. I'm sure he will speak to you in due time."

"And the lion, I believe you called him Reaper. I've never seen such a beast. What is he? Why is he so big?"

"Yes, Reaper. Reaper is my animal companion, my familiar. He brings me news from the forest and does my bidding when I ask him. He may look rather fearsome, but he's really just a big sweetie."

"And the big one? What is that Dobbohk thing?"

"Dobbohk is his name. He is a stone golem."

"A golem is something I have only read about in books. I never thought they could exist. Is he really made of stone? What is his purpose? How do you even control something like that?"

Lavina smiles. "Yes, he is made of stone. His purpose is to serve me, for I gave him life. It's a complicated process I may, perhaps, teach you some day. It requires powerful magic to create a golem. Every golem is born from a single stone. This stone is the golem's life force, its heart, if you will. Once I created Dobbohk, I locked his heart in an ornate box, which I keep in my private chambers. Thus, he will live and serve me until his heart is destroyed. Sometimes the best protection comes from having a golem at your side."

I'm intrigued seeing the power magic can grant someone. I wonder what impressive feats I might perform if I learn to master this power.

"Is there anything else you would like to know?" Lavina asks.

I shake my head. "That's all for now. I suppose I have some reading to do and even more to think about. Thank you for taking the time to answer my questions."

"It was no trouble at all."

Lavina rings a small bell, and Ruven enters the room. "Please escort Valessa back to her room, Ruven. Enjoy your reading, my dear. We will talk again soon."

I nod and rise from my chair. "Thank you. Thank you for breakfast as well."

I follow Ruven. Once in my room and seated at the desk, I open The History of Magic and Its Uses in the World. The book appears to be ancient, with pages made of thick parchment. Its words are written in an elegant and airy manner, which sends a shiver down my spine as I wonder what secrets it will teach me. I can't fight the feelings of curiosity and excitement rising inside me. I make myself comfortable and begin absorbing the knowledge contained within its pages.

Chapter 7

Days bleed into weeks as I learn the skills that will allow me to survive this world. True to her word, Lavina has been an invaluable teacher. I spend my mornings learning and practicing various incantations and spells and have learned how to conjure fire in the palm of my hand and how to bend the flora of the forest to my will. I'm well on my way to mastering the power contained within me. Lavina has taught me the benefits of potion making as well, and I have become adept at creating healing draughts, as well as poisons, and everything in between. I spend my evenings reading countless texts that provide me the knowledge I need to forge a place for myself in Sheonaetara. In the past few months, I've read many books on magic and its uses, the history of this world, the creatures that inhabit it, and the people that call it home, as well as the structure of their societies. I've gotten to know Ruven better, too. He still hasn't opened up to me, but he talks to me now. Our conversations are brief and to the point, but I hope he will trust me soon. I have also come to appreciate both Reaper and Dobbohk and the safety they afford us. Neither is as frightening as I once thought.

"Do you care for any more?" Lavina's voice rouses me from my reverie.

"No, thank you. I've eaten my fill for tonight. I think I'll retire to my room and continue my reading."

"Very well, dear. Have a wonderful evening."

I make my way down the hall to my quarters. Once there, I change into a nightgown and settle onto my bed with my latest book, Conquering the Worst of the World. It's a gripping text outlining the weaknesses of the mysterious creatures found in Sheonaetara, at least the ones that have been studied and documented. I'm sure it doesn't contain everything about every living entity in this world, but I feel it will prepare me for many of them.

I'm not sure how long I've been asleep when I'm awakened by a familiar sound. I sit up in disbelief. It's a soft whinny, much like the horses of my world. And I hear the faint murmur of talking, but can't make out who the voices belong to. I should ignore it, but my curiosity gets the better of me, so I rise from bed and exit my room. A sigh of relief escapes me when I see no one around as I tiptoe down the hall to the main chamber. Here I can hear Lavina's silvery voice, and a deep, raspy hissing voice I have not heard before. Still unable to make out what is being said, I inch closer to the entrance.

"Oh, but the trip was warranted," says the unknown

voice. "You were supposed to send word if you succeeded in your endeavor or if you discovered anything of note."

"I would have notified you if I had," says Lavina.

"They demanded I make the long journey here because we felt a great power emanating from the forest, a far greater power than anything we have felt before. Are you sure you were unsuccessful in opening the portal? Are you sure you have not found the one we seek?"

I feel this unidentified person is referring to me, so I ease into a position that allows me to observe Lavina and her visitor. Lavina is standing in the cave's doorway. In front of her stands a tall hooded figure wearing a long black cloak. He has taken great care to conceal his identity, making it impossible to see his face.

"If I opened the doorway, then I am ignorant of it. I never saw it open. I am unaware if I was successful or not."

The hooded figure crosses his arms over his chest. "And have you come across any newcomers to our realm?"

My breath catches in my throat, and a shiver runs down my spine. Now I know the mysterious visitor is referring to me. *Why would he choose to visit in the middle of the night? Does he mean me harm?*

"I found a young girl who claims she appeared here from elsewhere. She seems quite ordinary but may have potential. I would have sent word once I determined if she is the one," says Lavina.

"Where did you find here?"

"With the Crimsonclaw Nightwalkers. They intended to bond her with the Alpha's son."

"And you thought it wise to cause conflict with those monsters? You could start a war that we will not protect you from."

"Oh Jizurza, I think you know me better than that." Lavina chuckles. "None of us will suffer their wrath. I took care of that. They viewed her as family, so I killed them, every one of them. Couldn't have them trying to steal my prize."

I want to launch myself at Lavina. *How could she kill the pack? Worse than that, how could she convince me I had killed them?* It takes everything in me to stay hidden, but I calm myself and resume my observation of the scene before me.

"Good, good. Creatures like those will never come into the fold," says the mystery figure.

"Glad to be of service," says Lavina.

"Continue to observe and work with the girl. Determine if she is indeed the one we seek. If this becomes clear, do make sure you inform us immediately. Don't make me undertake this journey again. It is rather long and arduous."

"Understood, Jizurza. And what would you have me do with the boy?"

"Do with him as you wish. I'm sure he can be useful to you."

"Oh yes. His sacrifice could power many great spells."

"Very well." The hooded figure mounts his horse. "We look forward to hearing from you."

Lavina nods as the hooded figure gallops into the night. I return to my room, feeling relieved knowing I am not responsible for destroying the Crimsonclaw, but I'm angry Lavina killed the closest thing to family I have known since arriving in Sheonaetara and I fear for Ruven. *He doesn't deserve to be a sacrifice. I will save him. There has to be a way.* But for now, I must behave as though I know nothing of this night visitor. These thoughts run through my mind as I drift to sleep.

Come morning, I dress and make my way to the main chamber for breakfast. Lavina is present as usual, but wearing her foraging attire.

After our meal, Lavina addresses me. "Today will be a free day for you. You can read, practice or just relax. Whatever you want, Valessa."

"Thank you. I appreciate it."

"Of course, dear. I must go foraging to gather some reagents I require for a powerful hex I wish to work. I shall return by dusk. Enjoy your day." She leaves, Reaper following at her heel.

I'm itching to make a hasty escape, but I must take my time. *It's possible Lavina knows I eavesdropped on her conversation last night. This could all be some elaborate setup to catch me off guard, so I need to play my hand in a smart and measured manner if I have any hope of success.* I return to my private chamber and prepare myself for what is coming.

Midafternoon arrives and Lavina has been gone for

five hours, so I feel it is safe to leave. I gather my few belongings and stash them in a small travel pack before exiting my room and making my way down the hall where I enter Ruven's room. He is sitting on the floor surrounded by parchment and pencils.

"Ruven, I know you don't trust me, but I need you to listen and do exactly what I say. Can you do that for me?"

"Yes, Valessa."

"Good. I need you to gather only what you can carry, then put on your shoes and meet me in the great chamber. Do it now. Do it quickly. Wait for me there. Got it?"

Ruven nods, then stands and begins his preparations. I dash down the hall to Lavina's private quarters and begin searching the shelves lining the walls. *It should be here.* I'm losing hope of finding it when I spot it in the center of the shelf opposite her bed, a large blue lockbox inlaid with golden filigree. I rifle through the drawers of her nightstand, hoping the key is also in the room, and breathe a sigh of relief when I find what I'm looking for. My heart races as I take the ornate key to the lockbox, open it and peer inside. On a small decorative pillow sits a stone, pulsing as if beating. Even though I've never seen it, I know this is Dobbohk's heart. I lift it out of the box and wrap it in some linen before placing it in my pack and leaving the room.

When I enter the main chamber, Ruven is waiting for me. He looks puzzled and scared.

"It's okay, Ruven. We're leaving. We need to be far

away before Lavina returns. I know you're scared, but it's a matter of life and death. Please, just trust me." I attempt to comfort him. Ruven nods and stretches one hand out to me. I take it and we exit the cave together.

Outside stands Dobbohk, waiting in his usual position when he has no task to fulfill. He looks down at me and I gaze into his blue eyes. "We're leaving, Dobbohk. Come." Ruven and I walk into the trees.

After thirty paces, I glance back and see Dobbohk is following us. I'm glad he obeys my commands. He will be an invaluable asset on our journey. I take a last gaze at Vauxsard Overhang behind him. It's been my home for the past few months, and I didn't think I would leave it so soon. The journey before us seems daunting, but I'm happy we could make such a clean escape.

We must get as far from the Overhang as possible before Lavina returns, so I encourage Ruven to keep up the pace, walking several hours and taking no breaks. I've spent all my time in Sheonaetara in the Chatsraine Forest and have never seen the edge, but I intend to find a way for us to leave this cursed place. As dusk approaches, I hear the shrillest scream of rage I have ever heard, and I know Lavina has returned from foraging to find us gone. I know she will send Reaper after us, and I'm sure a terrible fate awaits if he catches us. I grab Ruven's hand and run faster than I ever thought possible.

Chapter 8

Ruven and I tear through the foliage as fast as our legs can carry us. Without losing a stride, I open my bag and look for a vial I brought with me. *Ah, here it is.* I remove the stopper and douse myself and Ruven in its contents. The foul smell of wolfsbane fills the air, which should mask our scent if Reaper picks it up. I'm unsure if it will work, but we must try something if we are to escape. Our best chance for survival is to leave the Chatsraine. We can't stop running, but I don't know how much longer we can keep it up because I can see Ruven tiring, and I won't be far behind him. We need a miracle, but I've never believed in such things.

I hear the snapping of twigs, and freeze, waiting for the nothingness I know will come any second. There is no fear, only disappointment for having failed Ruven. *How was I so blind to Lavina's true nature?*

"What are you doing? Don't stop. Come with me. I can help," says a soft and lilting voice.

I open my eyes and find a young woman standing in the trees to our right. She is tall and has feline-like features with one yellow eye and one blue eye and thin black slits for pupils. Below her eyes is a small pink button nose, and on top of her head sit two large triangular ears with tufts of fur extending beyond the points. Instead of hair, she has tawny fur covering her head and running down her arms, but unlike the Crimsonclaw, it does not cover her entire body. As I lead Ruven toward her, she smiles and I see she has sharp fangs, just like a cat. She reaches out, offering me her hand, which has retractable claws instead of fingernails. I take her hand and allow her to lead us through the woods.

"Who are you?" I ask.

"My name is Prizu. I only wish to help. You need to leave this place, but the exit is difficult to find. The magic will keep you wandering in circles, but I will take you to the forest's edge. I know the way. All you need to do is trust me."

If nothing else, my time with Lavina has taught me not to trust anyone I meet in this world, and now I'm being asked to trust someone I just met. But I know Ruven and I must escape the Chatsraine if we are to survive Lavina's wrath, so I follow Prizu. I only hope we can trust her and that she will help us leave. If following her is a poor decision, at least there is Dobbohk.

"How much further?" I ask. "We've been running for a long time, and I don't know how much farther we can go without rest."

"It shouldn't be too far now. She will not catch you, not today, not if I can help it."

"But what about the lion? She will send the beast after us."

"She will not. You have her golem. She will not risk the lion."

"How do you know? What makes you so sure we can escape?"

"My people have known the witch for some time. We have watched her and learned her ways. That's how we have avoided her all this time. We also know you have become somewhat talented at the gift. The witch will not risk pitting the lion against you. Not when you control the golem."

"That doesn't make me feel any safer. If you've been watching, then why have you not helped before?"

"We could not. My people are peaceful. We dared not interfere."

"Then why help now?"

"I could not live with myself if I did not."

We continue to run as fast as our legs will carry us until Prizu comes to an abrupt halt. I look around, knowing if we tarry too long, we will not survive the night.

I look at Prizu. "Why have we stopped? We must keep going."

"We are here."

"Here? There is nothing here. It's just more forest."

Prizu looks at me and smiles. "The well shrouds the Chatsraine Forest in magic. It creates a shimmer that masks the edge of the woods, making it appear as though the forest continues on. At this location, the shroud is thin which will allow you to traverse it, thus exiting the forest. Pass through here, cross the Wrentcona River and follow the road north. It should bring you to a settlement. You may find help there."

"If Lavina finds you, she will kill you for helping us. Come with us, Prizu."

"I cannot. A terrible fate awaits my people if we leave the forest. Those who leave never return. I will remain here."

A loud crack and blinding flash of light fills the air, stunning us. I see Lavina standing between two fallen trees. She has found us. My eyes widen in fear and I freeze.

"You will go nowhere, Valessa. You will return Ruven and Dobbohk to me here and now," Lavina says, her voice filled with rage.

"No. I heard your conversation last night, and I know you plan to sacrifice Ruven. I can't let that happen."

Lavina shrieks and walks toward us, and I ready myself for the fight I know will ensue.

Prizu grabs my arm and pulls me toward the edge of the forest. "You won't beat her. The only thing you can do is run."

I shake my head and turn my focus back to Lavina, who is approaching faster than I thought possible. I look at Ruven and see he is afraid. Prizu is right. If I have any hope of saving Ruven, I must flee now.

"What about you?" I ask.

"Just go. Run. Cross the river and don't stop. Don't even look back. Go. Now."

I grab Ruven's hand and turn to flee, but I can't just leave Prizu, who said her people were peaceful and abhor violence. She will be defenseless against Lavina. I have to try something, so I plant my feet on the ground, take a deep breath, clear my mind, and focus all the energy I can muster. It courses through my body and pools in my hands, which I raise and force away from my body toward Lavina, and she stops dead in her tracks. Her eyes widen with surprise, and I know I've done it. It's a simple stun spell holding her in place, but I don't know how long it will last, so I grab Ruven and turn to flee.

"Get out of here, Prizu."

I lead Ruven through the trees and pass out of the forest. The atmosphere feels different here. Gone is the oppressive nature of the Chatsraine. It's replaced with a remarkable sense of freedom. We make our way forward and ready ourselves to cross the river as I take one last look back at the Chatsraine Forest. I inhale when I see Lavina has already broken free from my stun. She is holding Prizu in a levitation spell. I know Lavina will kill Prizu for helping us escape. My eyes fill with tears, knowing there is nothing I can do to help her. I can only watch as Lavina tosses her aside with inhuman strength. Prizu strikes a tree and her lifeless body falls to the ground.

Lavina turns her gaze to me. "I will find you,

Valessa, and I will end you and everyone you hold dear. You will curse the day you turned on me, you little bitch."

I say nothing as I turn and make my way across the Wrentcona River with Ruven and Dobbohk. I don't know what fate awaits us now, but I'm glad to have left the Chatsraine behind.

Chapter 9

We have spent two days following the road northward, as Prizu instructed. At night we stop and rest, but the journey is exhausting none the less. We've eaten what little food I could bring and are tired and hungry, and I fear we won't make it to our destination if we don't find help soon. We march ever onward, hoping the next rise will reveal the reprieve we long for.

As the sun drops below the horizon, I know we must find shelter for another night, so we move off the road and into the trees to search for this night's safety. That's when I see it. A light appears through the trees ahead of us, shifting and flickering like a fire. I motion for Ruven to stay put and keep quiet, then creep through the foliage in the light's direction to determine if this light means friend or foe. I am wary of both, but we need sufficient food and shelter if we are to survive. In a few hundred yards, I arrive at a clearing containing a small structure made of stone, a tall steeple rising from its roof. The faint singing of hymns comes from the building, and I breathe a sigh of relief as I walk to the door. I knock and I'm greeted by a short, elderly woman dressed in a dingy gray habit.

"Can I help you, child?" She smiles at me.

"My companions and I seek asylum. We require shelter, food and rest for the night."

"You may find that here. Come in. Come in. We will prep some soup for you." She beckons me forward.

I motion for Dobbohk and Ruven to join me, and the three of us enter the church. Six nuns are kneeling on the floor, all of them elderly women dressed in gray habits like the woman who greeted me. At the far end of the room opposite the door stands a pulpit made of chestnut, which is occupied by an elderly gentleman in a black robe who leads the chanting. He must be the head of the congregation. No one looks at us. The woman who invited us in approaches him and whispers something in his ear, to which he smiles and nods. She then motions for us to follow her through a nearby door.

The room we enter smells wonderful. It's been two days since Ruven and I have had a proper meal. We drop our packs and take a seat at the table. The soup placed in front of us smells divine. Once we finish eating, the woman takes our empty bowls away, then seats herself opposite me at the table.

"Thank you. That was very good. What was it?" I say.

"You are quite welcome, dears. It's vegetable soup. We eat no meat here."

"Thank you for taking us in. We just need food and rest. We will leave in the morning."

"Nonsense. You stay as long as you need. We are always happy to help the less fortunate."

"We appreciate it. I'm Valessa and this is Ruven. What should we call you?"

"You may call me Almedha, Mother Almedha."

"Thank you, again, Mother Almedha. Like I said, we'll be on our way in the morning. We don't want to inconvenience you."

"Oh, it's no inconvenience at all, child. Our congregation chose this location to help unfortunate travelers such as yourselves. Now come, I will show you to your room for the night." She walks to the door. "Come children. No need to be afraid." She motions for us to follow.

I take Ruven by the hand and follow Mother Almedha into a short corridor, where she opens a door a few feet away. She smiles as we enter the room. Against one wall sits two beds, a small window sits in another. A single candle on the nightstand between the beds illuminates the room, revealing that the walls, floor, and ceiling are all made of stone. There is nothing else in the room.

"I hope this is sufficient," says Mother Almedha.

"It will do."

"Good. We serve breakfast in the morning. Simply come to the room we just left when you are ready. Now, there is just the matter of your golem. We ask that he remain outside. We don't know how well you control him and would rather not risk an incident. I trust you understand."

"I do. It's not a problem. Dobbohk will stay outside for the night." I turn my gaze to Dobbohk, who nods, then exits the room. I don't like the idea of not having him here with us, but he will still be close if we need him.

Mother Almedha smiles. "Have a good night, dears. Do try to get some rest."

"Thank you. We wish the same for you."

Mother Almedha leaves the room and closes the door behind her. I rush to it and turn the lock. I don't think it will do much good, but it makes me feel safer.

"We should get some rest, Ruven. I want to leave as soon as possible in the morning."

Ruven nods and hops in a bed as I blow out the candle, plunging the room into darkness, and settle into the remaining bed, my mind racing as I drift into slumber.

I wake with the sun the next morning, rubbing my face to wipe the sleep from my eyes. It felt great sleeping in an actual bed last night, making me hate we must leave. I don't know when we will have another restful night like the last. Ruven is still sleeping, so I take the time to reflect on everything I've been through. After growing up so meek, I'm amazed I've been able to overcome so much in such a short time. I wonder what adventures still await me and if I will ever return to the world I left behind.

A tap on my shoulder brings me out of my reverie.

Ruven has wakened, so I hop out of bed and put on my shoes to prepare for leaving.

"Make sure you are ready to leave, Ruven. I want to head out after breakfast."

Ruven nods. "I'm ready."

We make our way to the room from the previous night. No one is present, but someone has set places for us, complete with plates piled high with eggs, pancakes, biscuits, fruit and large glasses of orange juice. Ruven and I take seats opposite each other and begin eating. I wonder where the members of the congregation are. Last night, the church seemed so active and this morning it appears deserted. It's strange, but I decide not to dwell on it since we are leaving as soon as we finish breakfast.

After consuming everything on our plates, we prepare ourselves for the journey ahead. I don't know how much farther it is to the settlement Prizu mentioned or when our next meal will come, but we cannot delay our departure. The main room of the church is also empty. Ruven looks as puzzled as I am, but we continue to the front door. I push the door, and it doesn't budge, so I push harder and still nothing. My heart races as I look at Ruven and see his eyes widen in fear. I take a deep breath and throw all my weight into the door, but it still shows no signs of opening.

"Dobbohk," I say. "Dobbohk, we can't get the door open. Can you open it for us?"

Dobbohk grunts and I back away as the door shakes violently, but continues to stay sealed. He beats on the door with more force, but is still unsuccessful in opening it. It's as if some magical force is keeping it sealed.

"That is quite enough," says a voice behind us.

I turn and see Mother Almedha and the priest standing at the pulpit. "What is going on here?" I ask.

"You are causing a scene, child. There is no need for this."

"Open the door and we will go, like I said we would last night."

"I can't do that."

"You can't keep us here. Open the door."

"That will not happen, dear. You came seeking help, and we provided. You ate our food and enjoyed our hospitality and may continue to do so, but you will not leave this place."

The priest steps forward. The skin on his face appears wrinkled and his eyes clouded from age. "I am Father Vossler. At this establishment, we offer succor to those in need, but request payment for our services. Once you pay your debt, we will consider allowing your departure. We would have made this known to you had you asked, but you, like so many others, accepted the help we offered without question. Now, we grant you free range of the facility. When the time comes, we will let you know what we require of you in order to repay your debt to us." He and Mother Almedha disappear through a door behind the pulpit.

"What will we do now?" Ruven asks.

"I don't know."

"How can they do this?"

"I don't know."

We return to our room, where I take extra care to ensure the door is secure before crossing to the tiny window. I examine the window, which appears easy to open, but is not. No matter how much I try, I cannot unseal it, so I settle onto my bed to think. There must be a way out of here. We didn't come all this way to give up now.

It's late afternoon when I look at Ruven sitting on his bed. "Stay here. Don't open the door for anyone but me." He nods and I exit the room.

I'm determined to find an escape for us, so I make my way down the hall, checking each door as I go. They are all locked, except the one we ate in which has no window. I enter the main room and begin checking the windows. There are eight, two on either side of the door and three lining each wall. None of them open, but I didn't expect them to, anyway. I make my way to the pulpit, remembering the hidden door Mother Almedha and Father Vossler disappeared into earlier. It is so well hidden I can't even make out its edges, nor can I open it. I take a deep breath. We may have to work off our debt, like Father Vossler said.

I return to the room where we ate, thinking I might find something that can serve as a weapon within. I search the shelves and drawers lining the walls, but find nothing heavy or sharp. The only thing I discover is a strange looking key hidden in a drawer with a false bottom. Its entire length is black as crude oil. An intricate nine-pointed star adorns one end. Each point of the star ends in a thorn that is tipped in red. In the center of the star sits a tiny glass ball, similar to a marble, that contains a dark substance that twists and swirls like inky black smoke. The opposite end of the key has four prongs of varying lengths sticking up on one side of it. I pocket the key and sprint back to my room.

I knock twice on the door. "Open up, Ruven. It's me."

A few seconds later, he opens and I step inside, locking the door behind me.

"Did you find anything?" Ruven asks.

"No way out, but I found this." I remove the key from my pocket and show it to him.

He steps away. "Get rid of that."

"It is quite elaborate and was well hidden. It's obviously of great importance. Maybe it can help us get out of here."

Ruven backs into a corner as far from me as he can get. "Nothing good ever comes from something like that."

"How do you know that?"

He says nothing in response, just stares wide eyed until I put the key away.

We wait in silence until late evening, then make our way down the hall to dinner. Again, our food is waiting for us, but no one is present. We eat the same vegetable soup as the previous night before returning to our room and readying ourselves for bed.

I don't know how long I've been asleep when I hear it, low and distant. I sit up in the dark room and hear it again, the low rumble of murmuring. It's strange after seeing no one all day. Beside me, Ruven has heard it, too. He's sitting up, knees raised to his chest, rocking back and forth.

"Stay here," I say.

"No. Don't go, Valessa."

I ignore his pleas and exit the room. The murmuring is louder, but I can't make out what is being said, so I glide down the hall and into the main room. Here the voices are even louder, but I see no one as I scan the dark room. My eyes land on a sliver of light resting behind the pulpit, and I know it's coming from the hidden door I failed to find earlier. I nuzzle the door open to find a narrow set of stairs leading downward into a basement. I can hear the voices but can't see who is speaking, so I creep down into the shadowy room and hide behind some barrels and crates.

As my eyes adjust, a large circular room with a raised stone platform in the center appears before me. The room is lit by nine torches spaced around the outer walls. Father Vossler is standing behind the platform, wearing a dark tunic and hooded cloak. Seven figures stand in a semicircle opposite Father Vossler, all dressed in dark tunics and hooded cloaks. I assume these are Mother Almedha and the other nuns. Lying on the platform is a woman I've never seen before. She is bound and gagged, her eyes wild with fear.

Father Vossler raises his hands and speaks. "Sisters, we gather here tonight to both offer and accept a magnificent gift. We do as he bids and so we reap the rewards. We are blessed of late, for so many weary travelers have stumbled upon us, granting us many gifts to offer our God. He will be pleased. Amjir, God of Shadows, accept this gift we offer you here, for we are but your humble servants."

I watch as Mother Almedha steps forward and bows. "I have a modest request, Father."

Father Vossler nods.

"If it please the Lord, my skin grows thin and will be insufficient soon. Can we preserve this one so that I might make it mine own?"

"Of course, Mother. If there is nothing else, then it is time. We shall feast well tonight, sisters. Very well indeed."

I watch in horror as Father Vossler raises a large ritual knife above his head, then plunges it down into the chest of the woman lying on the platform. Her muffled screams pierce the air as he slices her skin and flesh from her chest to her navel. He removes her heart and raises it to his mouth, dripping red with the woman's blood. My eyes widen and my breath catches as he takes a bite of the quivering muscle. The sisters move in and begin sampling various parts of the woman's flesh and organs. I gasp and flee up the stairs.

"I knew that one would be trouble. After her. We must deal with her." Father Vossler shouts behind me.

I race up the stairs and through the door, slamming it shut behind me. It won't stop them, but maybe it will slow them down. I dash down the hall and into the room.

"We're leaving, Ruven. Now!"

Ruven springs off his bed and grabs my hand. "What happened? What's wrong, Valessa?"

"We have to go."

We run out the door and down the hall, freezing dead in our tracks when we enter the main room. Father Vossler and the seven nuns are there. Huge grins spread across their bloody faces.

"You go nowhere," Father Vossler says.

"You can't stop us."

"Look around, you foolish child. Your power, the golem, is outside. He can't enter and so he cannot protect you. We outnumber you, and you are defenseless. Stand down and return to your room. You're only making things worse for yourself and the boy."

"You're right. I am outnumbered." I bring my balled fists together in front of my chest. "But I am far from defenseless."

I bring my fists apart while uncurling my fingers and a tiny spark of flame dances between my palms. The congregation, save for Mother Almedha, backs away from me.

Mother Almedha points a gnarled finger at me. "Stop her. She has the key."

"Ruven, the door!" I shout as the nuns lunge in my direction.

I follow on Ruven's heels as we sprint for the door, opening my right hand and pushing it out in front of me. A jet of fire springs forward, so hot it melts the bolts on the door. The door falls open and we rush through it.

I look at the golem. "Dobbohk, help."

Dobbohk steps between us and the congregation as Ruven and I make a break for the road, but I stop and turn back.

"What are you doing?" asks Ruven.

"I have to do this, Ruven. Just wait there."

I walk toward the church, determination in my step. When I'm ten feet away, I stop, take a deep breath and focus all of my energy, drawing it from my very core. I raise my hands and shove them out in front of me. A huge orange fireball flies forward, causing a massive explosion upon contact with the church. The screams of the congregation fill the air as my head spins and my legs fall weak. Ruven rushes over to me and catches me before I fall. He slings my arm over his shoulder as we turn to the road and away from the nightmare of the past two days. As we reach the road, I glance back at the ruins of the church and see I have reduced it to rubble, thick black smoke billowing into the sky. Beside the church lies a pile of smoldering stones. In my haste to leave, I forgot Dobbohk's heart. It was still in the church when it exploded, forcing the same fate onto the golem, which fills me with sadness. Then I see it, there in the trees, and my sadness turns to curiosity and fear. Just inside the treeline stands a figure wearing a dark, hooded cloak. I can't see its face, but I know it is watching us. A shiver runs down my spine as Ruven and I head northward down the road.

Chapter 10

The fireball I conjured to destroy the church is the most powerful spell I have cast, and it has taken its toll on me, leaving me dizzy and lightheaded. My legs quiver and it is now a chore to keep them moving. It's a miracle I'm still conscious. Were it not for Ruven, I fear I would be lost. It feels like we have been walking forever, Ruven supporting me the whole way. I don't know how much farther we must go or if we will even make it. As day bleeds into night, I drift in and out of consciousness.

Ruven jars me as I slip back into darkness once again. "Stay with me, Valessa. We're almost there. Look."

I raise my heavy head and peer into the gathering dusk ahead of us. I think I see light brightening the horizon, but my current state makes me unsure.

"Just a little further," Ruven says.

As we grow closer, I see the source of the distant light is a town lit up with hundreds of candles and torches. A nine foot tall stone wall dotted with guard towers encircles the town, and a large wooden gate bars the road into the settlement.

A guard posted above the gate raises his hand as we approach. "Halt. Come no further."

"Please, we need help," says Ruven.

"We have sealed the gates for the night. Return on the morrow."

"Please let us in. My friend needs help. She can't keep going. Please. I beg you."

"Listen, kid. We don't know you. We've sealed the gates and they will remain so until morning. You may enter then if you so wish, but not before. Now, away with you."

Ruven sighs in defeat. The clop of hooves over dirt rises behind us, followed by the soft nicker of a horse.

"Heyo, Darby. I'm weary from my travels and seek a warm bed for the night. Might I enter, good sir?" says an unknown voice.

"Aye, Quimby. Glad to see you have returned, my friend. Hold a second and I'll see they open the gate for you," says Darby.

The heavy gate swings open, and Quimby urges his horse past us.

"May we enter as well?" Ruven asks.

"I already told you, we don't know you or your companion. You can enter in the morning like the rest of the riffraff. Now beat it, the both of you."

Quimby looks at us. "Let them in, Darby. I will vouch for them. If anything untoward occurs, it'll be my neck on the line."

"So be it."

Ruven gathers my weight and proceeds into the town as darkness overtakes me.

I awake later lying on a soft feather bed in a small room. Beams of sunlight stream through the only window in the room, and Ruven sits on a chair beside my bed.

"How long was I out?" I ask.

"Only through the night."

"Well, I'm thankful for that. Where are we?"

"The Silver Swan Inn."

"We don't have any money. How did you get us a room?"

"That guy at the gate last night, Quimby, he paid for us."

"Why would he do that?"

Ruven shrugs. "He says he knows who I am."

I give Ruven a puzzled look. "And who are you?"

"Quimby said he would explain things to you himself. He said to have you meet him at the Drunken Seahorse Tavern next door when you woke up."

I swing my legs over the edge of the bed, panic rising inside me. "Why? What's going on?"

"He says things are stirring. Remarkable things." Ruven leaves the room.

I dress, exit the room, and head downstairs. People stare as I wind through the lobby of the inn and join Ruven on the cobblestone street outside. I take in the surrounding activity. It's been so long since I've seen civilization that I'm overwhelmed at first. People walk the streets, making their way to some destination or another, while others stand behind stalls laden with goods they are trying to sell. I can only focus on one thing at a time, but it's such a welcome change from everything I have experienced since finding myself in this world.

Ruven takes my hand. "Come, Valessa." He pulls me in the tavern's direction.

Wooden tables fill the tavern, each with four chairs, while dirt and straw litter the floor and the smell of ale fills the air. Ruven leads me to a secluded table in the far corner of the room where an ordinary-looking man sits. I assume this is Quimby. His straight, golden brown hair ends right below his ears. He smiles, his clear honey eyes surrounded by laugh lines and round cheeks topped with dimples. He's wearing traveling attire in shades of brown. As Ruven and I approach, he motions for us to take a seat. I hesitate, but Ruven smiles and nods, spurring me to lower myself into a chair opposite the man.

"Ah, it's so good to see you up and about, fair lady," Quimby says. "Would you care for something to eat?"

I nod, and he motions to a serving woman who brings a tray laden with bread, fruit and mugs to our table. I take a hunk of bread and a mug. "Ruven said you wanted to speak to me. He said you know who he is. You're the reason they admitted us to the town, and you paid for our room at the inn. Who are you? Where are we and what do you want from us? What is going on here?"

My voice breaks.

Quimby smiles. "Stay calm, girl. You have nothing to fear from me. I can help you, both of you."

"I will determine if you can help us or not after you explain yourself. Start talking."

Quimby chuckles. "Where shall I begin? First, an introduction, my name is Quimby Carver, and it is a pleasure to meet you. Where are we, you ask? We are in the seaport town of Wolford. If you like, I can show you around a bit before you depart."

"And what do you expect in return for this help?"

"The only thing I ask is that you allow me to accompany you when you leave town. I require nothing else in return."

"I don't know you, so why would I let you come with us?"

"You are right to be wary. It's sometimes best to distrust others. But I mean you no harm, Valessa. I only wish to help. I know a great deal about this world, and I may prove an asset to you on your journey."

"Did Ruven tell you my name?"

Quimby nods.

"What makes you think you could be an asset to us?"

"I'm a minstrel who travels back and forth across the land, spreading music and news to the locations I visit, and so have gained a vast amount of knowledge about the places and people of the world. I know much about its history as well and can impart this wisdom to you, thus granting you the insight you may require to survive what is coming."

"I've read books. I know enough."

"Books are wonderful, but they cannot give the understanding needed to complete your journey."

"You keep talking about my journey and what is to come. What are you referring to? What do you know that I don't?"

Quimby looks around. "Finish your meal and we will return to your room at the inn. It's best we continue our conversation away from prying eyes and ears."

After eating, the three of us return to our private room at the Silver Swan Inn. I lock the door and settle on the bed. "So you were going to explain about a journey and things to come." I glare at Quimby.

"Indeed," he says. "Everything is because of him." He points a finger at Ruven.

"I don't understand."

"You will. Ruven here happens to be someone of great significance and in so being he needs to get somewhere important. You and I will see that he gets there."

I roll my eyes. "I've known Ruven for quite some time and he has yet to present himself as someone of great importance. He's done nothing significant since I met him. Hell, he barely speaks most of the time and would be dead if I hadn't saved him. He didn't have the courage or the skills to even get here without me. You must be daft, Quimby. I'm sorry, but what you're saying is not possible, and I'll be going now."

I rise, ready to leave, but Ruven grabs my arm and

pulls me back down into a chair. "You must listen, Valessa. Everything will make sense in time."

"Yes, Valessa," says Quimby, "listen and gain clarity. I'm not trying to fool you. Through my travels, I have heard a great many tales. I did not think them true until I saw the two of you at the gate last night. Hundreds of years ago, there was an uprising which led to a terrible war. This uprising began when an ancient force awoke and granted a primitive people the mental fortitude of the more advanced. With their new found intelligence, these beings enslaved the people of this world, and those they could not enslave, they destroyed. Among those destroyed were the Elves, who we believe to be extinct, the result of the genocide of their people for their resistance to enslavement.

"But it's possible they have fled instead, hiding in some faraway place yet to be found. For this one here," he points a finger at Ruven, "this one is Ruven Keldan, the lost elf prince who has long been thought dead. Rumors said he was in hiding somewhere, but there was never any evidence to prove them true. The subjugators believe he can lead them to the elves if they are indeed hiding. They believe he may know where to find them, so they made the minstrels of the land aware of his description and instructed us to keep an eye out for him."

"But I know nothing about the Elves," says Ruven. "For as long as I can remember, I've been with the witch of the Chatsraine. I don't know how I ended up there or where my people might be. The witch viewed me as a servant, and so I was her dutiful servant and, in return, she kept me safe."

I shake my head. "This is too much. The two of you want me to believe Ruven is some long-lost elf prince and his people are thought to be extinct, but in actuality, they are probably just hiding?"

Quimby and Ruven both nod, serious looks on their faces. All I can do is laugh. The story they are telling sounds unreal.

"So let's say I believe you. Why have these subjugators, as you call them, not found Ruven since he left the forest?"

"I believe they don't yet know of his heritage," says Quimby. "But now that he has entered society, they will learn of him soon, for they have spies everywhere and are always looking for those that oppose them."

"So what do we do?"

"I will return home," says Ruven.

"Great. Home. Do you even know where that is?"

Quimby leans forward in his chair. "I do. Across the continent, far to the east, lies the ancient Elven city of Naren Thalore. That is where you must go. I don't know if it is occupied or not, but I'm sure if it is empty, it will provide us with clues of where its residents have gone."

"How do we get there?" I ask.

"I know the way. If you will have me, I will take you."

"Fine. I accept your help, Quimby."

"Very good."

"You also mentioned something about things to

come. What is that about?"

"Oh, there are many things brewing in the world. Tales abound of peoples who are weary of being opposed, and murmurs of revolution ride the wind, a great uprising, and cries for freedom. In time, war will come once again. I believe you both have a part to play in this."

"Ruven, maybe. But I'm not from this world. These aren't my problems. I only wish to return home."

"No one has ever appeared in this world the way you did, which leads me to believe that you have a role to play in the struggles to come, as does Ruven," says Quimby.

"I'm no one special. I'm just a lost girl looking for a way to return home."

"You have already proven yourself invested in Ruven's survival, so accompany us to Naren Thalore. Once we arrive there, you will be free to do as you wish, Valessa. Neither Ruven nor I will try to stop you. Besides, if there is some way for you to leave Sheonaetara, the Elves will surely know of it."

Ruven nods. "Yes, once I have returned home, you will be free to go if that is what you wish."

I look from Quimby to Ruven and back again. "Okay. I'll help you get to Naren Thalore, and once you're there, I will search for a way home."

Quimby clasps his hands and rises. "Great. Now that we've settled that, would you care to tour the town?"

"Sure."

We leave the inn and head out onto the cobblestone

street once again, making our way through a crowded market which contains numerous stalls with many things available for purchase. Quimby delights in pointing out all the things Wolford offers, which include food items, clothing, potions, medicine and other concoctions. I'm in awe of all the goods on display and wish I had the coin to make purchases. We leave the market and wind our way through streets lined with small brick houses, each identical to the next. People fill every street, scurrying back and forth on some errand or another. In front of several of the houses we pass, children play and pets sun themselves. It's almost enough to make me forget the constant danger I've faced since arriving in Sheonaetara.

After passing through the Residential District, we make our way down a sloping street. In the distance lies a harbor filled with ships of different sizes, some with sails raised to catch the wind, while others are being loaded or unloaded with goods at the docks. Steep white cliffs topped with beautiful green grass encircle the harbor. One cliff juts out into the bay and holds a gold and white lighthouse. The sea rolls into the harbor and out again. Gentle waves crested white above clear cerulean water. Beyond the harbor, water rolls toward the horizon as far as the eye can see.

"It is quite a beautiful sight," I say.

Quimby nods. "Oh, yes, it is indeed. That is the Crescana Sea, a major transportation route, especially for ships carrying goods to the capital. The Saltstone Bay, named for the stark white cliffs that surround it, provides a safe harbor for ships to anchor. The salt in their stone gives them their white color and their name. Gaullita Lighthouse guides ships into and out of the harbor during times of low visibility, such as night or during storms. They named it after the family that maintains it. The Gaullitas have kept the lighthouse for hundreds of years."

Ruven smiles. "Almost makes you forget the troubles of the world."

"Make no mistake, my dear boy, these people are oppressed, just as others who are far less fortunate. The ships that come into the bay carry materials that are taken to the Sweatshop District, where they fashion many goods to be sent back out on another ship bound for the capital. The sole purpose of Wolford is to provide for the capital."

I gasp. "That's terrible. To think such a beautiful place can have such a dark purpose."

"Indeed. As the hour grows late, we will make our way back to the Drunken Seahorse for some supper, then it's off to bed for you two. We set out at first light on the morrow."

"It's so beautiful and peaceful here. Can't we stay longer?"

"It's best if we don't. The longer we stay, the more likely it becomes that someone gets wind of Ruven's true identity."

He turns and heads back in the direction we came from, Ruven and I following behind. When we reach the tavern, we seat ourselves at the table in the corner once again. A serving woman brings ale and meat pies, which we devour. Once finished, we return to the street. Ruven and I turn toward the Silver Swan next door, as Quimby turns in the opposite direction.

"You're not staying at the Silver Swan?" I ask.

"You two go get some rest. I will see you in the morning."

"Where are you going?"

"That is my concern, not yours." He disappears into the crowds.

"Well, how do you like that, Ruven? He wants us to trust him, but he runs off without telling us where."

Ruven shrugs. "Let's just go get some rest, Valessa."

We head into the Silver Swan and climb the stairs to our room. Ruven undresses and dives into bed. I do the same, doubting I will sleep, having learned so much today.

"Why didn't you tell me who you are?" I ask.

"I didn't know. I was young when the witch took me in. The Chatsraine is all I know. I remember little of my time before Lavina. She always made it clear I was in danger. I didn't know that danger might come from the very woman that raised me, though. I didn't even know I was a prince until Quimby told me."

"And you believe him?"

"I don't know. He seems to know what he's talking about, but he's a stranger. He could lead us to Naren Thalore, or he could deliver us to my enemies. But if we don't go, we'll never know, so let's travel with him for now."

"Okay, Ruven. I don't know him, but I know you and I trust you. If you wish to travel with Quimby, that's what we'll do, at least until he gives us reason not to. Let's get some sleep." I blow out the candle on my nightstand.

"Good night Valessa."

"Good night Ruven."

Chapter 11

Ruven and I wake the next morning to the sound of knocking. I spring out of bed and rush to the door.

"I said we were leaving at first light. I brought breakfast," says Quimby from the other side of the door.

I breathe a sigh of relief and open the door to allow him entry. Quimby enters carrying a tray laden with eggs, bread, and fruit.

"I brought you something to eat before we head out. I also brought you something to wear, Ruven, to help conceal your identity." He sets the tray on the table, then tosses a long black riding cloak to Ruven. "Eat, dress, then meet me downstairs. The day is waking, and it's time we set out." Quimby leaves the room.

I close the door and see Ruven has already helped himself to breakfast, so I join him. We finish our meal before making ourselves ready for the journey ahead, which I suspect will be long and arduous. Once on the street, we follow Quimby to a stable near the East Gate, where Quimby speaks with the stable master, then returns leading a white and brown paint, followed by two stable boys, each leading a horse.

Quimby pats the paint's neck. "This is my most faithful companion, Breezy. I spoke with Darby and secured a horse for each of you as well. I thought they might make our journey a little easier."

One stable boy hands Ruven the reins of a bay with a white stripe down its face, while the other stable boy hands me the reins of a beautiful dapple gray.

"I know Ruven has never ridden and believe it is likely you have not either, Valessa, but it's easy. Just put one foot in a stirrup, then swing your other leg up over the horse's back and settle into the saddle. I had Darby choose horses that are patient and have calm temperaments. Both of you should be fine." Quimby mounts Breezy to show how it's done.

Ruven and I do as we're told and swing ourselves up into the saddle of our horses.

"What are their names?" I ask.

Quimby points a finger at the bay under Ruven. "That one is Dava, and yours is Sky Blossom. Now, I gathered us some supplies for the journey." He pats the saddlebags slung over Breezy's rump. "We have many, many miles to travel before we reach our destination."

The three of us ride through the East Gate of Wolford and onto a wide dirt track, which is mottled with hoof prints and grooves from the wheels of wagons. Trees line both sides of the road as it cuts through woodland. This forest is quite unlike the Chatsraine. It's not gloomy, but bright and cheery, and the songs of birds fill the surrounding air. I take one last look at Wolford as we make our way down the road and gasp. In the trees just outside the gate, stands the same dark hooded figure I saw as Ruven and I fled the church. Again, I can't see its face, but I know it is watching us. I don't know who it is, but I'm sure we're being followed now. I decide not to mention this to the others.

We ride until sundown before stopping. Just within the trees, we make camp for the night. My body aches from spending all day in the saddle, and I welcome the respite. Quimby builds a small campfire, providing us with light and warmth. The three of us sit around it and nibble bread and jerky. It's been a long day, so after eating, we settle onto our bedrolls for the night. As I drift off to sleep, I can't help but feel as though we are being watched but shrug it off as an aftereffect of seeing the hooded figure again as I close my eyes and welcome some much needed sleep.

The next day, we rise with the sun and prepare for the next leg of our journey. After eating our breakfast ration, we break down camp and mount our horses before Quimby leads us out of the woods and back onto the road.

After a few hours of riding in silence, I urge Sky Blossom up beside Breezy. "How long will this journey take?"

Quimby shrugs. "An uneventful trip from Wolford to Naren Thalore can take anywhere from two to three months, depending on how fast you ride and how often you stop. It can take longer if a traveler meets trouble along the way."

"Two to three months?"

"Yes. I hope nothing waylays us. The sooner we get young Ruven to Naren Thalore, the better."

"I agree. Can we take this road all the way there?"

"The Golden Road does indeed connect the West Coast with the East Coast. In a few day's time, the forest will end and you shall see our first obstacle."

"What obstacle is that?"

"The Golden Road leaves the forest and crosses an open plain. Once we are free of the trees, the Cresford Range shall darken the horizon. The Golden Road dips southward and skirts around the southernmost tip of the Cresford Range. Within three weeks' time, we will be past the mountains. Then it's another six weeks to the city."

"Is there no faster route to Naren Thalore?"

"There is no safer way to get there."

"You said no safer way, so there is a faster way then?"

"Oh, there is a faster way, but that is not a route one should want to travel."

I fall back to ride beside Ruven. I can't believe the trip to Naren Thalore will take so long. It's only day two and I already feel the ache of muscles I'm not accustomed to using. I don't want to think about spending that much time on the back of this animal.

"He says the journey could take as long as three months if we meet trouble on the road," I say.

Ruven sighs and we continue onward in silence.

Every day since leaving Wolford passes in the same manner. We rise at first light and have a quick meal, then break down camp and mount up to proceed further down the Golden Road, inching ever closer to Naren Thalore. We ride until dusk, then set up camp off the road. Another quick meal follows, then it's off to bed, just to repeat more of the same when the sun breaches the horizon again. Most of our time passes in silence, and so the days crawl by one after another.

It's midmorning on the fourth day when we leave the forest. The land opens up into a great plain, shimmering a vibrant green in the morning sun. Ahead of us, a vast mountain range rises out of the earth, reaching upward into the sky where cloud and fog shroud the mountain peaks. This must be the Cresford Range that Quimby mentioned. It makes the horizon look ominous.

Quimby points into the distance. "There lies our first obstacle, the Cresford Range. It's as beautiful as it is dangerous."

Ruven and I gaze at the massive mountains in awe. I have seen nothing like them before, and a sense of foreboding washes over me as we begin our trek across the plain laid out in front of us.

We ride in silence as usual for a few hours before Quimby sings in a somber, melodic tone.

Come gather round and I'll spin you a tale
'Tis one that is old and made grown men wail
All was quiet in the midst of night
When the mountain burst and spewed forth a light,

The sky grew bright as fire did rain
Man, woman, child knew not the bane
With power that none would dare to defy
The beast so large rose into the sky
Death and destruction was all they could see
Forever more it is called Mount Misery

When Quimby finishes his song, Ruven bursts into applause. Quimby bows atop Breezy and smiles.

"That song seemed so sad. What is it about?" I ask.

"It's about a mountain in the northernmost reaches of the Cresford Range. They say that long ago, the mountain exploded in a rain of fire, and when this happened a great and terrifying beast was born into the world and this monstrosity caused death and destruction of a magnitude never seen. Rumors hold the behemoth was the torch that ignited the Great War which decimated the land and its peoples, causing thousands to become enslaved by the subjugators and others to be exterminated by them. Many believe extermination was the fate of Ruven's people. No one has seen an elf in hundreds of years, and it is widely accepted that they are extinct."

"Then why are we taking Ruven to this Elven city if there are no elves?"

"Naren Thalore was the last great stronghold of his people. If any of them still exist, the clues to finding them may lie there."

"Has anyone ever gone there and looked for these clues?"

"Oh, many have gone in search of clues and many

are never heard from again. The few that have returned report that they found nothing of interest there. Perhaps there are clues and perhaps there are not. Perhaps only Ruven's people can interpret the clues, if these clues exist at all. At least that is what I would do if I left clues to be found. Wouldn't want just any old goat showing up at my hidey hole, if you catch my drift."

"I suppose it makes sense when you put it that way."

We continue the rest of the day's journey in silence.

We take four days to journey through the forest and another three days to cross the plain. A week after leaving Wolford, we finally make it to the base of the Cresford Range where the Golden Road dips to the South.

"I told you before, Valessa. The mountain pass is not safe. We will continue on the Golden Road," says Quimby.

"But why spend two weeks going around the mountains when we can cross over them in a few days?" I ask.

"As I have stated, crossing over the mountains is not safe. The weather would be the least of our worries. It is dangerous."

"What makes it so dangerous? Would you just tell me that?"

"I don't know."

"But I thought you were well traveled. That's what you said. You told us you had seen much on your travels and you know things about the world that could help us reach Naren Thalore."

Quimby sighs. "I do, but no one knows what lies in that pass. People enter the pass and are never heard from again. There's a reason they call it the Passage of Bones."

"I thought the reason for our journey was to get Ruven to Naren Thalore. This will get him there faster."

"Yes, but we also want to get him there alive, you stupid girl."

"For the love of all the Gods, would the two of you please stop arguing!" Ruven says.

Quimby and I freeze and look at Ruven. He has never spoken in such a manner before, and I can't recall ever hearing him raise his voice.

"You are wasting time with all the fighting. Quimby, you say we should follow the Golden Road around the mountains. Valessa says we should take the Passage of Bones through the mountains. What about how I feel? What about what I want? Do I even get a vote?"

"Of course, dear Ruven," says Quimby. "What would you have us do?"

"I've seen what Valessa is capable of. I believe she may conquer whatever lies in the pass, and the pass is a much quicker route than the Golden Road, therefore I say we take the pass."

Quimby hangs his head. "I see I am outnumbered on this. Very well. We will take the Passage of Bones and see what it has in store for us."

We mount our horses and proceed forward, leaving the Golden Road behind. The pass is narrow and requires that we ride single file. It winds its way upward into the

Cresford Range. As we ascend, the air grows colder and snow thickens on the ground. We rise ever upward into the mountains, into the cold thin air, and it becomes harder to breathe. As the wind and snow swirl around us, I see what has given the pass its foreboding name. Skeletons of all shapes and sizes, human and animal, litter the surrounding ground. Snow buries some, while decaying pieces of wood I assume were once wagons bury others. The thought that corpses carpet so much of the pass sends shivers down my spine.

"This is horrible," I say.

"I told you it's called the Passage of Bones for a reason. People do not return. I hope we are not the next to disappear here," says Quimby.

"Look. Over there." I point into the swirling snow.

In the distance, a dim light brightens the pass ahead of us. It flickers like fire, and I wonder how it stays lit in this wind and ice. We approach the light and find a tall stone wall blocks the pass, which reflects the firelight from a large torch jutting out of the mountainside. Opposite the torch lies the entrance of a large cave. The sounds of grunting echo throughout the cave, filling me with dread as I wonder what mess we have stumbled into now.

I watch in horror as a massive creature stomps out of the darkness within the cave. The creature is tall and robust, and given his height and build, I assume he's not human. He's much taller than any human I've ever met. His entire body ripples with hard muscle, and his skin has a slight pale blue tint to it, giving him a wintery appearance. Thick black facial hair that reminds me of sheep's wool covers his wide square jaw. His nose is square and wide as well. Disheveled sable hair tops his head, then runs down his back, narrowing into a sharp V above the tawny striped furs he wears. He stares at us with piercing cobalt eyes, so piercing that I feel he is looking straight into my soul.

"Who are you?" He asks.

His great booming voice echoes off the surrounding peaks and startles the horses, causing them to rear. Quimby and Ruven ride the rear out, but I fall out of the saddle and land on my back in the powdery snow, throwing the creature into a fit of laughter.

"It's not funny," I say, picking myself up out of the snow.

"You speaking to me in that tone, are you?"

"I am. Who are you? What are you?" I ask.

"How dare you stumble into my abode and start demanding answers from me?"

"Now, now," says Quimby, "there's no need for anyone to get hostile right off the bat."

The creature shifts his gaze to Quimby. "Now this one thinks he can speak to me as well, huh?"

"I meant no offense, my good sir." Quimby's voice is smooth as butter. "We were only passing through is all. We mean you no harm. One such as yourself demands respect, and we should all stand in awe of you. Ogres are so very rare in Sheonaetara. What should we call you, great one?"

"Ogre!" Ruven and I say in unison.

"Aye, I'm an ogre. Name's Eizrog," says the ogre.

Quimby bows. "Ah, Eizrog, the three of us are quite pleased with the opportunity to make your acquaintance. Please excuse my companions. They are not so well versed in the culture of polite society as I."

Eizrog turns his icy blue gaze to Quimby. "I like you," he says, pointing a massive finger at him. "Why don't you come in and have a rest? I'll even let you bring your disrespectful runts. How does that sound?" Eizrog retreats into his cave.

"Why it is rather kind of you, my wise friend?" Quimby motions for us to follow him into the cave.

The cave is enormous and empty, save for a pile of furs on the floor by one wall and a large fire in the center. I'm surprised by how warm it is inside, so warm that one might forget about the raging snowstorm outside.

Eizrog plops himself down on the pile of furs and motions for us to take seats on the stone floor around the fire. "You are free to enjoy the warmth of the fire, but I fear I have no food to spare for you," he says. "I must keep what food I have for myself. I never know when I might get another meal."

"That is quite all right, friend. We came well prepared," says Quimby.

I roll my eyes and shake my head. "What kind of host doesn't feed his guests?"

Eizrog grunts. "That one is rude," he says, pointing in my direction.

"Please excuse her, sir," says Quimby, "she knows

not what she says." Quimby leans over to me. "Please stop insulting him. You do want to leave here, I assume."

"Are you saying he killed all those people whose bodies litter the passage?"

"I cannot answer that." Quimby turns back to Eizrog. "It's settled then. We thank you for the blessing that is the warmth granted by your fire, and we will eat our own food. We won't take too much of your time. If you'll only open the gate, we'll be on our way, good sir."

Eizrog lets out a bellowing laugh that echoes around the cave. "That I cannot do. Go back the way you came."

"But we came so far, sir. It would be quicker and safer for us and the horses if we continue onward."

"Sorry, tiny man. Like I said, I won't be doing that."

"Why?" I ask. "Why can't you let us pass? Are you keeping us here to serve as your next meal? Is that it?"

Eizrog smiles at me, then releases his bellowing laugh to echo through the cave once more. It's unsettling given the size of his mouth and the teeth that lie within. He leans forward. "You might find it hard to believe, you little brat, but I don't eat people."

"I do find that hard to believe, given the bones lining the passage."

"It is true those bones belong to unfortunate travelers. But it was exposure to the elements and injuries that caused their demise, not me. That is the truth."

"I will only believe that once you allow us to be on our way. You're big and you look strong. I'm sure you could tear a hole in the wall and let us pass?"

"Okay, girl, since you want to be so persistent. Long ago, they tasked me with protecting and maintaining this passage to prevent travelers from reaching the valley on the other side. They erected this wall for that purpose. The Passage of Bones exists because unfortunate travelers thought to shorten their journeys, but, being unable to pass, had to return the way they came and fell before they reached the base of the mountain. I am not the monster you think I am. I'm only doing as I was bid and will not harm you. But I tell you what, since you're so spunky, I will allow your passage, but only if you perform a minor task for me. I bid you bring me a very special, very rare item."

"Who do you keep referring to? Who instructed you to keep the gate here?" I ask.

"Them that own the world now. They make the rules, and I do as I'm bid so I can live in peace."

"If the oppressors charged you with preventing people from passing, then why allow us to pass when we return? Why risk their wrath?" Quimby asks.

"Oh, I do not fear their wrath, tiny man. I give you my word that should you provide the service of bringing me the item, then I will provide you with the service of allowing you to pass."

"Fine. Let's say we believe you will keep your word," I say, "what stops us from going down the mountain and taking the Golden Road around to the other side? Why should we return after leaving this place?"

Eizrog smirks and points at Ruven. "Well, since I

want that item, your quiet friend there will stay here with me until you return."

Ruven's eyes widen and he shakes his head. What fate may befall him if we leave him here? I don't wish to consider it.

"What if we refuse?" I ask.

"If you refuse my offer, then you are free to stay here unharmed until the end of your days. The quiet one will not leave until I get the item I desire."

"We could just kill you here in your cave and be done with you all the same," I say.

"You don't frighten me, little girl. I am an ancient being. My people are few and very rare. Killing one of us would see you cursed and shunned until your death, if you even succeed in the first place."

Quimby places a hand on my shoulder. "He's right, Valessa. It's well known that one does not kill an ogre. Doing so would grant you a lonely life, no friends, no help, just you alone in the world forever."

I rise to my feet. "I refuse to agree to your terms. We will take our friend and leave the way we came."

"You won't." Eizrog shakes his head, icy blue eyes peering at me. "Your friend will stay here with me. If you choose to leave, so be it, but you won't be taking the quiet one with you unless you do as I have bid."

"If you won't allow Ruven to leave with us, then I will kill you. I don't care how terrible the consequences are, you will not keep my friend here."

Eizrog cracks his knuckles, all the while staring at me. "You may try, small fry."

Quimby grabs my arm and holds me back. "Don't do this, Valessa. You won't succeed, and he will kill us all if you attack him."

I stare at Eizrog, stunned because I know both he and Quimby are right. Deep down, I know attacking this creature would spell our doom. It would mean we failed our mission, and that I had failed Ruven. Heading off on some mission to locate a rare item may add a considerable amount of time to our journey, but we have no choice. It's a task we must undertake if we are to see Ruven delivered to his homeland. An immense feeling of defeat washes over me as I realize Eizrog has bested me. We have lost and must now do his bidding in order to resume our journey and complete our task. The fear on Ruven's face makes me hate myself for dragging him into this and for giving in to Eizrog. I hope Ruven understands. Quimby's face is full of resolve. He knows we have no choice and has accepted our fate. I look at Eizrog, sitting on his pile of furs, looking as smug as ever. He knows he has beaten us.

"Fine," I say. "We will do as you wish. Quimby and I will go retrieve your item. Any idea where we might find it?"

"Far to the south lies a great expanse of sand called the Twisting Desert. Somewhere within the desert stands a small village. The village's inhabitants are the ones that hold the item. That is where you shall find it," says Eizrog.

"And what is this item you so desperately need?"

"It's a goblet, very ornate, carved entirely from red

diamond."

"A cup. Got it. How do you even know this cup exists?"

"I've heard marvelous stories, girl, and I want that cup."

"What can you tell us of this desert?"

"I know nothing of the desert except that it exists."

"Is there a trick to getting down the mountain that will save us from the fate of the others?"

"Don't get lost or injured." Eizrog laughs.

"I'm warning you, Eizrog, if you harm a single hair on Ruven's head, I will see that the day we return is your last."

Eizrog grunts. I embrace Ruven in a deep hug, then follow Quimby out of the cave. Once outside, we mount our horses and turn them back toward the Passage of Bones.

"Tell me you know how we can get back to the Golden Road," I say.

"I know many things, dear girl. These people panicked and got injured or their mounts got injured or wagons broken. Slow and steady is the key here. Always keep your wits about you. Now just follow me."

Placing a hand against the mountainside, Quimby urges Breezy down the path. I urge Sky Blossom to follow, and we begin our descent. Quimby keeps his hand on the side of the mountain throughout the entirety of our trek, all the way until we reach the vast green plain far below. We turn south and head off in search of the Twisting Desert

Chapter 12

Once back on the Golden Road, I bring Sky Blossom beside Breezy. It's great to be out of the frozen environs of the Passage of Bones.

"After seeing what lies in the pass, I didn't think we would see the plain again, yet here we are," I say.

Quimby smiles. "It's easy if you stay calm and go slow. Panicking only causes mistakes and injury. Keep one hand on the mountainside at all times so you don't get too close to an unseen cliff. If one can do these simple things, then he can always get back down the mountain. Most travelers lack the discipline though."

"Well, I'm glad to have you with us then."

I smile at the bright shining sun, hanging yellow in the clear sky like a giant sunflower upon a vast blue field. My thoughts are with Ruven. I hope leaving him was not a mistake and that he will be safe with Eizrog. My thoughts turn back to the task at hand, and I spur Sky

Blossom to pick up her pace until she is moving at a smooth canter. The breeze on my skin feels refreshing, like a dip in a cool pool on a hot day. I don't know how long it will take us to retrieve the ogre's goblet, but we must not tarry. I hear Breezy break into a canter behind me, and soon, Quimby is riding beside me.

"You know, for someone who's never ridden before, you ride that canter very well," he says.

"Thank you."

He gives me a single nod. "Well, we want to make good time, don't we?"

"I'm eager to complete this errand and return to Ruven."

"The Twisting Desert is a day's journey south of the Cresford Range. Even at a gallop, it takes time to get there. Rushing can lead to injury and is not wise. Don't worry. Ruven will be fine with Eizrog."

"How do you know that? Because the ogre gave us his word?"

"In my travels, I've seen and heard many things, but I know so little about ogres. They are extremely rare. Most texts describe them as wise, but I have no firsthand experience of the matter. I know the ones who set Eizrog on his task, though, and it would displease them if he allows us through the pass. This goblet must be more important to him than fulfilling his duty to them. That fact alone tells me Eizrog will do nothing to jeopardize getting it. He knows if we return with the goblet and he has harmed Ruven, he will not get this thing he so deeply desires."

"What do you know of this desert?"

"Enough to know I'm not thrilled to be going there."
Quimby emits a weak chuckle.

"So you've never been there."

"No one alive has been there. It's called the
Twisting Desert, because the landscape shifts and
changes, making it impossible to follow any landmarks
within it, so those who enter never come back."

"Then why would Eizrog send us there to get his
stupid cup if he knows no one returns?"

"He hopes we don't. He hopes it's a suicide
mission."

"Why would he keep Ruven and send us to die?"

"He may know who Ruven is and plans to turn him
over to the ones that seek him."

"Did you know this was a dead end when you
agreed we leave Ruven there?"

"I did, but what choice did we have?"

"You are unbelievable." I pull hard on Sky
Blossom's reins, bringing her to a swift stop.

Quimby slows Breezy and trots back to where I sit
motionless in the road. As he approaches, I dismount and
run over to Breezy. I grab Quimby and yank him off his
horse. He tumbles onto the ground and stares up at me
from his place in the dirt, a look of alarm on his face. I
lose myself, falling down on top of him with my fists
clenched. My entire being is fire stoked by my rising
anger. My right fist connects with Quimby's nose and he
laughs at me, causing me to pound on his chest, each
blow landing with more force than the last.

Quimby continues laughing. "Stop, Valessa."

"Don't laugh at me!"

"You need to calm down. I know you're angry, but this rage will not help us complete our mission." He pushes me off of him and rises to his feet.

I leap to my feet. "How could you do this, you bastard? If you knew people never return from the Twisting Desert, how could you allow me to agree to this impossible feat? What will become of Ruven if we don't return? You should have let me kill the ogre and be done with it."

"I couldn't allow that. Ogres are so strong they're almost invincible. Attacking Eizrog would only lead us down a dark spiral of disaster, which we don't need. It would have ended with our deaths, all of us. I told you this already."

"What would you have us do, then?"

"The only thing we can do. We must complete the task set before us. Just imagine the songs they will sing of us when we return. Surviving the Twisting Desert will make us famous beyond belief." Quimby beams.

My mouth drops open. "I don't give a fuck about fame or glory or riches. I only wish to survive, and I want to see Ruven survive. You endanger that by not giving me proper intel. The only reason I allowed you to join us is to provide information, to help us. This is not helping us, you asshole. I should kill you where you stand and take my chances on my own." I ball my hands into fists as fire rages inside me.

"You're upset. The things you say are out of anger."

Quimby flashes me a charming smile. "Take some time to cool off, and we can discuss your concerns later."

I take a deep breath and release it in one big whoosh before mounting Sky Blossom. Quimby mounts Breezy, and we set off again at a brisk canter. The miles roll away under us as the horses glide over the plain, carrying us to our meeting with destiny. We spend the rest of the trip in silence, the beating of hooves the only sound on the air. I can't bring myself to look at Quimby because I know doing so would only stoke the fire still raging inside me. I think of Ruven on the mountaintop, alone and frightened, and I hate myself for leaving him there.

As dusk falls upon us, we stop and set up camp for the evening. It's risky to continue on in darkness, and the horses need rest. We eat in silence. I'm lying on my back, gazing up at the stars like so many bright, tiny dots on a dark canvas when Quimby breaks the peace.

"You could apologize, you know," he says.

After our fight and spending the rest of the day without a word uttered between us, this is how he addresses me. I can't believe the audacity.

I roll my eyes in the darkness. "I don't owe you one."

"What makes you think that?"

"You joined us, saying you could help and you're not. All you've done is put us in danger by withholding valuable information. You said you could advise us about the world, then you kept quiet about a crucial decision. You have not proven yourself worthy. I owe you nothing."

"That is unfair. I'm not the reason we've found ourselves in this predicament. If you care to remember, I suggested we stay on the Golden Road even though it was longer. It was you and Ruven who voted against that, which led us up the Passage of Bones, and that landed us here. If it wasn't for me, you would have attacked Eizrog and you both would be dead, lying in the Passage of Bones until you turned to dust. You should thank me."

It's infuriating that I cannot disagree with his assessment. I sit up, pull my knees to my chest, and wrap my arms around them. I feel ashamed of my behavior, but I refuse to apologize.

"I understand your reasoning, but I won't thank you, nor will I apologize. I still believe you could have done more to help our situation with Eizrog."

Quimby settles himself onto his bedroll. "Fine. I will accept that. Let's get some rest and we'll continue on in the morning."

I continue staring into the fire, the orange and red flames flickering like they're dancing in the cool night breeze. In the distance, I hear the howling of wolves, which reminds me of my time with the Crimsonclaw Nightwalkers. It reminds me of Alkin, and I think maybe being his mate would not have been the worst fate for me. I'm saddened by the thought of the beautiful lives that were lost, cut down before their time by that wicked witch of the Chatsraine. *Has Lavina given me and Ruven up as lost or does she still hunt us? Who was the hooded stranger I overheard her with? And who is the cloaked figure following us?*

The snapping of a nearby twig jolts me from my thoughts. I look at Quimby, but he is fast asleep, having not heard a thing, so I peer into the darkness, concentrating with all my might, hoping I can glimpse what might lurk there. I hear nothing more, but for a split second, I think I see movement in the bushes just outside our camp, so I watch and listen even more intently, trying to pick up something, anything, that may help me identify what might prowl the night nearby. After several minutes of staring into the darkness without seeing or hearing any additional clues, I decide it was only the sound of the horses as they graze nearby. I'm certain if anything dangerous was near, they would alert us to its presence. I take solace in this thought, settle myself onto my bedroll, and drift off into dreamless sleep.

Quimby and I awake with the sun the next morning. After breaking down camp, we mount our horses and ready ourselves to continue our task. We journey southward until midafternoon. With the sun aglow in the cloudless sky above, we top a small rise and I get my first glimpse of the Twisting Desert laid out in front of us. All I see is golden orange sand stretching into the distance in every direction. There are no signs of life, fauna or flora, as far as my eye can see.

"Seeing the desert makes me feel even more hopeless," I say. "How will we do this?"

"Have faith, Valessa. Don't give up. We must never lose hope. You don't know how much depends on it. It's so much bigger than you or me or Ruven."

Quimby urges Breezy forward and I have Sky Blossom follow. The task before us seems more impossible as we inch ever closer to the sea of sand in the distance. As we near the boundary between plain and desert, the idea of finding anything in the nothingness ahead becomes more daunting. Fear rises inside me. I'm afraid I will fail and never see Ruven again and that this desert will become my tomb.

At the edge of the plain, just where the Twisting Desert begins, Quimby comes to a stop. "We will camp here for the night." He dismounts and begins setting up camp.

"But why? We still have several hours of light left. We should keep going."

Quimby shakes his head. "Valessa, I know you want to get back to Ruven as soon as possible, but it would be best if we wait until first light to enter the desert."

I ignore Quimby and drive Sky Blossom forward. Let Quimby stop if he wants to. I will complete this task with or without him.

"Valessa, stop!"

I turn in Quimby's direction. "How dare you raise your voice to me after what you've done?"

"You can disagree with me, but just hear me out. Please. After I've said my piece, you can continue. I won't stop you."

"Speak fast then," I say through clenched teeth.

"Valessa, once we enter the desert, whether daylight or darkness, we will be lost. There is no doubt about that. But I believe tis better to be lost in daylight than in darkness."

I sit atop Sky Blossom, staring down at Quimby. I hate to admit it, but what he says makes sense. Darkness would only make our impossible task that much more impossible. I dismount and join him in setting up camp. I suppose it will feel good to have a decent rest. We hobble the horses then lay out our bedrolls before setting about gathering what wood we can find to build a fire.

As afternoon turns to dusk, I return to our little camp with my meager haul of sticks, twigs and dried grass. I drop it onto the small pile Quimby has amassed and take in our surroundings one last time as the light fades. I see nothing but sand ahead of us and grass behind us. As I stare down the road, I think about Ruven and hope he's okay. That's when I see a hooded figure top the rise on the road behind us. The distance makes it hard to distinguish any features, but I'm sure it's the same person I saw at the church and again when we were departing Wolford. *Who is this mysterious person and what does he want?*

"Quimby."

Quimby raises his eyebrows as if to ask what.

"Do you see that figure coming over the rise there?"

"I do."

"I think he's been following us."

"What makes you think that?"

"Before Wolford, when Ruven and I were leaving the church that waylaid us, he was there. I saw him again as we left Wolford all those days ago. I'm sure it was the same person both times."

"That is quite curious. Do you have any idea who it could be?"

I shake my head. "I do not. It could be several people. I have made some enemies during my time here. At camp last night, I swear I heard someone or something lurking in the darkness, just out of view. No matter where we go, I always feel as though unseen eyes are upon me."

Quimby takes a deep breath. "That is quite concerning indeed. We shall keep an eye out for this mysterious shadow you have. Since he has yet to attack, maybe he means you no harm."

The rest of the evening passes in silence as I reflect on past, present and future.

Chapter 13

As the sun wakes the following day, so do we. We pack our paltry belongings, then mount our horses and take our first steps into the Twisting Desert. The desolate landscape with its golden brown sand is beautiful and for a few fleeting moments, I forget how dangerous it is. Great mounds of sand, like tiny mountains, surround us. As the ground passes under Sky Blossom, I note the ripples in the sand caused by the gentle breeze on the air. Above us, the rising sun paints the dim sky a bright pale blue. The day wears on, and it becomes hotter, and I grow weary.

"How will we find anything out here?" I ask.

"I'm not sure. We need a methodical way to search this wasteland."

"Well, at least our footprints will show us where we've already searched. That should prevent us from searching the same area multiple times."

Quimby sighs and shakes his head. "That will never

work. Look behind us."

I glance behind us and see the hoofprints of the horses have already disappeared, covered by the shifting sand. Even the dunes have changed size and shape since we set out. No landmarks dot the terrain with which to find our way, but Quimby does not appear alarmed by this.

"How will we find one tiny cup amid all this sand with nothing to guide our way? Do we just wander aimlessly and hope to stumble upon it?"

"I'm thinking we travel in one direction every day. Today we head south, tomorrow we head back north, but several paces to the right. Then so on and so forth until we find something that can point us to this goblet."

"But how will we know which direction we are traveling in?"

"The sun will guide us, dear girl. It's the only reliable landmark we have out here."

"So, using the sun, we search in a grid pattern? Is that the best way to find what we are looking for?"

"I think it is. There is no way to know what direction we are heading in other than the sun."

"Right. So we wander through an ever shifting barren landscape and hope we stumble into something."

"Well, if we will wander through this desert for the rest of our lives, I suppose it's best to hope we stumble upon something."

I laugh. "When you put it that way, it sounds ridiculous."

Quimby chuckles. "That's just my opinion, mind

you." He nudges Breezy into a trot. "Let's go have one last adventure, shall we?"

I nudge Sky Blossom into a trot and together; we start our trek across the ocean of sand laid out before us in search of something we may never find while the surrounding sands change the landscape into something new as each moment passes. This is how we pass the next two days, stopping to rest as the sun sets each evening.

"I know I'm stating the obvious, but if we don't find something soon, we're going to die out here," I say one afternoon.

Quimby sighs. "I know."

It's the third day of our wandering the Twisting Desert. The horses are tired, their pace slowed to a mere crawl. We were careful to ration our supplies, but the days were hot and long, and we consumed the last of our water yesterday. We hoped to find what we seek before that happened. Hope is great, but it won't save us from dehydration and certain death. We both know this.

I study our surroundings, searching for some sign that shows a break from the monotony that is the desert sand all around us. As I scan the horizon, a bright flash in the distance catches my eye, like clear sunlight reflecting off a shiny silver mirror. I blink and rub my eyes in disbelief before gazing into the distance once again. The same bright flash occurs once again and I breathe a sigh of relief.

I point into the distance. "There's something over there."

Quimby squints toward the horizon in the direction I have pointed out. "I don't see anything."

"Wait and watch."

The flash occurs again, and Quimby releases a cry of delight. "I can't believe it."

"I don't know what it is, but it has to be a good sign, right?"

"Good or bad, it's the only sign we've had in days. Let's check it out."

We turn our horses in the flash's direction and make our way over the sand. As we approach the general area where we saw the shining beacon of hope, we see the most remarkable sight. Nestled on the side of a dune is a tiny village. The buildings are small and made of orange brown bricks walls and thatch roofs. An oasis lies in the center of the village, complete with palm trees and a pond filled with cattails. The water looks refreshing, and I want to run and jump into its depths. But this would be reckless when we don't know what inhabits the settlement, so as inviting as the water looks, we wait and watch.

A few minutes of quiet observation passes and we have seen no people, so we assume the village is empty and advance. It's then that we realize the village is occupied after all. Animals of all shapes and sizes fill it, but they aren't animals one would expect to find in the middle of a desert. These are the animals one would keep as pets, such as cats and dogs. It's the most peculiar thing I have seen. It's puzzling.

"Something isn't right here," I say.

"Indeed. Be on your guard, Valessa."

We lead Breezy and Sky Blossom into the oasis and hobble them at the water's edge. They dip their heads and suck up the water. Taking this as a sign the water is good, Quimby and I do the same. It's unbelievable how cold the water is in the heat of the desert sun. We drink, then splash the cool water on our sunburnt skin to wash the dirt of the last few days off. It does wonders to quiet the burn caused by our time in the sun.

Once we have our fill, Quimby and I turn our attention back to the village, freezing in our tracks. Among the animals filling the village are several small creatures. They stand only three feet tall, their skin a shade of orange brown, like the desert sand. Many have skin patterned with spots or stripes, while others have no markings. They stare at us with large dark brown eyes. Short triangular ears flop on the sides of their heads like the ears of a dog. Loincloths fashioned from palm fronds are the only clothing they wear. Most of them have short protrusions extending from their heads, like spines or horns.

"What are they?" I ask.

"I don't know. Never seen anything like them."

"Are they friend or foe?"

Quimby shrugs. "Best we tread carefully until we find out."

Quimby takes a few steps forward and raises his hands. "Hello there. We mean you no harm."

One creature steps in front of the others, accompanied by a second. Quimby stops.

"Who are you?" I ask.

They give me a bewildered look. "We be Gobines."

"My name is Valessa and my friend here is Quimby. What he says is true. We are not here to cause you harm."

"I be Cheenik and Grilt be me wife," says the Gobine, motioning toward the one standing beside him.

Cheenik looks at us with large brown eyes. One of his ears has a ragged edge, as if torn in a struggle. Dark brown stripes run down his back and across his arms. Six horns adorn his head arranged in two rows of three. Grilt's eyes are smaller than Cheenik's, one of which is covered with an eye patch. Her dark orange brown skin has no markings, and her ears are whole. She has a spine protruding from her brow above each eye. They're almost cute with their small stature.

I bow. "It's very nice to meet you."

Cheenik looks at me, then glances at the Gobines gathered behind him. "Take them. Bind them. Bring them." A sneer spreads across his face.

My heart races as every Gobine we can see bolts forward much faster than Quimby and I could have expected, and before we have time to react, we are both ensnared in nets woven from palm fronds. We struggle to break free, but in our weakened state, we cannot muster the strength required to sever the strands of the nets. Our time in the sun and sand has rendered us helpless. Cheenik laughs at our futile attempts to gain freedom. He knows we are not strong enough. The Gobines drag us toward the largest of the buildings in their tiny village.

"What are you planning to do to us?" I ask.

Cheenik smiles. "I do nothing. Stossi gonna fix you."

"Who or what is Stossi? What do you mean, break us? Where are you taking us?"

"Calm down, girl," says Quimby. "This is no time for panic. We must keep our wits about us if we hope to escape."

Quimby is right. If I let panic and fear consume me, I can't think clearly enough to avoid whatever fate awaits us, so I take deep breaths and calm myself to prepare for what is coming as the Gobines drag us into the gigantic building on the outskirts of their village. We enter a rectangular room that is warm and dimly lit. My eyes adjust to the darkness within the room and I see orchids in various sizes, shapes and colors, line the walls of the room, filling the air with their scent. I don't recall seeing any flowers in the oasis and wonder where the Gobines have gotten so many beautiful flowers in such an uninhabitable environment. Rows of benches line a center aisle, reminding me of pews in a church. The Gobines place us on an altar at the far side of the room, then leave the way we entered.

"What do you think this place is?" I ask.

Quimby shrugs. "With the layout and this altar, a place of worship maybe."

"What do you suppose they intend to do with us?"

"I haven't the slightest idea. I guess we will find out, though. It's not like we can go anywhere."

Quimby and I lay in our nets on the floor until the

room darkens with the sunset. Two Gobines enter and light candles spaced throughout the room, causing the room to brighten. Once they accomplish their task, they exit, but return a few minutes later, followed by the rest of the Gobines. The creatures take seats around the room, filling it with their excited chatter. After a few minutes, an eerie silence descends upon the room and I give Quimby a puzzled look, to which he shrugs. Looking at the altar, I see the source of the sudden hush that has invaded the room. Cheenik and Grilt lead an old, weathered Gobine with a hunched back through a door to the right of the altar. She gazes at the gathered Gobines and I see age has clouded her eyes. Her skin is pale and covered with patchy gray spots, her head covered with dozens of tiny bumps like the skin of a toad.

Cheenik and Grilt lead the elder Gobine to the center of the altar, then leave her. She raises her hands above her head, and every Gobine in the room kneels. She must be an important member of their society. As she lowers her hands, she nods and the Gobines rise and reseat themselves.

"What is this?" I ask.

Cheenik walks over to me. He squats and gazes at me. "You don't speak. Stossi gonna fix you." He nods in the altar's direction.

I look at Quimby. "What does he mean, fix us?"

Quimby sighs. "I wish you would stop asking me. No one comes out of the desert. I have no answers for you."

Stossi looks at us lying on the floor. "This gift," she

says in a quiet, shaky voice. "I fix. Make new."

A few Gobines step forward and drag Quimby onto the altar, a look of alarm plastered on his face. Stossi approaches him and shoves something into his mouth. Quimby's eyes widen in fear, then his face twists in agony.

My mind comes alive with fear and anger. "You're not fixing him. You're killing him. He's in pain. Can't you see that?"

Cheenik laughs. "We no kill. Only fix. You watch. You see."

I look at Quimby and can't believe what I see. He lies on the floor of the altar writhing in pain as his body elongates and his limbs shrink before my eyes. I watch in horror as Quimby's arms and legs disappear into his torso and his hair vanishes to be replaced with scales. I rub my hands against my eyes, thinking I must be lost in the throes of some fever dream brought on by heat and dehydration. When I open my eyes, Quimby is gone. Lying on the altar in his place is a long coiled snake with shimmering golden green scales. I'm shocked by the disbelief of what I have just witnessed. It cannot be real. It must be some illusion.

I turn on Stossi. "What did you do with him?"

Cheenik steps in front of me. "Stossi fix him. Stossi fix you next."

A Gobine picks snake Quimby up and takes him away, before I am dragged onto the altar. I look at the Gobines seated in their pews, and terror fills me. My mind races as I try to think of a way out of this predicament. I attempt to tear the net apart, to no avail. Stossi approaches and shoves something into my mouth. It tastes bitter and its texture is smooth and thick, like a mouthful of peanut butter. I try to spit it out but try as I might; it is hopeless. It melts down my throat, and I understand why Quimby didn't spit it out. As the seconds march into minutes, the Gobines grow more agitated and murmuring rises in the room.

Cheenik approaches me. "What's this? Why you not fix?"

"I . . . Um . . . I don't know." I look into his deep brown eyes.

Stossi raises her arms once again, and the room falls quiet. "This one peculiar." She motions for Cheenik to release me.

"This one no fix?" He asks as he bends down to free me from the net.

Once free, I leap to my feet. The Gobines jump in their seats as if startled, puzzled looks on their faces. "What is this fixing you keep talking about? What did you do with Quimby?"

Cheenik steps forward. "You not in charge here. You not speak out of turn."

"You can't stop me." I snap my fingers.

The room fills with gasps of alarm and wonder as a bright blue flame erupts on my fingertips. Every Gobine face freezes in surprise as they leave their seats and bow in the aisles. Cheenik bows beside me. Stossi is the only Gobine not in complete awe of me at the moment.

"What . . . What is happening?" I say.

Stossi approaches me. "Human not do magic. Never. You magic so not fix. You not human."

"Oh no, I assure you I am human. Someone taught me some things. That is all."

"You special." Stossi takes my hand. "Come. We talk."

Stossi leads me through the door to the right of the altar and into a small room. A few small tables and chairs, a bed, a cooking area and many books fill the room. It seems this is her private quarters. She motions for me to take a seat in the chair opposite a desk, then takes a seat on the other side of the desk.

"Who be you?" she asks.

"Umm . . . My name is Valessa."

"You be God?"

"No, no. I'm no God. Just a girl trying to save a friend. Just a girl trying to survive." Tears build in my eyes as I think of Ruven alone with Eizrog.

"You not cry."

"Sorry. Just thinking of my friend. He's alone with a stranger, and I can't save him unless I complete an impossible task assigned to me by this stranger."

"What task?"

"It's nothing. I'm not even sure why I've told you so much already."

Stossi pours a glass of liquid and hands it to me. "You drink."

"What is it?" I ask as I take the cup.

"Tea. You drink. You feel better."

I take a sip. It has a fruity sweet taste like fruit

punch. "Why don't you tell me about your people?"

"We be Gobines."

"I know that already."

Stossi glares at me. "This place be Scorchhorn. People come. We fix. We keep."

I remember animals filled the village when Quimby and I arrived. I think about how no one returns from the Twisting Desert and how I watched Quimby turn into a snake right in front of me, and it all makes sense. People enter the desert and some of them perish, but some don't.

"When you say you fix people, you mean you turn them into animals. You keep them as pets. Those animals we saw when we arrived, they were all human once."

Stossi nods. "We fix."

"What do you mean, fix?"

"We feed paste. Splendid Rutilum. It's magic mushroom. Frees soul animal. We fix."

"The way you speak is so frustrating. Let me see if I understand. You feed humans that stumble into Scorchhorn a paste made from a magic mushroom called Splendid Rutilum, and it somehow transforms them into the animal that represents their soul. Then you keep them as pets."

Stossi nods.

"Why didn't I turn into some animal?"

"I not know. You be magic. Must be."

"Yeah, well, I don't feel magic. Can you turn my friend back into a human? Will you allow us to leave this place?"

Stossi nods. "First you tell what task."

I see no reason to divulge my secrets to this creature, so I look around the room in silence. There are many shelves stacked with many artifacts. Wonder upon wonder lines the walls of the tiny room. That's when I see it and my breath catches in my throat. A beautiful red goblet sits among several silver bowls and cups. It reflects the candlelight in magnificent shades of pink and red. I blink a few times, not believing what my eyes are seeing.

I point at the goblet. "Do you mind?"

Stossi shakes her head.

I pick up the goblet and twirl it around in the light. "Do you know what this red material is?"

"No. Glass not break though."

Thoughts flood my mind. *If this goblet does not break, could it be red diamond? Is this the object Eizrog tasked us with retrieving? Will this set Ruven free and see us continue our journey?*

"I don't suppose you would let me have this."

Stossi nods. "You want cup? Take cup. You magic God girl. You have anything you want."

"Anything?" My head swims with wishes I might demand of these Gobines.

Stossi nods again.

"Okay. I want Quimby back. But I want him returned to his original form. Is that possible? Can you turn him back into a human?"

"Yes, yes." Stossi nods.

"I want this cup, along with food and water, for our return journey through the desert."

Stossi picks up a quill and begins making notes on a parchment.

"I want our horses returned to us unharmed and all your pets returned to their human forms and released."

I don't know where Stossi's boundaries lie, but I can't depart with Quimby and leave all these other people to suffer their fate without trying to rescue them.

"I have remedy prepared. Take time. You wait." Stossi leaves the room.

I breathe a sigh of relief, unable to believe how quickly the situation has turned in my favor. Stossi is so willing to give me everything I'm asking for, and I'm filled with joy at the prospect of returning to Ruven and continuing our journey. As I reflect on recent developments, questions flood my mind once again. *Why does Stossi keep saying humans don't do magic? I saw Lavina perform many spells during my time with her. Hell, she taught me many spells as well. Are we not both human? Why do these Gobines believe I am some God? Are they going to let us go? Will they be true to their word and let the others go as well? How will we find our way out of the desert? But the biggest question of all... What's the catch? There's always a catch.*

Stossi enters the room, disrupting my reflection. "All arranged," she says. "Remedy ready in morning. You feast and sleep till then."

She motions for me to follow her and we exit the room, making our way outside. The Gobines have arranged tables around a bonfire, and the smell of food cooking fills the air, causing my stomach to do somersaults inside me. I had forgotten how hungry I am. Stossi leads me to the largest table and seats me opposite Cheenik and Grilt before taking the seat beside me. Servers bring food and drink and lay them out in front of us. Everything looks and smells wonderful. I eat under the watchful eyes of the Gobines. The servers clear the plates once we finish the meal and many of the Gobines retire for the night. Cheenik and Grilt motion for me to follow them, leading me across Scorchhorn to a small house.

"You stay here," Grilt says. "You guest my house."

She shows me to a room. As I take in my surroundings, she leaves, closing the door behind her. I'm left in the room, alone, wondering if this is some trap. I lower myself into bed and drift to sleep as thoughts of returning to Ruven dance in my head.

Chapter 14

The beams of sunlight through the small window make me feel refreshed the next morning, so I ready myself for the day, then leave the room in search of my hosts. I don't find them in the house, so I make my way out into the bright desert sun. No one is around. Not a single Gobine or animal seems to be in the village. My heart races and I break into a sweat as thoughts of abandonment fill my mind. On the verge of tears, I hear a familiar sound coming from the large ritual house on the edge of the village. I enter the building to be greeted by a joyous surprise. Stossi kept her word regarding the return of Quimby. He sits at the altar, no worse for wear, entertaining the Gobines with his melodious voice.

Task was doomed long before it began
We set out across the hot desert sand
Sun shone bright as we rode the land
Searching for a treasure to rescue a man
Stumbled on a village as we lost hope

Never to find what he sent us to seek
The outlook certainly did seem bleak
For soon they quickly tied us up in rope
Taken by surprise and fed a strange paste
Twisted me up and made my body ache
When it was over I had become a snake
Memory I would rather forget with haste

The Gobines cheer when Quimby quiets. It's clear they enjoyed his performance.

"Bravo!" I shout from the back of the room.

Everyone looks at me as the room falls silent.

"Oh, dear Valessa," says Quimby. "I hear I have you to thank for my freedom."

"Don't mention it." I approach the altar.

"Yes, yes. But thank you all the same."

"The others?" I ask, turning to Stossi. "Have you freed the others as well?"

Stossi looks at me with her clouded eyes and nods. "Remedy ready. Freed soon."

"Very good."

Grilt approaches and hands me a bowl of fruit, which I eat before joining Quimby on the altar.

"So, how did you convince them to turn me back?" he asks.

"It really took no convincing at all. The paste had no effect on me. I got angry and conjured a tiny flame, and now they think I'm some God or something because they don't believe humans can perform magic."

"Well, it is true. It's very rare for humans in Sheonaetara to use magic. Most of those who do are never proficient at it."

I look at Quimby in disbelief. It seems I'm some special freak from another world that can do magic when others can't.

"Regardless, it helped. They agreed to free not only you, but all the humans they're holding here."

"Remarkable."

"I have more remarkable news than that."

"Do tell, Valessa."

"I found a beautiful red goblet on a shelf in Stossi's private quarters. It appears to be carved out of gemstone. It may be the red diamond goblet Eizrog sent us out here for."

Amazement passes over Quimby's face. "Absolutely astounding how our luck has changed. How are we to get back, might I ask?"

"Don't worry. I'll take care of that, too."

"All human free now," Cheenik says as he approaches. "You leave. They leave."

I nod. "Yes, they will leave with us. And our horses?"

Cheenik smiles. "They ready. Have food and water."

I smile. "Great. We have one more tiny problem that requires a solution."

"What you want?"

"Is there someone in Scorchhorn who knows a way back to the plain? It would be terrible if we had to wander aimlessly again and ended up meeting our demise regardless of your help." I grasp Cheenik's hands in my own.

"Yes, yes. You get guide. I take you meself."

"That's fantastic. Give me a few minutes to take care of something and I'll meet you both outside." I rise to my feet.

Quimby and Cheenik smile as they turn to leave. I make my way to Stossi, who is standing just outside the door to her private quarters, wearing a huge, toothy grin. As I draw closer, she reaches out and I take her hands. Together we enter her private room, where she wraps the red goblet in cloth before handing it to me.

"How did you come by such a gorgeous object?" I ask.

Stossi smiles. "We find. Many treasures in sand."

"Well, again, thank you so much. You don't know what this means to me." My eyes fill with water.

"Welcome. God girl, you not cry. As she waves me toward the door, she says, "You do good things. You go. Safe travel."

I exit the building into the bright midmorning sun to hear cheering. My eyes adjust to the brightness, and I see many people looking at me and cheering. These must be the humans, newly freed of their captivity. I smile and wave at them.

"Savior. Savior. Savior." They chant in unison.

"Oh, no. No, no, no. I'm no one special." I shake my head from side to side.

Quimby laughs atop Breezy. I mount Sky Blossom. It's been an interesting journey. I only hope our return is less eventful. Quimby lifts Cheenik into the saddle in front of him and we set out on our return trip through the

Twisting Desert, followed by the humans.

With Cheenik's guidance, we return to the great plain by dusk. Quimby and I wandered the desert for two days and I can't believe how quick the trip back is. We stop just inside the desert's edge and Quimby lowers Cheenik to the ground.

"Will you be okay traveling back by yourself?" I ask.

"Yes. Yes. I be fine."

"Well, travel safe, friend. Thank you."

"Yes. Yes." He disappears into the sand.

I turn to the others. "You are free to return to your friends and families. No need to thank me. Just go live your lives."

They cheer as an elderly man steps forward. "You don't know the service you have done us, milady. We are, all of us, so appreciative. If the world was different, we would celebrate your coming. But alas, to do so in the world's current state would cause strife and death. Be well, milady. Safe journeys to you."

I watch the group disperse in different directions, then turn to Quimby and see he has dismounted and is setting up camp.

"Wait. What are you doing? We have to get back." Desperation coats my voice.

"It's getting dark, Valessa. We'll head out at first light. Same as when we came this way four days ago."

"We have what we came for, Quimby. We should get back as soon as we can."

"It's not up for negotiation. I'm not risking Breezy

by riding in the dark, and you shouldn't risk your mount either. If you want to go ride around blind, then I won't stop you."

Once again, Quimby is right, so I dismount and begin setting out my bedroll. Quimby builds a small fire and I settle onto the ground beside it. I look into the dark, starless sky. It looks like a sea of inky black oil. A gentle breeze rises and I smell nature in the air. It's quiet, and before long, I drift to sleep.

As the sun rises the following morning, we break down camp, mount up and begin our two-day trek across the vast green plain on our way back to the Passage of Bones and Ruven. We ride in silence for the entire journey. My thoughts are always with Ruven. It's been a week since we left him alone with the ogre. I hope he is safe, and I hope Eizrog keeps his word and allows us safe passage.

When we arrive at the Cresford Range, I'm so eager to get through the Passage of Bones that I can't contain my excitement at reuniting with Ruven. The temperature declines as we ascend the mountain, but the weather at the summit is milder than our last visit. Quimby and I dismount and hobble our horses next to Dava, who remains where we last saw her. Her dark brown coat speckled with fresh snowflakes.

"Hello?" I call out, but the only answer is the echo of my voice. I turn to Quimby. "Where are they?"

Quimby shrugs and proceeds into the cave. I enter behind him and see the cave is empty. Eizrog and Ruven are nowhere to be found.

"I can't believe this." Panic rises inside me.

"Let's take a seat and wait. I'm sure they will be back soon." Quimby comforts me.

I sit near the fire, which, although unattended, is raging, and pull my knees into my chest, wrapping my long arms around them, worrying about Ruven. I shouldn't have left him alone with this Eizrog, an unknown entity. Has some harm come to him? I could never forgive myself. Hours pass and still there is no sign of Eizrog or Ruven.

Dusk settles outside, and I leap to my feet. "I'm going to find Ruven."

Quimby grabs my wrist. "I can't let you do that. It will be dark soon. You'll freeze to death if you go out there now."

"I can't keep sitting here waiting for them to return. I have to find out what Eizrog has done with Ruven."

"Valessa, we don't know that Eizrog has done anything with Ruven. We must await their return. It's the only thing we can do."

I sit back down, knowing Quimby speaks the truth. We wait as the night deepens outside the cave.

A few hours after darkness sets in, heavy footsteps enter the cave and I see Eizrog and Ruven. Ruven throws his arms around me, pulling me into a deep embrace. Eizrog stands at the mouth of the cave, looking stunned.

Ruven releases me, and I rise to my feet. "Surprised to see us return?" I look Eizrog in his cold, cobalt eyes.

"I, uh . . . What . . . It's not that. Just didn't think you would make it back so soon is all."

"No." I step in his direction. "You didn't expect we would return at all. You sent us out there knowing it was a one-way trip. Whether or not you choose to admit it, you sent us out there to die. Why? Why would you do that?" And why keep Ruven here if you sent us to our deaths?"

Eizrog laughs. "Does it matter? You've returned."

"It matters, ogre. Answer my questions."

Eizrog seats himself by the fire. "This is my house, and I don't take kindly to your tone. Did you find the object I asked for?"

"We did."

Eizrog's mouth drops into a gape. "Let me see it."

I remove the goblet from my pack and unwrap the linen, holding it up for Eizrog to see. His eyes widen as the firelight dances off the goblet's exterior.

"Give it to me. Give it to me, please."

"No." I wrap the linen back around the goblet and stow it in my pack, and Eizrog gasps. "Here's what's going to happen. We're going to stay here tonight in the safety of your cave. You will provide us with the hospitality we deserve for retrieving your stupid cup. When the morning comes, you will allow as passage through the wall and upon doing so, you will receive the goblet for payment."

Eizrog grunts. "Yes, of course. I will do these things you ask."

I look at him, puzzled. "You agree too easily. Why is that?"

"You and the other one went to the Twisting Desert

and returned, which no one has done before. Not only did you return, but you returned, and brought with you a fabled goblet that should not exist. Therefore, you shall have safety, warmth, and succor here in my humble abode tonight. Come morning, I will allow you passage to the lands beyond this wall. It is the least I can do to help one so great as yourself."

I look at Quimby. "Why does everyone keep saying I'm so wonderful? I'm just an ordinary girl. There's nothing special about me."

Quimby raises an eyebrow. "Are you sure?"

I'm unsure what he means by his question. Remarkable things have happened around me since arriving in this world. I've performed feats I never thought possible and made friends, gained support and garnered adoration, and I'm filled with an odd sense of belonging that I've never felt before. But no, I'm sure it results from everything I've been through the past few weeks. My thoughts turn to the family I left behind. The belonging I feel turns to sadness as I think about how they must worry about me after my disappearance. I picture my mother and father, fear, sadness, worry and panic painted on their faces as they search for me. Unable to eat, I lay down on the hard stone floor and drift to sleep while salty diamond drops run down my face.

The next morning I wake to Ruven shaking me. I'm groggy and sluggish, but I know we must head out as soon as possible, so I rise and see Quimby and Ruven readied the horses while I slept. The three of us partake of some jerky and juice Eizrog provides before exiting the cave into the frosty white morning. It's cold as usual atop the mountain and I long for the warmth of the desert. We mount and turn toward the towering wall blocking the pass.

Eizrog walks in front of us, blocking our path. "You'll go nowhere, worms. You'll give me the goblet, then go back the way you came."

"We had a deal, ogre," I say. "You will let us pass or you won't see the light of another day."

Eizrog laughs. "You can't harm me, little girl. I'm strong and you are just a wee human."

In the blink of an eye, I raise my hand in front of me and lob a glistening blue fireball at Eizrog's face.

"Valessa!" Quimby says.

Eizrog stumbles. "What was that?"

"Consider it motivation to keep your word," I say. "There is plenty more for you if you continue to refuse. Now open the gate and let us pass as you agreed to do last night."

"Your spunk amuses me, so I'll do as you wish and allow you to pass. But I don't want to see you here again. I dislike you, small one, and I will kill you should I see you again."

Eizrog walks to the wall and pulls a large lever hidden inside an alcove carved into the stone of the summit. A sharp cracking sound like the sound of ice breaking off a glacier echoes off the peaks, and a huge icy gate swings open. Quimby nudges Breezy forward and passes through the gate, followed by Ruven. I stop beside Eizrog and remove the goblet from my pack. His eyes light up with joy. I toss the goblet in the snow in front of him and urge Sky Blossom through the gate, bringing her alongside Dava and look at Ruven, glad to see he's unharmed by his time with Eizrog.

"The ogre was kind to you?" I ask.

Ruven smiles. "Yes, Valessa. He was most kind. Glad to have you back, though."

"Likewise. I missed you more than I thought I would." I give his arm a light squeeze.

"I wish I could have gone with you. Quimby says it was quite the adventure."

"Indeed."

We spend the next few hours riding in silence along the narrow trail down the mountain. I'm eager to leave the Cresford Range behind and eager to feel warmth again. Before long, my wish is granted. As we descend the mountain, the wind and snow decrease and the air warms while the trail beneath us turns from snow to mud, then to dry dirt.

"Where will we end up next?" I call out to Quimby.

I receive no answer. He only turns in his saddle and raises a finger to his lips in the universal be quiet sign. I give Sky Blossom some heel and trot up beside Quimby, glaring at him.

"What?" He asks in a whisper.

"You shushed me."

"Because we need to keep our voices down."

"Why?"

He points to his ear, then out ahead of us. I listen

and hear the faint sounds of chains rattling and hammers pounding.

"What is it?"

"Soon we will pass by the Lower Cresford Mine. We don't want to make ourselves known when we do. If they detect us, there will be trouble."

"I understand." I drop back to my position beside Ruven.

By midafternoon we have descended to the location of the mine. The trail passes the vast pit on an elevated cliff. An enormous basin with a flat bottom dug into the side of a mountain lies below us. Several tunnels lead into the mountainside around the basin and hundreds of short, muscular beings toil in the great bowl. Some push carts filled with rocks out of the tunnels while others push empty carts into the tunnels. Many more swing hammers to break the rocks on the floor of the basin. They are sweaty and dirty and chained to each other, reminiscent of chain gangs I've seen in movies.

I move beside Quimby and stop. "What is this?"

"This is the Lower Cresford Mine. Its purpose is to unearth gold, gemstones and other precious metals to be sent to Thren Dorei, the capital of the Bleak Lands. The dwarves toil day and night. Their master's thirst is never satisfied."

As we watch, a man drags one dwarf to a wooden X-shaped structure, hauls him up onto it and ties him into place. A bare-chested man walks behind the dwarf and raises a club above his head. I watch in wide-eyed horror as he brings the club down into the dwarf, thrashing him.

Afterwards, they remove him and drag him back to his place in the chain gang.

"What did he do?" I ask.

Quimby shrugs. "Who's to say?"

"This is terrible."

As we turn to continue our journey, a blaring horn blast rings out below. We turn back and observe a gigantic monster of a man exit a tunnel at the far end of the pit. Muscles ripple under his dark skin, not an ounce of fat on his bones. His body has not one strand of hair on it, to show off the impressive red tattoos that cover his skin, reminding me of the markings I've seen on vikings in my history books at school. His visage is striking, but his mount is even more so. The massive man sits atop a tremendous bear, twice the size of a grizzly. Patchy dark brown fur as if it has mange covers its body. There's no doubt its long claws could tear a man apart. But the claws and the size are not the worst of him. That title belongs to his enormous head with its gigantic jaws and twisted muzzle. The beast is the stuff of nightmares.

"Holy hell. What the fuck is that?" Quimby's voice quivers.

Could it be that I know something our traveling minstrel friend does not?

"It's a bear," I say.

He looks at me with astonishment. "How do you know?"

"I spent some time with the Crimsonclaw Nightwalkers when I first arrived here. We ran across a bear like that one on a hunt. Those I was with were terrified of these bears. I can't imagine how this man tamed one."

"It is quite frightening."

We watch in silence as the man atop the bear makes his way through the basin, stopping to inspect the quality and quantity of the work being performed by the dwarves. He draws closer to our position on the cliff, and I see he carries a long leather bullwhip.

"This will not do." His voice is deep and thunders through the mine. "We won't make quota if you lot don't pick up the pace." He cracks a few of the dwarves with the whip.

The dwarves wince, and a gasp escapes me. I dismount and inch closer to the edge of the cliff.

"What are you doing, Valessa?" Quimby says behind me.

"I have to help them. I'm going to stop him."

A heavy hand grabs my shoulder and spins me around. I stop face to face with Quimby. "You can't do that."

"Like hell I can't. You can't stop me."

Quimby looks at Ruven as if asking for help.

"He's right, Valessa," says Ruven. "We can't let you do that."

I scowl at them.

Quimby takes me by the shoulders and forces me to look at him. "Listen, Valessa, I know you want to help them. I get it. I do. But our number one priority is seeing Ruven get to Naren Thalore. Everything else is secondary. Everything else. If you want to help these people, then you can do that after we complete our primary objective. If you present yourself or attack now, your rashness will cause us to fail and result in our deaths."

Ruven nods in agreement. "It's true, Valessa. It's unwise to do anything now. You know it is."

I sigh. "I know."

They are right. It would be stupid to call attention to us when we could pass by unseen. I mount Sky Blossom with reluctance and we continue down the mountain, eager to leave the Cresford Range behind.

When we reach the bottom of the mountain, the sky darkens as night settles across the land, so we find a suitable place to make camp for the night. After eating, we sit around the fire and I reflect on the horrors at the Lower Cresford Mine. I wish there was something I could do to lessen the burden of the ones enslaved there. But alas, that is not my saga at the moment.

"Where are we headed next?" I ask Quimby.

"Once we take the Golden Road up again, the next attraction would be Blackwick, and oh, what an attraction Blackwick is. It's such a great place with so much to see and do." Quimby exudes excitement and enthusiasm.

"How long for us to reach it?"

"It should be about a week's ride from here. The Golden Road goes right up to the gate. Blackwick itself is quite magnificent."

I stare into the distance. A few minutes pass before I leap to my feet, alarming both Ruven and Quimby. I grab a stick and march into the darkness.

"Valessa, come back," says Quimby from behind me. "What now?"

I ignore his pleas and continue forward into the oily blackness of the night, stopping by a large boulder to gaze into the dark. I know it was here. I just saw it.

"Who are you?" I call into the silence. "Come out. I know you've been following me. Show yourself."

I get no response, nor do I detect any movement. *Maybe there was nothing here after all.* I trudge back to the fire and take a seat between Ruven and Quimby.

"What was that about?" asks Quimby.

"I thought I saw eyes in the darkness watching us from behind that boulder. I thought maybe they belonged to whoever has been following us. But there was nothing there."

"Just because you didn't see or hear anything doesn't mean it wasn't there. Let's keep an eye out and get some rest. We'll head out again at dawn."

I settle onto my bedroll. My head is full of thoughts of the mysterious figure that's been tailing me since the church before Wolford. *I've made some friends since arriving in Sheonaetara, but also some enemies. There are several people who may have the motivation to pursue me from a distance.* These thoughts race through my head as I drift into a restless slumber.

True to Quimby's word, we mount up and continue our trek as the sun breaks over the horizon. Quimby and Ruven look well rested. Visions of mysterious strangers, monsters, and enslaved dwarves plagued me throughout the night. If it shows on my face, Ruven and Quimby don't acknowledge it. Regardless, I greet the day with a smile, eager to arrive in Blackwick and see what adventures it holds for us.

Chapter 15

As Quimby stated, it takes about a week to ride from the Cresford Range to Blackwick. The trip has been peaceful despite the eyes in the dark on the first night. We ride from dawn until dusk, when we stop for the night. The nights are somber and spent in quiet reflection. The landscape transitions from forest to grassland before morphing into farmland dotted with homesteads and fields ripe with crops or occupied by livestock. We see more people as we near the city. Many of them stop to gaze at us as we pass, some standing in fields while others stand on the roadside. Quimby greets them or waves at them, but I keep my head down. I've never enjoyed being ogled by gawkers.

"Do we need to know anything about Blackwick before we arrive?" I ask.

"Hmm. I don't think so," says Quimby. "It's just your typical bustling city, ripe with trade and entertainment. Don't worry. I'm quite familiar with it.

Blackwick is one of my favorite places to be, and I frequent it often."

"Good to know." I drift back into silence.

A few hours pass, and Blackwick comes into view. My first thought upon seeing it is how large it looks from a distance. There are so many buildings packed close together, all surrounded by a huge white wall and resting in the shadow of a large mansion atop a hill. The city lends a certain atmosphere of excitement to the air as we inch ever closer. More and more people meet us on the road as we draw nearer. Some are leaving the city, no doubt on their way home after a day spent in town. More are traveling toward Blackwick with goods to be sold in the markets.

"Blackwick houses some of the largest markets in the world." Quimby notes my interest in the various carts sharing the road with us.

"I've never seen such a place," says Ruven.

I realize there is a lot Ruven has never experienced. He lived with Lavina in the Chatsraine Forest for as long as he could remember until I absconded with him in tow. It gives me joy to experience these new and wondrous things with him, especially because he never would have if I hadn't stolen him away. Tears build in my eyes as I realize *Ruven would be dead by now if I hadn't saved him. Maybe I am a savior, just like the desert wanderers claimed. But no, I'm too brash and impulsive to be a savior. That would require skills I do not have, and I don't know how to gain such things.*

Ruven grabs my arm. "Look at that, Valessa." He

points at some carts nearby.

I look in that direction and see several carts laden with cages containing various large animals. They look like wolves, hyenas, lions and leopards, but are all much larger than any I have seen before, except for Lavina's familiar, Reaper. Reaper was a dire lion, so I assume these are also dire animals. These animals are terrifying.

"What are they?" asks Ruven.

"Dire wolves, dire lions, dire hyenas and dire leopards," says Quimby.

"What are they for?" I ask, a touch of fear coloring my voice.

"Most likely, they are for the arena."

"The arena?"

"Yes, the arena. Most say the arena is the best entertainment Blackwick offers."

"But you disagree."

"Well, it's my opinion the brothels hold that title, my dear."

A mental image of Quimby in a brothel invades my mind, causing me to shudder. I don't want to be thinking of Quimby in a brothel. Yikes.

Upon approaching Blackwick's gate, I notice the wall is a lot taller than I thought. It must stand at least ten feet tall. The gate is wooden planks of a striking red decorated with ornate carvings of flowers, birds and stars. It is quite beautiful. Cobblestones comprise the streets dyed red to match the roof tiles of the buildings that line them. The buildings are dazzling white stone with red doors and shutters. Both buildings and streets are clean and free of dirt and debris. It's clear the citizens of Blackwick take pride in their city.

Quimby leads us through the streets to an unadorned white building similar to many others we have passed. A wooden sign in the shape of a twisted serpent hangs from the building's eave. It's adorned with green scales and the words Ye Olde Snake Inn and Tavern in elegant black script. Quimby dismounts and leads Breezy around the side of the building. Ruven and I do the same, following Quimby at a brisk pace. Once around the corner, Quimby enters a stable attached to the inn. He has a brief conversation with a stable boy, then hands him Breezy's reins. The stable boy motions for others to take Dava and Sky Blossom's reins.

After seeing the horses stabled, the three of us enter Ye Olde Snake Inn and Tavern. The interior is bright and cheery, a stark contrast to the inn we stayed at in Wolford all those moons ago. Music and the smells of meat pie and ale fill the air. We seat ourselves at an empty table, and Quimby raises his hand to summon a barmaid. Her face beams as she approaches, as if she is reuniting with an old friend after some time apart. He requests three meat pies, two mugs of ale and two mugs of water, then inquires about lodging for a few night's stay. The barmaid says she will have rooms prepared for us, then hurries off to retrieve our food and drink, which is amazing after eating trail rations for so long.

"So why is this city called Blackwick when everything is so white?" I ask after we our meal.

"The city was established hundreds of years ago

when a bounteous onyx mine was nearby. That mine produced all the world's onyx. Hence the name Blackwick," says Quimby.

"That makes sense."

"What happened to the mine?" asks Ruven.

"The mine was destroyed long ago during the Great War. But it had long since gone dry," says Quimby. "When the war died and the ashes settled, they appointed the Darkmore family as guardians of the city, charging them with overseeing its reconstruction and they have ruled here ever since. They live at Shadowfield Estate, that enormous mansion on the hill we saw as we approached."

"Yes. I saw the mansion on the hill. The hill looked black from a distance. Why is that?"

"Ah, yes. They planted the fields around the house with black irises. They lend a shadowy appearance to the grounds around the mansion itself. Hence, the name Shadowfield Estate."

"Interesting. Who appointed the Darkmores guardians of Blackwick?"

"The oppressors, of course. They reshaped the world once the fires of the Great War stopped burning."

"Does that mean the Darkmores support the oppressors?"

"It's not clear whether they do."

"The oppressors gave them their power. They must hide their support for them."

"I said it's not clear, Valessa."

"These oppressors you keep mentioning. Who are

they?"

"The oppressors are a formidable people. They enslave all they can and force others to do their bidding. They seldom leave their city and do nothing for themselves."

"If they don't leave their city and they do nothing for themselves, then how do they survive?" I ask.

Quimby shakes his head. "Have you not been listening? They enslave people and force them to do their bidding. Most every settlement in the world supplies the oppressors with some good or service."

"There must be more people outside their city walls than within, so why don't people band together and fight against them?"

Quimby sighs. "Everyone knows what happened during the Great War. They are scared to turn against their masters. This talk is spoiling my joyous mood. Let's discuss something less depressing."

I scowl at Quimby. "Fine. Tell me about the governor."

Quimby bursts into laughter. "Oh, ho, ho. Claudius is wealthy, fat, and disgusting. Pray you never occupy the same space as him, at least for the sake of your nose."

Ruven explodes into bouts of laughter, causing me to develop my own case of the giggles.

"You mentioned entertainment on our approach?" I ask once the laughter subsides.

"Oh yes, yes. There is so much to do here," says Quimby. "I enjoy the brothels, but the two of you should check out the market. There are many wonderful things to purchase here."

"We have no money, Quimby."

"True. Try bartering or trading there instead. Merchants will sometimes do that."

I'm losing my patience with Quimby. "I barely have any possessions. What am I supposed to barter with?"

Quimby smiles. "You're a smart and capable girl. You can think of some way to get what you want from the merchants."

"What about the arena you mentioned? What is that like?" Ruven asks.

Quimby's eyes light up with excitement. "Oh, it's so grand. The Onyx Arena, as it's called, is a huge, round structure built during the onyx mine's prime. They built the arena entirely out of onyx and it can seat thousands. There are fights that range from man on man to man on beast, and anyone can enter. It's a magnificent spectacle to behold. The two of you should check it out while we're here."

Excitement crosses Ruven's face at the mention of visiting the arena and I make a mental note to wander that way over the next few days.

"What do the victors get for winning?" I ask.

"They say those skilled enough to win receive riches beyond measure. However, I don't know the truth to that since I've never spoken with any winners."

"And the losers?"

"Oh, they put those poor unlucky sods to death. They don't have to. That's just what Claudius finds the most entertaining these days."

I gasp. "That is despicable. Finding entertainment in another's misery. What does that say about a man?"

"Tis sport, dear girl. Many come to Blackwick to either take part in or observe the spectacle of the arena. These people often spend time in the markets. The arena drives the economy of this city. Besides, entry is voluntary. Every participant knows the cost of losing. If you don't like it, then don't partake of it."

An idea enters my mind. "Maybe I should enter. If I won, we would have all the money we'd need to see Ruven to Naren Thalore."

Quimby and Ruven both look at me, their eyes wide with fear.

"What?" I ask.

"You can't, Valessa. Please don't," says Ruven.

"He's right," says Quimby. "That's a terrible idea. What combat skills do you have that you could claim victory in the arena? You don't have any formal training. Not really, anyway. All you have is sheer luck, and we can't risk our mission based on luck."

"But—"

"That's enough, Valessa. I know you don't trust me. Hell, I feel you don't even like me, but for the sake of Ruven and reuniting him with his people, please do nothing brash like entering the arena competition. Besides, there's no guarantee you would win. It's more likely you would die like so many before you."

"He's right, Valessa," says Ruven. "I don't want to see anything happen to you, either. You're the only friend I've ever had, and I don't want to lose you."

I huff and fold my arms across my chest. "Fine."

"Very well," says Quimby. "If the two of you will excuse me, I have business to attend to." He rises and turns toward the door.

"Where are you going? What kind of business?" I ask.

"Private business. If you need me and I'm not in my room, check The Filthy Dog, the brothel at the end of the street. You'll find me there."

I shudder as I watch Quimby walk away.

Once Quimby exits the tavern, I plant my eyes on Ruven. He shrinks under my intense gaze.

"What?" he asks.

"I'm not happy with you. You could have backed me up about the arena, but all you did was turn against me and agree with Quimby. Why did you side with him?"

Ruven sighs. "On this I had to, Valessa. He's right. You shouldn't go anywhere near that arena. If you entered a fight there, you could lose. I don't want to lose you. It would devastate me."

"You flatter me, Ruven. But you've seen what I can do. I'm confident I can win an arena bout."

"Yes, I have seen what you can do, and it pains me to say it, but I'm not as confident in your abilities, Valessa. I've seen you conjure fire in the palm of your hand and make a few poisons and potions, but I don't feel that's enough to clench an arena win."

"You saw what I did to that church on the way to

Wolford."

"I did, and it weakened you almost to the point of collapse. You're not as powerful as you think you are, and you're not invincible, either. You perform parlor tricks, and I don't want to see you do something foolish."

"You and Quimby sound like you're trying to parent me." I rise to my feet. "The two of you will not dictate what I can and can't do."

I climb the stairs to our room, slamming the door as I enter, frustrated by the events of the past few minutes. *Of all the people I've met since coming to Sheonaetara, I thought Ruven was the one person I could count on, but I feel as though he has betrayed me by seconding Quimby's advice.* I lie on the bed and sulk. After some time, Ruven enters the room. I close my eyes and pretend to be asleep. Ruven sits on the edge of the bed beside me. He brushes his fingertips along my arm. His touch is almost imperceptible as he places a few strands of hair behind my ear before he rises and crosses the room to settle himself into his own bed.

What the hell was that? I think to myself.

Thoughts of Ruven and his gentle touch and what it means fill my head as I drift into dreamless slumber.

The rising sun wakes me the next morning. I'm eager to explore Blackwick and choose to not wake Ruven after the events of the previous night. I dress and hurry downstairs for some breakfast. A few minutes after seating myself, Ruven comes down the stairs. With my current mood, I would rather dine alone, but a smile spreads across Ruven's face and I know he has spotted me. He crosses the room, winding his way through the tables and seats himself across from me.

Ruven beams at me. "Good morning."

"Morning."

"Are you still mad at me?"

"I'm not mad anymore, just disappointed. You, of all people, should have my back."

Ruven takes my hand. "I have your back, Valessa. Always. I just refuse to stand by while you put yourself in unnecessary danger. That's something I can't do."

I snatch my hand away from him. It's clear Ruven has developed some feelings for me. I care about him, but I'm not sure I can reciprocate his interest. Being claimed by Alkin didn't thrill me, but I had grown close to him and the thought of how I lost him still pains me. I'm not ready to grow close to someone else.

Our food arrives and we eat, impatient to get out and explore Blackwick. The city is enormous and there are so many things I want to see. Ruven is just as excited as I am, so after finishing our meal, we race upstairs to collect our packs, then back downstairs and through the door, exiting onto the street. Outside, the day is bright and warm and the city is already alive with the sounds of its citizens going about their daily tasks. Rows of white buildings sparkle in the sunlight and add a cheerful vibe to the atmosphere. Blackwick's ambiance is a drastic juxtaposition to anything I have experienced so far.

Ruven and I walk over the cobblestones, taking in the sights and sounds of the city. An overwhelming number of people bustle here and there. We turn toward the market. Women in beautiful dresses with children in tow head in the same direction. I feel out of place amidst them, dressed in the same plain clothes I've been wearing since leaving the Vauxsard Overhang, and decide I will try to get some proper traveling clothes before leaving Blackwick.

The market lies in a large square. Stalls of all sizes line the outside walls with varied goods on display. In the center of the square, children play accompanied by pets and livestock. The market fills me with warmth and joy as I make my way to a stand occupied by a short elderly gentleman. Scarves, bags and cloaks in various colors and styles line his stall. I run my hand over a beautiful black velvet cloak trimmed with green stitching.

"Are you intending to purchase that?" the man asks in a gruff voice.

"I would like to, but I can't afford it."

"Piss off then. You're blocking paying customers."

"A friend of mine said some merchants might trade. Is there something else I could provide you in exchange for this cloak?"

The man rubs his hand over the scraggly beard on his chin. "There might be something, yes. My wife needs some aconite. She hasn't been able to find any. I don't suppose you have some with you, do you?"

I sigh. "No, I don't think I have that." I turn to leave.

"Wait, Valessa," Ruven says. "I think we have some aconite. Let me check."

Ruven rummages through his bag. He pulls out the

vial of wolfsbane that we stole from Lavina during our exodus all that time ago.

"Ruven, that's wolfsbane, not aconite."

"But it is aconite, Valessa. You should know that. Did Lavina teach you nothing?"

He turns to the man. "Is this what you're looking for? Will it do so my friend can have the cloak?"

The man inspects the vial. "Aye. This'll do." He pockets the wolfsbane.

Ruven takes the cloak and walks behind me, throwing it over my shoulders. I smile and pull it around me. It's soft and warm and the most beautiful thing I have ever possessed. In that moment, I am so thankful that I embrace Ruven and whisper a thank you in his ear. When I release him, he is blushing and beaming.

"Is there anything here you might like?" I ask. "Maybe we have something else we can trade."

"The only thing I want is a nice hot bath."

I realize how long it's been since my last bath and agree with Ruven that we could both use one. We search the streets for a bathhouse, thinking a city as large as Blackwick must have one. As we search, we take in all the sights and sounds within the city. There is more activity here than in Wolford. We walk past children playing and women completing household chores, such as washing clothes or baking bread. We stroll past a myriad of workshops where men toil for their day's pay.

We turn down a street that runs beside an aqueduct. "This looks promising," I say.

We continue looking for a bathhouse on this street

until we reach a large establishment with a sign that reads, The Warm Spring Sinkhole, hanging outside it. I shrug at Ruven before entering the building. Steam and a flood of perfume invade my nose, and I know this is what we were looking for.

I greet the young woman standing at the counter. "How much for a bath?"

"For the two of you, I would say eight copper," she says.

"I'm sorry. We don't have that kind of money."

She waves her hand in the air, showing that we should leave.

"Now what?" Ruven asks once we are back outside.

"I'm not sure."

"Things would be easier if we had some money."

I sigh. "Yes, they would. I guess we'll go check out the arena."

Ruven smiles with excitement and we head toward the outskirts of town and The Onyx Arena.

Chapter 16

My first impression of The Onyx Arena is how extravagant it is. Its inky blackness stands in stark contrast to the rest of Blackwick. Its height must be equivalent to a seven story building, and the curve of its outer wall tells me it is oval. To support its grand design, arches run around the walls like the ancient roman coliseum. Throngs of people crowd the streets surrounding the arena, no doubt there to partake of the entertainment offered within. I approach a guard standing outside the entrance and ask about the price for entry and am met with the wonderful news that anyone can watch the bouts for free.

"Why is that?" I ask growing suspicious. "How does allowing people to watch for free help the city?"

"The entertainment provided here is for the fun and joy of the people and so the governor deems it be free to all to allow the masses to enjoy the show. The activity here draws crowds to the markets, which is where

Blackwick makes its profit," says the guard.

I return to Ruven. "He says it's free."

"Strange."

"Yes, very strange indeed."

We enter The Onyx Arena through the main gate with the masses, then follow the flow of foot traffic up three flights of stairs to a seating area. Men, women and children gather here, some standing while others sit. Ruven and I stand at the wall for a better view of the activities taking place below. Excited chatter fills the surrounding air, making it hard to distinguish the topics being discussed by those nearby. Delight dances in Ruven's pale blue eyes and I return the smile he gives me before turning my attention to the event getting underway in the oval bowl below us.

On the floor of the arena, men use rakes to smooth the dirt and fashion it into a racetrack, which lends me a hint of confusion because I assumed only fighting took place here. When the men finish, beautiful painted chariots make their way into the arena drawn by two horses each, themselves decorated similarly to the chariot they pull behind them. The charioteers move into a rudimentary starting block and await the start of the race. My breath catches with anticipation as a horn blares throughout the stadium, and the horses spring into action. They jostle for position as they gallop around the track, their hooves creating a mighty thunder and throwing up thick clouds of dust.

"Can you believe it, Valessa?" asks Ruven. "This is amazing."

"Yes, it's incredible, Ruven. The horses are beautiful."

"They are." Ruven whoops and cheers with the surrounding crowd.

We stand shoulder to shoulder and watch as the charioteers complete a lap and move onto a second. A golden chariot drawn by two ebony horses pulls into the lead and the crowd erupts into cheers and applause. This charioteer must be the favorite.

The race continues below when one chariot crashes against another. The cheering around us turns to gasps as the chariots collide, sending them toppling over one another. Screams of horses and the sounds of wood splintering fill the air, but the remaining racers drive their horses onward, jostling for the top position. I wait for the dust to clear with bated breath, hoping the horses and racers who collided are unharmed. When the dust settles, we can see men leading the horses away from the wreckage and it's clear the six of them have escaped a gruesome fate.

As the remaining racers make their way across the start line once again, the cheers from the crowd grow in amplitude. The rumble of the horse's hooves dies, and the air clears to reveal that the golden chariot has won, sending the crowd into celebration. The charioteer removes his golden helm, revealing a true Adonis hiding behind and the women in the stands surrounding us swoon. Ruven rolls his eyes as I shake my head.

Ruven laughs. "Ridiculous."

"Indeed. He is clearly a crowd favorite."

Ruven nods in agreement.

"I thought they only held fights here. The chariot race took me by surprise," I say.

"Oh, there are many competitions here," says a gentleman standing beside us. "They hold chariot races, horse races and sprints for men. It helps break up the monotony of watching people beat each other to death."

"Interesting." I look at Ruven.

"No, Valessa," he says.

"I didn't say anything."

"You don't have to. I know what you're thinking. You don't ride well enough to compete in a horse race, and you know nothing about driving a chariot."

I scowl at him before turning away to watch the arena workers set up for the next bout. They uncover pits filled with spikes on the arena floor and set out weapon racks which contain different weapons before arranging large wooden posts throughout the grounds below and setting them ablaze with torches. When the men clear the field, a large, muscular man enters through a door at one end of the oval. He strolls to the racks and looks over the weapons laid out there. He ponders his choices, then picks up an enormous axe and raises it above his head. A chilling howl which originates from deep within the tunnels under the stands interrupts the crowd's cheers. One of the tunnel gates opens and a giant dire wolf charges into the silent arena. The warrior and the wolf eye each other before the wolf springs into action. It charges the warrior as he stands in place, raising his axe as the beast draws closer. Once it is within range, the man brings the axe down in one swift movement, cleaving the head clean off the animal. I wince and look away.

"That was terrible," says Ruven. "It wasn't even a fight, just senseless slaughter."

"I agree."

"I don't think I want to watch anymore."

"Me neither."

We turn away from the carnage below and wind through the crowd to the stairs.

Once we descend to the ground floor, I turn to Ruven and say, "Wait for me here. I'll be back soon."

"Where are you going?"

"The bathroom. Just wait here. I'll be back soon."

"Don't do anything stupid, Valessa. Please."

I raise my hand in a half-hearted wave and weave through the people crowding the corridor. Ruven and Quimby have warned me not to get involved in the arena, but it seems such an easy way for us to get some gold. Besides, I'm sure I can conquer any opponent with my wits and my magic. I reach the end of the corridor, locate a guard and ask for help in joining an arena match.

"Take the staircase here to the sublevel. You can find Dodrik Bloodaxe in a small room on the right. That's who you want to speak with," he says.

I thank him and make my way downstairs, where I knock on the wooden door I find there. There's no response, so I enter the room and find a short, rotund man sitting behind a desk. He has long dark red hair on his head and face, all of it gathered into braids, and weathered skin surrounds his dark brown eyes.

"What you want, girl?" he says, eyeing me.

"Sorry. I was looking for Dodrik Bloodaxe."

"Aye. You found em. What you want?"

"I was told to speak to you about entering the arena competitions."

He laughs. "You think you can do that? You think yer a badass, do ya?"

I glare at him. "I've seen some bouts, and I believe I can do well enough."

"Have I offended ya, lass?" Dodrik strokes the trio of braids on his chin. "You don't know what ya getting into entering this arena. You wouldn't last a minute against this lot."

I place my hands on my hips and stomp my foot. "Why does everyone keep telling me what I can and can't do? I can make my own decisions. What makes you the authority on who can take part here?"

Dodrik sneers. "I'll tell you, ya brat. You just listen close and I'll outline it nice and clear for ya. Long ago, the ones known as the oppressors enslaved my people. I was born into a life of slavery. Never knew nothin else but bein a slave. But one day, me master sold me to the arena here, so I fought. I fought harder than I ever had before. Became the master of me own fate. Won a bunch and became a grand champion. I killed so many me axe was always stained with the blood of the fallen. That's how I got me name Bloodaxe. So I know better than most what it takes to win here, and you," he points a crooked finger at me, "you ain't got what it takes. Now get outta me office. Go on, get."

I stare him down. "Your people are enslaved?"

"Aye. What of it?"

"On the way here, we passed a mine filled with men and women who looked a lot like you. They toiled in the dirt, and I saw some of them beaten. It was horrible, and I wanted to stop it, but my companions wouldn't allow it."

His breath catches in his throat. "This mine? What's it called?"

"The Lower Cresford Mine. Is that important?"

"Aye. My family still be there. Well, that be if they still draw breath." Dodrik sighs.

"I'm sorry to hear that. Truly I am. It's a horrible fate for any man, woman, or child to endure."

"Aye. Tis. You want to free those at the mine, do ya?"

"I did. But like I said, my traveling companions put a stop to it."

"Go back and free them. Do it, please. Don't let me family go another day in that hellhole."

For a brief second, I consider returning to the Lower Cresford Mine, but then I remember my priority is seeing Ruven safe among his people in Naren Thalore. "I'm sorry, Dodrik, but I can't do that because I have prior commitments that I must see through. I feel for your family and your people, but I cannot return to the mine just now."

"So the plight of me people was horrible, and you wanted to help, but now I ask you to help and you refuse? Okay. I see how it is. You want to compete in the arena? Go right ahead and compete in the arena. Come tomorrow at noon and I'll make sure you get a shot in there."

I clasp my hands in front of my chest and smile. "Oh, thank you. Thank you so much, Dodrik. What contest will I take part in?"

"Does it matter?"

"I suppose not. I just wanted to prepare for it."

"Come tomorrow. I'll have something special lined up for ya." Dodrik laughs.

"Okay. I'll be here at noon tomorrow. See you then."

"Aye. You be here. Can't wait to see ya. And I hope you die in that arena tomorrow. That's what I want to see. I hope you die a grisly death, ya bitch." Dodrik calls as I climb the stairs outside his office.

I return to the main level above, reunite with Ruven, and we exit The Onyx Arena together. The sun has set, and the day has ended, so we trek back through Blackwick and return to Ye Olde Snake Inn and Tavern for dinner.

After our meal arrives, so does Quimby, who joins us at our table. "How did you get along today? I hope you saw some of the city." He beckons the barmaid over.

"We did. The city is quite nice," I say.

"Yes," says Ruven. "We visited the market and the arena today. It was very exciting."

"The arena, huh?" Quimby eyes me. "I hope no one did anything stupid today."

I meet Quimby's gaze. "No one did anything stupid, Quimby. We kept a low profile. How was your day?"

"Fine. Fine indeed. Nothing of great import to note."

Something in Quimby's voice sounds off, leading me to believe there may very well be something of great import he wishes not to divulge. But having chosen to not divulge my secret plans for tomorrow, I let it go. We finish our meal to the sounds of Ruven regaling Quimby with the tales of our arena adventure, then head upstairs to bed. I lower myself onto my mattress to prepare for my big day on the morrow.

Chapter 17

Before sunrise, I dress and head downstairs without waking Ruven. Ruven will worry when he wakes and finds me missing, but I know both he and Quimby would attempt to put a stop to my so-called foolishness. I'm far too nervous to eat, so I skip breakfast and exit the tavern, wrapping my new traveling cloak around me in the brisk air outside. The streets are empty save for a few citizens getting a head start on their toils for the day. I make my way down the empty streets toward The Onyx Arena. As I grow closer to my destination, I see more and more people traveling in the same direction. No doubt some of these are other contenders for glory in the arena today. I study each one I pass, sizing them up as potential opponents.

When I reach the arena, I traverse the entrance, then realize I don't know where to go, who to speak with, or what to do. I observe the others. Many of them make their way down a set of steps near the entrance, so I follow and find the steps lead to a medium-sized room already occupied by others. I join them and await what comes next.

Before long, Dodrik enters the room. He climbs onto a chair and looks around, his face lighting up as his gaze settles on me. Of course, he's happy to see me. After my refusal to help his family, he is more than ready to watch me die in the arena today. I have no doubts he will pit me against a powerful adversary and hope I meet a gruesome fate for all to see. The thought doesn't shake me, for I have the hidden advantage of my magic and I feel confident I can pull off a victory.

Dodrik raises his hands and the room quiets. "All right. Listen here, you lot. Some of ya will be lucky enough to win today. Good for you. Others will lose and die horrible honorless deaths. Sucks to be in that camp. But hey, your participation is voluntary and since ya showed up this mornin, I assume ya don't value your life too much. Now, this fella here," he says as he points to a man standing nearby, "he's gonna take yer names. Then yer gonna wait here till yer name is called. When it's yer turn, make yer way through the tunnel over there," he points to a door at the side of the room, "and into the arena. Choose yer weapon from the ones provided ya and wait for the horn to signify the start of yer match. After that, it's whatever you feel will help ya survive. Got it?"

The men scattered around the room nod to signify they understand.

"There aren't rules to govern these fights?" I ask.

Dodrik gives me an intense scowl. "You daft, girl?

Was you not listening? I just explained the rules to ya."

"I . . . Um . . . Those sounded more like instructions on entering the arena for our match. I guess what I'm asking is what is and isn't allowed once the match begins?"

"Like I done said, once the match begins, you do whatever ya can to survive. There ain't no rules, ya dumbass."

I say nothing more, only nod as the men around me laugh and Dodrik leaves the room. The man Dodrik left behind collects the names of the participants. After writing every name down on his parchment, he leaves the room, and a quiet murmur descends as the others pick up their quiet conversations where they left off when Dodrik entered.

The number of men in the room decreases as the day progresses. Many leave and do not return, while a few leave and come back beaten and bloody. I assume those that return won their fight and have opted to press their luck a little more because they wait until their name is called a second time before disappearing once again. With every hour that passes, I get more anxious as I wait with anticipation.

While I await my turn, I watch the others leave. When I'm the final combatant left, a man sticks his head in the door to tell me it's my turn. I take a deep breath before exiting the room and making my way through the tunnel. As I draw closer to the tunnel exit, the cheers of the crowd grow louder. Apprehension fills me as I step out into the bright afternoon sunlight. The crowd cheers and applauds upon seeing me. It's clear they don't see many women compete in The Onyx Arena. I approach the weapon rack and glance at the choices provided to me. I've only had training with a bow, but it's been a long time since I've used one and I'm sure my skill has suffered for it. The sun dances off the blade as I pick up a short sword and decide it will do. I don't have experience wielding the weapon, but it's only for show since once the match begins, I will use my magic.

The tunnel opens opposite me, revealing a large, muscular man. He enters the arena with an air of confidence and chooses a large hammer from the weapon rack. A smile spreads across his face when he sees me, sending a tickle of fear through me. I know he sees me as an easy win.

A horn blares throughout the arena, causing the crowd to quiet and adrenaline to course through me. My huge opponent walks toward me at a steady pace and I feel the fingers of panic close around me. My heart races as I watch him close the distance between us, my breath catching in my throat with every step he takes. I give my head a vigorous shake to clear it, then drop the short sword to the ground. The crowd gasps and the man approaching me, grins and raises his hammer. I raise my hands in front of me and clasp them together, gathering all my energy into my core to prepare for channeling it into a focused attack. The man approaches a few paces more before I throw my hands forward to release the energy, and nothing happens. I concentrate harder and try once again and still nothing. My eyes widen with the realization that my magic has failed me and my opponent is within reach of me. He lets loose a deep, bellowing laugh as he grabs me by the hair and drags me to the center of the arena. Still laughing, he tosses me to the ground where I spring into action, throwing punches that don't phase him and kicks with no effect. He grabs my arm and raises it above my head. My captor looks at the stands and I follow his gaze to an elaborately decorated box filled with several people. In the center of the box sits a gargantuan man, his pale white skin glistening with sweat. He raises one meaty paw and makes a thumb down gesture as he gives a single nod of his head. The man standing over me raises his hammer into the air, and I close my eyes against the coming blow.

Chapter 18

"Stop! Don't do this, I beg you!" shouts a voice I recognize.

I open my eyes and see Ruven and Quimby running toward the fat man in the extravagant box.

"Please, stop this," says Quimby. "She didn't know what she was getting herself into."

The fat man eyes Ruven and Quimby, then looks back at me.

"It's true," says Ruven. "She didn't know. We begged her not to enter these competitions, but she's stubborn. We will do anything if you spare her. I will do anything for you if you would only spare her. Please, sir."

"If you spare her life, I will see that she repays your kindness in full, Claudius," says Quimby.

Claudius waves his hand in the air and nods. My opponent tosses me into the dirt and stomps away with a scowl.

Claudius turns to Quimby. "Very well. Have your friend cleaned up and brought to Shadowfield Estate. Her boldness is intriguing. I'd like to spend time with her."

I breathe a sigh of relief and rise to my feet. Ruven leaps over the wall of the seating area, landing on the dirt of the arena floor. He races to me and folds me into an embrace.

"I was afraid when I woke to find you gone this morning. I knew you had gone to do something stupid." Ruven's voice breaks as he embraces me. "You had me so afraid I was going to lose you."

"I'm fine." I push Ruven off me as I exit the arena.

"You have some friends that really care about ya," says Dodrik as I leave the tunnel. "Sure is a shame, that. I was looking forward to seeing your brains decorate the ground out there." He laughs as he walks away.

"He is an asshole," says Ruven as he catches up with me. "Come on, let's get you back to the inn and clean you up."

I pull away from him. "I don't need your help or anyone else's."

"You don't mean that. You're just embarrassed and angry."

I huff at him and begin the journey back to Ye Olde Snake Inn and Tavern, Ruven following close behind me. Once in our room, I lower myself onto my bed. I feel beat down and defeated. Ruven seats himself beside me and places his hand on my back in a caring manner.

"It's okay," he says. "We all have setbacks."

"I was so confident I could win." I wipe the tears

from my eyes. "But I almost died. Magic failed me, Ruven. How is that possible?"

"I didn't even know it was possible for magic to fail."

Quimby enters the room, shutting the door behind him. "Well, that was quite the embarrassing display."

The twinkle in his eyes tells me he finds the situation amusing. "It's not funny, Quimby. I could have died."

"Would have too, if it wasn't for Ruven. He found me just in time for us to come rescue you. I told you not to enter the arena. I told you would die if you did. What were you thinking?"

"I just wanted to make us some money so our journey would be easier. I thought I could win by surprising my opponent with magic, but the magic failed me."

Quimby shakes his head. "Of course it did. They ward the Onyx Arena against the use of magic. It would be unfair to allow combatants to use magic when their opponent may not have the gift."

I leap to my feet and stomp toward Quimby. "And you didn't think to tell me this?" I ask once I'm face to face with him.

"I did not think you would attempt to enter the arena. I should have known better, given your propensity for brashness and your failure to listen to sound advice."

I roll my eyes. "You really are an asshole, you know that? It's almost like you don't care if I live or die."

"Oh, that is unfair, Valessa. I was there with Ruven,

begging Claudius to spare you. Or have you forgotten that fact already?"

"No, I haven't forgotten. It's just not clear to me whether you were there for me, for Ruven, or for yourself."

Ruven steps between us. "Please stop this. We can't fight each other. We are all we have right now."

I continue to eye Quimby, but back down for the sake of Ruven. He's right. We shouldn't fight amongst ourselves when we have enemies without. But I can't shake the feeling that Quimby isn't in it for Ruven or for me. The more time I spend with him, the more my distrust of him grows.

"Ruven is right," Quimby says. "It's more important now than ever. Claudius has requested that you visit Shadowfield Estate, Valessa. He wishes you honor him with your presence in return for sparing your life today. He's a powerful man here in Blackwick. You will fulfill your duty and you will be grateful."

"Why does he want me to come see him?"

"Oh, Claudius has a great interest in unique and pretty things."

"Great. Just great. Will either of you be coming with me?"

"Claudius requested your presence alone. Ruven and I will stay here. Just mind your manners and you should be fine. We will be here when you return."

"What if I refuse to go?"

"That would be very unwise, Valessa. Very unwise indeed."

The thought of visiting Shadowfield Estate alone does not thrill me, but I know I must, regardless. I comfort myself by accepting it's just one more thing I must do to keep Ruven safe and make sure he reaches Naren Thalore.

I sigh. "I suppose I'm as ready as I'll ever be."

"A carriage will pick you up in half an hour. Make sure you're ready when it arrives." Quimby leaves the room.

Once we are alone, I turn my attention to Ruven. "I'm sorry I went against your wishes. I just thought . . . It doesn't matter what I thought. I made a choice. It was a stupid one and now I must accept the consequences of my actions."

Ruven grabs my hand. "It's okay, Valessa. I'm just glad you're still here with us."

Ruven exits the room, leaving me alone with my thoughts. Although I abhor the idea of spending time near Claudius, I'm grateful Ruven and Quimby saved my life and vow to repay them someday. I spend the next half hour reflecting on my recent decisions and mistakes, and contemplating my current situation. I wish to get my visit to Shadowfield Estate over as fast as possible so I can rejoin my friends.

Outside Ye Olde Snake, the evening air is chilly. True to his word, Claudius has sent a magnificent carriage to transport me to Shadowfield Estate. The gold trimmed carriage shimmers like opals in the rising moonlight. As I take a seat inside, I marvel at the deep red crushed velvet seats. It's a smooth ride over the cobblestones as the powerful black horses pull me ever closer to my date with the governor of Blackwick. We pass through a wrought-iron gate and begin our ascent up the hill to the main house, the fields of black irises passing by outside the window.

The carriage stops at the top of the hill, and the footman opens the door, allowing me to exit. I climb the stairs to the door alone, startling when the door swings open on its own. A butler dressed in formal attire greets me and bids me to enter. With reluctance, I pass through the door into a grand foyer with a marble tile floor below and crystal chandeliers above. The walls are the same shade of red as the seats of the carriage. I take in my surroundings, never imagining a building decorated in such a glorious fashion might exist in this hostile world. The butler leads me to a small washroom on one side of the foyer and motions me inside.

"The master asks that you change into the garb he has selected for you before joining him for dinner." He closes the door.

The room houses a privy and a washbasin and nothing else. The most stunning dress I have ever seen hangs on a peg on the wall. Its vibrant blue color is the first thing I notice. Not a color I would choose for myself. The bodice is thin with black ribbon crisscrossing its way down the front and back, and the long full skirt is gathered into ruffles accented with black lace. I disrobe and pull the dress over my head. My whole life I have preferred casual jeans and a t-shirt and have never worn something so formal before. The gown is strapless with a sweetheart neckline, which adds to my level of discomfort, having never exposed so much of my chest and shoulders before.

After dressing, I step out of the wash closet to be greeted by an older woman wearing a plain brown dress. She motions for me to turn around, then pulls and yanks the ribbons in the back of the dress, taking care to tighten the corset as much as possible before tying the ribbon at my lower back. I can barely breathe when she has finished. The butler then leads me through a door beside the staircase at the far end of the foyer and into a long dining room with a table I'm sure could seat twenty people or more. He motions for me to take a seat, then exits the room.

A few moments later, Claudius enters, followed by another man and a young boy. Claudius walks to the head of the table while the others seat themselves across from me. The governor takes his seat, then rings a small bell, signaling the servers to enter. They place large plates piled high with meat and vegetables in front of the four of us, then pour us each a glass of wine before leaving the room. Claudius and the others eat with greed while I take my time observing my companions.

Claudius sits at the head of the table, his remarkable girth spilling over the sides of his chair. Thinning gray hair tops his head, and his tan skin glistens with sweat, much as it was earlier in the arena. The seams of his maroon tuxedo struggle to hold his substantial mass. The skin of his face creases and wrinkles as his oversized hands shovel food into the black hole of his mouth. I find him quite repulsive.

Claudius takes me in with his honey eyes. "Eat, girl, eat."

The boy seated across from me laughs, his freckled face beaming. The candlelight dances in his green eyes as the curly ginger hair atop his head shakes back and forth with each movement he makes. He notices my gaze and returns it with a bucktoothed grin. I glance away.

"Don't mind him," says the young man seated beside him. "Zeke is a little simple."

I lock eyes with the man and realize I have seen him before. "You competed in the chariot race at the arena yesterday. You won."

He smiles, revealing a mouth full of perfect teeth, and his green eyes twinkle. He runs a hand through his dark brown hair and blushes.

"Yes, well. I've had loads of training and practice."

"Your adoring fans filled the stands."

Claudius laughs. "Ha! Those fans adore Zayn because they think he's handsome and every one of them believes she could be the next Mrs. Darkmore. Now, enough of this drivel."

"Yes, father," the boys say in unison.

Claudius returns to stuffing his face as silence descends once again. There's no conversation for the rest of the meal. Once Claudius and his sons have finished eating, Claudius dismisses Zeke and Zayn while servants take the empty plates away. A sense of unease rises within me as I realize Claudius and I are now alone in the room.

"So tell me, what is your name, my dear?" Claudius asks.

"Valessa."

"You look quite ravishing in that dress, Valessa." His eyes give me a once over. "I see it fits you well, considering I had to guess your size."

"Thank you. It's beautiful. I've worn nothing like it before."

"Is that so? Well, as long as you're with me, you will always have things as lavish as this."

I smile. "That isn't necessary."

"But it is. The governor of Blackwick is the most powerful person in the city, and I won't allow riffraff to surround me."

"I meant no offense."

Claudius sighs. "You have not offended me. I was merely stating facts."

"I see." With every moment that passes, I grow more uneasy.

"Would you care for desert, Valessa?"

"No, thank you. I thank you for the wonderful dinner, sir. It was quite delicious. I appreciate your hospitality, but I must go. My friends are awaiting my return." I rise to my feet.

Claudius shakes his head and rings his bell once again. The butler enters the room.

"Show our lovely guest to her quarters," Claudius says. My heart races as fear and panic fill me. "That's not necessary. I'm not staying. My companions and I are just passing through your beautiful city and will continue on our way soon."

"You are staying. I can't let a treasure such as you escape me, now can I? Bertram will show you to your quarters."

The butler, who I assume is Bertram, takes me by the elbow. "It's best you come with me, my lady."

"No." I attempt to fight Bertram off.

Bertram releases me and claps his hands twice. Two armored guards enter the room at his beckon. They grab my arms and lift me off the floor, then carry me from the room. We return to the foyer, and the guards carry me up the grand staircase and down a dark hallway. Bertram runs ahead, motioning for the guards to follow him. At the end of the hall, he opens a door and the guards carry me into the room. They lift me onto the canopy bed inside and exit before Bertram closes the door, leaving me alone in the darkness.

I know they have locked me in this room like a prisoner, but I try the door, anyway. As I suspected, I find it locked. I cross the room to the large window and look out into the night. Twinkling diamonds sprinkle the dark sky and below the hill I can see the torch light rising from the city. My thoughts turn to Quimby and Ruven. *What will they think when I don't return? Did Quimby know my trip to Shadowfield Estate was one way? Maybe he has been trying to get rid of me all along.* I take a deep breath to clear my mind and focus on my current situation. I have to escape this mansion and the governor, but it's late and I am so tired after such a long day. My best course of action is to get some rest. After all, I can't fight, nor can I flee if I'm exhausted. I slip out of the blue velvet gown and into a plain white shift that someone has left for me, climb into the bed and wrap the thick warm covers around me, then drift to sleep as my mind races through ways to break out of this prison.

Chapter 19

The next morning, I wake with the sun as usual and dress in the clothes I was wearing when I arrived at Shadowfield Estate last night before donning my new traveling cloak. I break a leg off the small table beside the bed and use it to smash the window then lay the blue dress over the windowsill and pull myself out the window, lowering myself into the tall shrubs below. I hop out of the shrubs and make a break for the wall that surrounds the estate grounds in the distance, hoping I can scale it and disappear into the city before anyone realizes I have escaped.

Before long, I reach the inn and fly upstairs to the room I share with Ruven. I slam the door shut behind me, startling Ruven and causing him to bolt upright in bed.

Ruven rubs the sleep from his eyes. "Oh my God. Valessa. Where have you been?"

"Shadowfield Estate. Claudius wouldn't let me leave

last night."

"I was worried, but I thought maybe you had stayed because it had gotten so late."

"I didn't intend to stay. He kept me locked in a room all night. I don't think he had any intention of allowing me to leave."

"If that's true, then he's going to come looking for you. We have to get out of here."

"Yes, I know, Ruven. We'll need to leave Blackwick immediately."

Ruven jumps out of bed and dresses before we race down the stairs and out onto the cobblestones beyond. We hurry down the street, leaving Ye Olde Snake behind us and pass through the market, then enter The Zealous Knight Bar on the other side, keeping a low profile as we seat ourselves at an empty table in the corner. I pull the hood of my cloak up over my head as Ruven informs the barmaid that we require privacy.

"What are we going to do?" Ruven asks.

"I don't know. Have you spoken to Quimby since I left last night?"

"He left after you. He's probably at the brothel."

I nod in agreement. "It may take Claudius's goons some time to locate me here, but I'm sure they'll find me eventually. They're probably already looking. We need a contingency plan for when they find me."

Ruven nods. "I agree."

"We need to find . . ."

"Valessa?" Ruven waves his hand in front of my face, trying to rouse me from my frozen state.

"Don't turn around. Raise your hood and keep quiet. Don't draw attention to us," I say, keeping my eyes trained on the figure that just strolled through the door.

Ruven raises his hood as I instructed. "What is it?"

I pull my hood lower over my face and slouch further into my seat. "It's Lavina. She just walked through the door."

"Are you sure?"

"Absolutely."

"We don't need more problems. What are we going to do?"

"We're going to stay quiet and inconspicuous and see what she is up to."

"And if that doesn't work? What will we do then?"

"We will fight, Ruven. We will do everything we can to maintain our freedom."

Ruven nods in agreement.

Lavina, looking as radiant as ever in a ruby red traveling cloak trimmed in gold thread, crosses the room and takes a seat at a table behind Ruven, forcing me to retreat deeper into the shadows of the corner. She orders no food or drink, nor does she speak to anyone. With her head down, she sits quietly. A tall man in a black cloak joins her, his face covered in a black cloth. Lavina's face twists into a forced smile. I'm unsure if this is the man who has been following me, the man who met her at Vauxsard Overhang all that time ago, or someone new. I only know I must remain hidden in the shadows, still and quiet, and observe their meeting.

"So good to see you again, Lavina," a deep, gravely

voice growls. It's the voice of the man I heard eavesdropping those many moons before.

"Wish I felt the same, Jizurza," says Lavina in her sweet honeyed tone.

"Come now, witch, you know how much I hate leaving the safety of Thren Dorei to come speak with you. However, your incompetence forces me to do so yet again."

Ruven's eyes widen in surprise, as do mine. If this hooded figure came from Thren Dorei, he could be an oppressor Quimby goes on about. I use my eyes to instruct Ruven to keep his composure before returning my attention to the meeting taking place behind him.

"I hardly call it incompetence," says Lavina. "The girl outsmarted me is all. I will find her along with the boy. Once I do, you can have either of them or both of them. I don't care anymore."

"Oh, I think you care a lot more than you let on. We know the girl is powerful, and we know you wish to train her as a weapon you could wield against your enemies. You will both come to Thren Dorei if you find her. You will train her to be this weapon you desire. But she will be our weapon, not yours. Do I make myself clear?"

"Crystal," says Lavina through clenched teeth. "But what of the boy?"

"Bring the boy, keep the boy, dispose of the boy. It matters not to us. I'm sure he would make a nice snack for your dear kitty." The mystery man releases hissing laughter.

"Then you no longer wish to use him to locate his

people?"

"If the girl does indeed prove herself as powerful as you claim, then we would have no need of the boy. After all this time, it's clear his people no longer exist. If they do somehow survive, we're sure their numbers are so few that they are not a threat to us anymore."

"I don't wish to keep him after this betrayal, so should I find him, he will make a delightful meal for Reaper."

"Then it's settled. Capture the girl and bring her to us. Feed the boy to your cat."

Lavina bows her head. "As you command, my liege."

The hooded stranger rises and starts toward the door. "Oh, and Lavina," he says, turning back, "do not fail us again. The consequences would be dire."

Lavina nods and the hooded man exits the bar, who is shaken. I never took her as one to exhibit fear. But it's not fear, I realize as she slams her fist down onto the table. It's anger. She is hot-blooded and angry and I know she will stop at nothing to find and capture us. A few moments later, she rises and walks to the door. She takes one last look over her shoulder, then exits and disappears into the crowded street.

Ruven and I remain at our table for the next few minutes, giving Lavina time to leave the area. I think about all the things we've been through since fleeing the Vauxsard Overhang and our current situation regarding the governor. Doubt rears its ugly head inside me, but I push it back down. Now is no time to doubt we will make it to Naren Thalore, and it certainly isn't the time to doubt we will even survive.

"Well, that was both frightening and insightful," I say once the coast is clear.

Ruven nods. "Indeed. I think we need to leave as soon as we can."

"I agree. Let's collect Quimby and the horses and make haste toward Naren Thalore. The sooner we get there, the better."

Ruven nods, and we leave The Zealous Knight Bar and wind through the streets to The Filthy Dog. I inquire after Quimby upon entering. The house madam informs me she has not seen Quimby all day. I thank her then return to the street with Ruven.

"We should take the horses and leave without him," I say.

"We can't, Valessa. He's our friend. We can't leave our friend behind."

"But what if he's not our friend, Ruven? What has he done that screams friend to you?"

"He saved you. You would be dead if it wasn't for Quimby. I know you don't trust him, but I do and you owe him, Valessa."

"Fine. Fine. He may be at the arena, but there will be guards there, so I can't go anywhere near it. You'll have to go check without me."

Ruven nods. "Okay, Valessa. You should stay hidden as best you can. I'll return soon."

Ruven leaves me, rushing toward The Onyx Arena as I take shelter in the alley between The Filthy Dog and the building next to it, hoping I can stay hidden until Ruven returns. My only hope is he finds Quimby fast so we can leave Blackwick before Claudius recaptures me. I survey everything around me on the constant lookout for Ruven or for those coming to return me to Claudius. As I sweep the alley, I notice a cloaked figure standing in the shadows several yards behind me. I'm sure it's the same person I've seen several times since leaving the church on the way to Wolford and whoever has been following me this whole time. He slips around the corner, disappearing from view. Against my better judgment, I walk to the end of the alley to follow him, hoping to unmask my stalker at last.

"Hey. Who are you? Why have you been following me?" I say as I round the corner.

I stop to avoid colliding with the stranger. His presence puzzles me, since he has avoided confrontation for so long. He could have escaped me once again, but we now stand face to face in the alley. I still cannot see his face hidden deep within the shadows of his cloak, but I can hear the whoosh of air as he breathes, his shoulders rising and falling in a steady rhythm. I don't know who this man is, but he is clearly angry at me or something I've done.

I take a deep breath. "Who are you, and why have you been following me? What do you want?"

The strange man says nothing. He just stands frozen in front of me, watching from within his hood.

"Who are you?" I ask once more, taking a step toward him. My muscles tense as I prepare to turn the confrontation physical.

The stranger reaches up with his long fingers and grasps the edges of his hood. All I can do is stare, frozen by anticipation. As he lowers his hood to reveal his face, I stumble back a few steps, gasping in shock. Golden eyes look down at me from above a sneer lined with sharp teeth.

"Surprised to see me?" He asks in a deep voice laced with hostility. "I'm sure you thought I was dead after that stunt you pulled."

"But how . . . I didn't . . . Yes, I did."

"Well, I'm very much alive. No thanks to you. I looked for you after the explosion, but you were gone. When I found you again, you were unreachable, but now you're alone and I can finally exact my revenge for what you've done to me." He steps in my direction.

I stand my ground, throwing my hands out in front of me. "Stop. We can discuss this. You don't know the entire story."

"I know enough, and there's nothing you can say that will sway me." He runs his hands through his shaggy black hair. "There was the explosion, then darkness. When I woke, everyone I knew and loved was dead and you were gone. Why would you run if you did nothing wrong?"

"It wasn't like that at all."

"I claimed you to provide you protection. We had a connection, I thought. I felt a connection. You felt it, too. I loved you, Valessa. Why? Why did you do it?" His anger melds with his sadness.

The hurt coloring his voice moves something inside me, causing tears to fill my eyes. "I swear to you it was not me, Alkin. I loved you all like you were my family. Although I did not ask for your protection, I was happy to have it. Even after I learned what it meant, I was still happy to have it. When I learned I had lost you, it devastated me. I felt so much guilt for losing control and destroying the pack. I know you're angry and upset with me, but at least give me the chance to tell you the truth of what happened. Please, Alkin."

"What makes you think I would believe anything you say, Valessa?" Scorn drips from Alkin's words.

"I'm not asking you to believe me, Alkin. I'm only asking that you allow me to tell you what happened that night. Please."

"Fine. I'll listen to your words, but I make no promises of withholding the revenge I aim to exact on you."

"All I ask is that you listen, Alkin. Let's sit."

I lead Alkin to a bench beside a building in the middle of the alley. I take a deep breath before I begin.

"After that night, I spent a week lying in bed, unconscious. When I awoke, I didn't know where I was. It turns out I was in a cave inhabited by a woman, Lavina, who calls herself the witch of the Chatsraine."

"My people knew her. She was an enemy to us all."

"Indeed. Only I didn't know that. The only thing I knew was I had seen her in the woods the night the lion attacked, and what she told me had happened. Lavina told me she believed you held me captive, so she set the lion upon us in order to save me. She said that in my fear, uncontrolled magic had exploded from me and that the explosion had killed all of you and destroyed the encampment."

"And you believed her?"

"I did not, not at first anyway. She wouldn't allow me to go back to the camp and see for myself. She kept me confined to my quarters, her golem standing guard. Left no choice, I mourned the loss of my family and you. Although I could not forgive myself for what I had done, I accepted what destiny had written for me. In order to survive, I accepted Lavina's help, and so she taught me about this world and its people. As time passed, I learned how to create potions and poisons, but the most important thing I learned was how to control my magic.

"I spent many weeks with Lavina and her young ward, Ruven. Then one night, I heard strange noises coming from the main chamber, and my curiosity led me to investigate. I eavesdropped on Lavina and her mysterious midnight visitor, and that is when I learned the truth about everything. Yes, I had an uncontrolled magic outburst, but that isn't what killed the Crimsonclaw. Lavina admitted to the visitor that she had slain you all as you lay unconscious and that she had convinced me I was to blame for your deaths, convinced me that the explosion had killed you. She informed the stranger that she would notify him if I showed promise of being the one, whatever that means. The stranger told her she could do as she wished with Ruven, and she claimed she would sacrifice him to power a hex or something.

"I couldn't stand to see Ruven harmed, so I vowed I would escape with him the next opportunity that arose, which I did. The first time Lavina was gone after that night, I took Ruven and her golem and we ran. We lost the golem at a roadside church outside Wolford. Man-eating monsters parading as nuns and priests filled that church. They used the church to lure unsuspecting victims, so I destroyed it. We met an ogre, who sent us on a suicide mission to The Twisting Desert, which we survived. Now our path has led us here to Blackwick. Through trials and tribulations, we've come this far and I don't plan to stop until I see him safe."

A few minutes pass before Alkin stands, runs his hands through his hair and sighs. He looks stressed and I can't help but feel sympathy for him. After all, we had grown close before fate tore us apart, and deep down, part of me has missed him.

"I didn't realize you had been through so much," Alkin says.

"It was never more than I could handle, and besides, I've grown from it. I'm not the same person I was when I arrived here."

"Oh, I know, Valessa. I've been following you all this time. I couldn't just let you go."

"I know. You don't know how happy I am to see you."

I look Alkin deep in the eye and see so much emotion there that it pains me. I rush forward, throwing my arms around him in an embrace. A look of alarm passes over his face and he throws me off him. I stumble backwards, falling and landing on the ground. Alkin looks down at me and scowls. I scramble to my feet and meet him toe to toe.

"What was that for?" I ask.

Alkin laughs. "Oh, Valessa, I think you got it a little twisted. You think I couldn't let you go because of some feelings I have for you? Is that it?"

I stare at him, shocked. "After recounting everything I have endured, I thought we could reunite, but I guess I'm wrong."

"Yes, you are. I couldn't let you go because I need to avenge what you did to my people, not because of some feelings I have. Those don't matter anymore."

"But I just told you what happened. It wasn't me that killed your people. It was the witch. I heard it from her own mouth."

"I heard everything you said, but there's no one here that can corroborate your story. You could be feeding me lies in order to save yourself."

"I wouldn't do that to you, Alkin. What I've said is the truth, I swear it. I would never have harmed you or your people."

"I don't believe you." Alkin screams with rage.

Alkin lunges at me. I escape him by stepping out of the way, causing him to run past me. I spin and look at him. Saliva foams in his mouth, giving him the look of a rabid dog. He lunges at me again, and as I attempt to dodge him a second time, I stumble and fall to the ground. He stands over me, laughing.

I look up at him. "Don't do this, Alkin. Please."

As I lay on the ground below him, he falls down on top of me, his fists clenched. I brace myself for the blows I know will come soon. He raises a fist above his head and brings it down into my stomach, hard. All the air in my lungs whooshes out at once, leaving me in pain and gasping for air. There's nothing I can do to defend myself. Alkin rises to his feet and kicks me in the shoulder before lifting me off the ground and throwing me into the wall of a building that lines the alley. He stands several feet away, admiring the beating he has already given me, which allows me the time I need to catch my breath.

"I mean it, Alkin. Please don't do this." Tears fill my eyes.

My appeal only triggers him to continue his assault. He walks to where I lie slumped on the ground.

"Alkin, if you continue this, you will force me to defend myself and I don't want to hurt you."

"You're not strong enough to stand up to me and you can't hurt me anymore, Valessa."

As Alkin approaches, I look for an escape route. Finding none, I clench my fists and prepare to face my attacker. When he reaches me, Alkin bends down and grabs me by the throat, lifting me into the air and looking deep into my eyes. He slams me into the wall behind me and pulls his fist back to prepare for another blow.

"Please." Tears run down my face.

My plea goes unnoticed once again. I wince as Alkin slams his fist into my jaw, causing my head to connect with the wall behind me. A blinding white light fills my vision and fog clouds my mind as I realize Alkin will kill me if I don't fight back. I pull my leg back, then deliver a swift, hard blow to Alkin's manhood. He buckles with the attack but does not drop me. The thought that I cannot beat him flashes through my mind before I understand what I must do.

As I dangle in front of Alkin, suspended by his hand wrapped around my throat, I pull all the energy I have into my core and focus it there in preparation. I place my hand on Alkin's chest, then force the energy down my arm to my hand with as much force as I can muster. The magical shock wave catches Alkin off guard, causing him to stumble and fall backwards onto the cobblestones. I hear a sickening crack as his head slams into the ground and I fall on top of him. The blow causes him to release me. I roll off him and climb to my knees beside him.

Tears flood my vision. "Oh no. Please be okay, Alkin. Don't die. You can't die on me a second time. I won't survive losing you again."

Alkin moans and opens his eyes. He glances around before settling his gaze on me. I look at him, tears streaming down my face.

"What the fuck was that, Valessa?" he asks.

"I . . . I had to stop you. You would have killed me."

"I told you that's what I planned to do. Don't act so surprised."

"I know you don't believe me, but I told you the truth. The witch is a threat I will have to deal with. You want revenge for your pack? Why don't you come with us? You can exact your revenge when the moment presents itself."

Alkin sits up. "Whether or not you speak the truth doesn't matter." He rubs the back of his head. "I won't come with you. I want nothing to do with you and I never want to see you again, Valessa."

Alkin rises to his feet and turns away from me. I wish he wouldn't go, but I don't know how to stop him.

"You don't mean that. I know you don't," I call after him as he exits the alley and disappears into the crowd.

I take in my surroundings as I rise to my feet, hoping the commotion in the alley has drawn no unwanted attention. Ruven turns into the alley and freezes as he catches sight of me. I realize he is looking past me and I see fear and panic wash over him. I glance over my shoulder to see what has alarmed him. Advancing down the alley behind me is a trio of Blackwick guards. After my bout with Alkin, I'm too bruised and battered to evade them or fight them off. As they close on me, I command Ruven to run. The last thing I see before the guards encircle me is Ruven leaving the alley and vanishing into the multitudes of people in the streets beyond. I breathe a sigh of relief at seeing him go as I resign myself to my fate.

Chapter 20

Two days ago, guards trussed me up in chains and dragged me through the streets to the mansion on the dark hill. I remember the cries of alarm and looks of pity I received from the citizens we passed as they whispered about Master Claudius finding another one. Once back in Shadowfield Estate, Claudius confined me to a windowless room and chained me to the bedpost. I have seen no one save for the doctor who treated my wounds and the servants who bring my meals. The guards stripped me of the belongings I possessed. That includes the clothes I was wearing, which they replaced with a plain brown shift. I've spent the past two days lying in bed, too sore to move. Thoughts of Alkin and the hurtful things he said to me fill my head. My heart aches for him and what he has lost at the hands of the witch, and I vow to avenge the wrongs she has wrought. I wonder if Ruven escaped that day and I think about Quimby and my distrust for him grows. He said we could find him at

The Filthy Dog, but when we needed him, he wasn't there.

I abandon the thoughts running through my mind when the door opens. A short round woman wearing a simple white dress enters carrying a tray of bread, honey, fruit and wine. She sets the tray on a small table near the bed.

"Wait," I say as she turns to leave.

She stops. "Yes?"

"How long will I be stuck in this room?"

She shakes her head. "I cannot say."

"Can I at least be unchained?"

She leaves the room without answering, locking the door behind her. I prop myself up with the many pillows covering the bed and pick at the breakfast before slipping off to sleep for yet another nap.

Three days later, I receive my first real visitor. After I finish breakfast, the door opens wide and Claudius waddles into the room dressed in an ivory tunic and brown pants, his thinning gray hair slicked back off his forehead in a poor comb over and sweat glistening on his skin as usual. He shuffles across the room and seats himself in a chair beside the bed.

Claudius smiles. "I offer my apologies for the delay in visiting you, my dear, but it pained me to see you so bruised and battered."

I roll my eyes. "Now that my bruises have faded to yellow, you can look at me?"

Claudius frowns. "You are too beautiful to be marred. I did not wish to be haunted by that vision."

"Whatever you say."

"Don't be like that, Valessa. I saved you. You should be appreciative."

"You saved me? I wasn't in need of saving."

"The guards told me you were lying injured in an alley. They brought you here under my direction so I could provide you the best medical care available in Blackwick and this is how you show gratitude?"

"You want gratitude? From me?" I lift my arm to show off my shackles. "You have me chained to a bed, and you keep me locked in this room with no visitors save the servants that bring my meals, and you think I should show you gratitude? You're insane."

"I know you're angry, dear, but there is no need for name calling. I only wish to provide for you and take care of you. That is all."

I raise my cuffed hand again in response.

"If it will please you, I shall have those removed. But should you do harm to yourself or any of my servants, you will see yourself back in those chains and worse. Do I make myself clear?"

"Crystal."

"Is there anything else I can do to lift your spirits?"

"You could let me go."

"Now, now, my dear sweet Valessa, I can't do that. I wouldn't want to lose you again."

"Fine. Then I would like to see my friends, Ruven Keldan and Quimby Carver, if they are still within the city and you can locate them. We had rooms at Ye Olde Snake Inn and Tavern."

"I'm sorry, my dear, that is something I cannot allow. Wouldn't want you to plot an escape with them, now would we?" He wipes the sweat from his brow.

"If that's what you're afraid of, then post a guard. Hell, attend the meeting yourself. I don't care. I just want to see my friends." Tears fill my eyes.

Claudius sucks his teeth at me and shakes his head. "I still won't allow it and crying will not sway me. It's not a chance I'm willing to take. Sorry, girl. If it's conversation you desire, I will have Zeke visit you. That is all I will allow."

"Until when?" I ask. "What do you have planned for me? Will you ever allow me to leave this room?"

"You're not completely healed yet and you still require rest. I won't burden you with my plans. Now get some rest. I'll have Zeke attend you later this afternoon."

Claudius heaves himself off the chair and crosses the room, his notable bulk swaying back and forth, then disappears through the door. The guard he leaves behind unlocks my shackles, then follows Claudius, locking the door behind him. I rub my wrist where it has become sore from being chained for five days while I pace the floor. It feels good to stretch my legs, but I yearn for true freedom. It's clear Claudius has some grand plan in the works and the curious part of me wants to find out what it is. But the rest of me only wishes to reunite with my friends, then watch Blackwick disappear behind us as we continue on to Naren Thalore. I must escape my current predicament and decide my only course of action at this point is to persuade Zeke to help me flee captivity.

Several hours later, a quiet knock at the door causes my muscles to tense. During the five days I've been in this cage, no one has knocked before entering.

I take a deep breath. "Come in."

The door swings open, and I breathe a sigh of relief when I see it is only Zeke coming to pay me a visit, as his father promised. He stands in the doorway, grinning.

I motion him inside. "Come in, Zeke. It's okay."

As he crosses the threshold, the door closes behind him and I hear the click of the lock I have grown so accustomed to.

"Hey Zeke. Your father said you would come to visit me. I'm glad to see you. Please have a seat."

"Hi pretty lady." Zeke seats himself. "I like you. We'll have nice talks."

"Yes, I look forward to getting to know you better. I have little in my room, but what can I do to make you more comfortable?"

"I'm fine like this. What do you want to do?"

"I don't know. Being locked up alone has made me lonely. I'm just happy to have someone to talk to."

"Okay, then let's talk. Why are you locked up in here?"

"Your father tried to keep me here, so I left without his permission. He wants to make sure I don't leave again."

Zeke's eye widen in disbelief. "My dad is a good dad. He's a nice man. He would never do that."

I realize Zeke may not be as smart as I thought. He's disillusioned about my plight, and I doubt he will provide much help to escape. I get the sense this is why Claudius agreed to send Zeke to entertain me during my time here. He thinks Zeke won't be useful to me. I decide to befriend him none the less and see what information or help I can get out of him, but doing so will require tact for speaking to Zeke is like addressing a young child.

"How old are you Zeke?"

"I'm fifteen. How old are you?"

"Sixteen, but I'm getting close to my seventeenth birthday."

Zeke's eyes light up. "I hope you have a party. I like parties. Can I come to your birthday party?"

"Of course you can, Zeke. You'll be there if I have one."

"You better have one. I'll tell my dad that you need to have one."

"What do you enjoy doing for fun?"

"I like watching fights at the arena. I like to watch my brother compete."

"Do you explore the city alone or are you accompanied by guards?"

"I always have guards, but sometimes I run away from them. I don't like them following me and telling me what to do."

A light bulb flashes on inside my mind. "Do you think you could do me a favor?"

He nods. "Anything for you, pretty lady."

"Listen carefully, Zeke. The next time you go to the arena, run away from your guards. Go to an inn called Ye Olde Snake and ask to speak to a boy named Ruven.

If he's there, tell him where I am. Tell him I need help. Do you think you can do that?"

He smiles. "It's like a game."

"Yes, just like a game."

Zeke rises. "I'll go now."

"Okay. That's good. What are you to do?"

"I'm supposed to leave the guards, go to the inn and tell Ruven where you are."

"Yes, very good. Thank you, Zeke."

"Don't go anywhere, pretty lady. I'll be back soon."

He exits the room and the lock clicks behind him. My only thought is that I hope he can accomplish the task I have set before him. I know I cannot escape Shadowfield Estate for a second time, at least not as easily as I did before, so I must use what cunning and wits I possess to break out of this place and continue my task to return Ruven to his people.

I spend the next four days locked in my room with no visitors. The servants continue to bring my meals, but none of them speak to me. I eat alone and receive no more visits from Zeke, so I don't know if he contacted Ruven. I entertain myself the best I can, but I'm bored all the same, so I spend most of my time sprawled on the bed, sleeping or crying. My loneliness grows more intense with each passing day. I have to leave this room soon.

The door opens, causing me to spring upright from my prone position on the bed. The butler enters and tosses a dress on the bed next to me.

"You will dress and meet Master Claudius for

dinner. I will await you in the hall so I may escort you to the dining hall." He exits the room.

I change into the dress provided to me, which is black and form fitting. It shimmers in the candlelight. I step into the hall where the butler is waiting, accompanied by a pair of guards. I know the guards are present to prevent me from escaping in some foolish manner. The butler leads me to the foyer, where we descend the stairs and enter the dining room where I had my first meal at Shadowfield Estate. Claudius sits at the head of the table, eyeing me as I enter the room. I'm disappointed he is alone and annoyed that he has already begun eating after having invited me to join him.

I take the seat to his left. "So you invite me to dine with you, but don't wait for me to join you before you stuff your face."

"There's no reason for you to be rude, my dear Valessa. After all, I unchained you and I sent you Zeke just like I said I would."

"It's true that you did those things. I won't deny it. But I only saw Zeke once, and you continued to keep me locked up in my room alone."

Claudius nods. "Aye, I did. The most curious thing happened. After visiting you, Zeke left the grounds, where he ran away from his guard and disappeared into the city. Hours later, he returned with that strange boy who so adamantly pleaded for your life at the arena trailing after him. I suspect it was something you put into his head. Therefore, Zeke will not be visiting you again."

I'm unsure if I can outsmart Claudius and escape

him. I stare at him as he continues to shovel food into his gaping mouth.

"Are you going to sit there gawking or are you going to eat? I had the cooks prepare this meal for you." He says after some time.

"I just don't understand what your game is here. What is it you want from me?"

Claudius sets his fork down and turns his attention toward me. "What do I want from you?" He laughs. "I want nothing from you. I want you."

His implication makes me shudder.

"I'm sure your dear Quimby told you all about me, about how I like rare and beautiful things. I like to collect oddities. There is something quite odd about you, and I mean to have it. Upon the closing of autumn, we will be wed and you will be mine." He gives me a disturbing smile.

"That will not happen. I will be leaving."

I leap to my feet, pulling my hands in close to my chest. Near the door, the guards step in my direction, but Claudius raises one fat hand and waves them away, leaving me puzzled.

"I know what you're planning in that head of yours and you don't frighten me, girl. I meet many people here, so the same wards that seal the arena also seal this estate. Your magic won't work while you're on these grounds. Take your seat and let's enjoy our dinner, shall we?"

I lower myself back into my chair, my mind racing as I try to work out a way to escape the fate Claudius has outlined for me.

"It's no matter. I still refuse to marry you and you can't make me. You hold nothing over me to sway me."

Claudius throws his head back and releases a bout of raucous laughter from deep within his gullet. "Is that what you think, you stupid bitch? I already told you Zeke returned with your little friend. You believe I just let him leave?"

Fear and panic burst inside me. "What have you done to him?"

"Oh, don't worry. He is quite safe and enjoying his new accommodations in the basement dungeon. It's strange how he wears his chains with such pride. Would you like to see him?"

I nod. "Yes, of course. Show him to me."

Claudius waves a hand at the guards, who leave then return a few moments later with Ruven in tow. True to Claudius's word, Ruven wears chains. His expression is one of fear and sadness, but his eyes light up when he sees me.

"Valessa, I'm so sorry," says Ruven. "I hope you're okay."

Tears flood my eyes. "I'm okay, Ruven. We'll get out of this somehow."

Ruven nods.

"You bastard." I turn on Claudius. "Let him go. He has nothing to do with this. Nothing at all."

"I will let him go after we are wed, and you have accepted your fate. Until then, he will remain chained below, no matter how long it takes for you to acquiesce."

I shake my head in disbelief. "That will never

happen."

"So be it." Claudius nods at the guards holding Ruven.

A guard raises his hand and brings it across Ruven's face and a resounding slap fills the air. Ruven winces. Claudius waves his hand in the air, and the guard strips Ruven of his shirt and turns him away from us. The guards then take turns striking Ruven on his bare skin. Tears fill my eyes and flow down my face as Ruven cries out in pain and large red welts form on his back. Ruven falls to his knees on the floor as the guards continue their brutal beating. They look at Claudius, who waves his hand in a carry on manner again and the guards return to their work of beating the helpless boy lying on the floor, raining blows upon him with their fists and feet.

I jump to my feet. "Stop this. Stop this now. I'll do whatever you want. Just don't hurt him anymore."

Claudius nods to the guards, and they pick Ruven up and carry him away.

"I want to see him," I say as liquid silver tears stream down my face.

"I can arrange that, my dear," says Claudius. "But only if you behave and do as I bid. Now, I apologize for that show. I do so hate to see you cry. Please eat with me. After all, that's why I asked you to join me."

I look at the plate in front of me. The food looks appealing but, having lost my appetite, I only pick at it to appease my host. Dread fills me now that I know what I must do if I hope to leave this place. I must do whatever Claudius wants, hoping it will gain me his trust and more freedom within the estate.

A few minutes pass before Claudius looks up from his plate and smiles at me. "You look radiant in that dress, Valessa."

I glance down and take in how the dress accentuates my body. "Thank you." I feel my cheeks warm from a sudden blush. "It is rather plain, but beautiful all the same. I really like how it shimmers in the candlelight."

"Yes, yes. It was quite expensive to give it that shimmer as well. It's no easy feat to grind diamonds into powder to mix into dye, but I will spare no expense for you."

"I wasn't aware such a thing was even possible."

"Well, nothing is impossible if you have enough riches. This is a lesson you will soon learn."

Claudius raises his hand and waves the servers over. They clear our plates, then return with dessert. The sweet smell of chocolate invades my nostrils as they set a plate before me. Lying on the plate is a large slice of chocolate cake, topped with chocolate frosting and sliced strawberries. My mouth waters as I dig into it. The richness of the cake is intoxicating, and I consume the whole thing.

"How has your stay here been, my dear?" asks Claudius.

"It's been okay now that I'm no longer chained, but I get bored alone in my room all the time."

"Is there something I can do to help?"

"There may be. As I have had time to reflect on my pitiful performance in the arena, I was hoping you might allow me to learn a little swordsmanship. For self-defense only, of course."

Claudius studies me, no doubt looking for some sign of deception. "Very well. If it will make you happy, so be it. I shall instruct Zayn to see that you receive some proper lessons."

Overcome by what little joy I can find in this wretched place, I smile at Claudius and thank him for his consideration.

Our meal draws to a close, and I'm excused and escorted back to my room. After hearing the familiar click of the lock, I disrobe and climb into bed. Sleep does not come easy for me this night as thoughts of Ruven and my plight dance through my head, sometimes accompanied by excitement for learning another skill I'm sure will serve me well.

Chapter 21

I have lost count of how many days I've been a prisoner at Shadowfield Estate, because each day is the same. Most days I spend several hours with Zayn practicing slashing, dodging, parrying, deflecting, lunging and pivoting. Zayn says I have nice form and a good grip, but although I have learned a lot, I still have much more to learn. After proving my proficiency with the training swords, Zayn gifts me with a sword of my own. The blade is long and thin, with a slight curve to it. Black leather wraps around the simple hilt. It is now my most prized possession. Besides swordsmanship, I convince Zayn to help me improve my skill with the bow, too. With the Crimsonclaw Nightwalkers, I learned enough to be an efficient hunter, but I lack true skill with this weapon. I have improved, though.

Most nights, I join Claudius in the dining hall for dinner. The food is great, but the company isn't. Sometimes Zeke and Zayn attend dinner, but often it is

only me and Claudius. I behave well enough that
Claudius allows me to see Ruven, but only once, and he
forbid me to speak to him. His time in the dungeon is
taking its toll on him. He has grown ragged and thin, his
pale skin and silver hair turned dark by dirt and bruises.
Upon seeing him, I begged Claudius to free him, but he
refused and I have not asked again. The fateful day of
my wedding approaches, and I must play my part if
either of us is to get out of this place.

I have followed the rules laid out for me, so
Claudius now allows me to leave my room if I wish to,
the only stipulation being that I cannot leave the house. I
take advantage of his offer when I can, strolling through
the corridors and investigating some rooms I find. On
one such escapade, I find the most curious locked door
decorated in designs I remember seeing at some point,
but cannot remember where. Centered near the top of the
door, a nine-pointed star is carved into the ebony wood.
A red thorn adorns each tip of the star, and the middle
houses a glass ball that appears to be filled with dark
swirling smoke. The carving is frightening yet beautiful.
I place my hand on the door and a shiver runs down my
spine, causing me to gasp and back away.

A few days later, I remember where I saw such
symbolism before. I rummage through my belongings
and find the strange key from Father Vossler's church.
When I presented the key to Ruven, he was frightened. I
take the key to the imposing door and slip it into the
lock. I turn the key and hear a faint click, then nuzzle the
door open and enter the dim room. My eyes adjust to the

lighting and I gasp, realizing the room is the same as the shadow altar room in the church's basement. There are nine torches lining the walls at even intervals and a raised stone dais, which is discolored in a dark brown I know is dried blood. On one wall hangs a dark, hooded cloak the size of a bedsheet. I know it must belong to Claudius.

I lock the door behind me as I exit the room. Claudius is in league with or has some agreement with the beings from the church I destroyed. Regardless of the circumstances, the danger Ruven and I are in is clearer now. My first instinct is to escape with Ruven, but this would likely be a death sentence for us both. I decide to continue my charade of complying with Claudius's requests if we are to survive and see ourselves delivered to Naren Thalore. I return to my room to reflect on our situation and await my summons to dinner, but my summons never comes, so I eat dinner alone in my room for the first time in weeks, wondering if Claudius knows I discovered his secret room.

The days linger on, and I remain confined to my room with no visitors. I practice my sword play with the sword Zayn gifted me wondering what I have done to receive this punishment once again. I've had no word of Ruven's fate, nor do I know what has become of Quimby. In my room without windows, I have lost count of how long I've been sequestered. As each day bleeds into the next, I lose hope of seeing my friends again and of escaping Shadowfield Estate.

I'm in the middle of my swordsmanship practice

routine when the door opens and a short round woman enters. She nods and motions for me to join her in front of the vanity.

"Who are you?" I ask.

"Why, I'm the seamstress, milady. Now come, we have to get you measured," she says in a sweet voice.

I approach the chair, puzzled. "Measured for what?"

"Your gown, milady. Master says it must be perfect and so has sent me to gather your measurements."

I hesitate. "What gown is that?" I'm certain I already know what gown she's referring to.

"The gown you will wear on the magnificent day when you wed our great governor and become our governess, milady."

I walk to the chair, dragging my feet. I can't tell if this woman is excited or if she's being sarcastic, but it doesn't matter. The day is fast approaching and I see no way out of marrying that fat slob Claudius. I stand in front of her, holding my arms out beside me, and wait while she takes my measurements. Once she has finished, she gathers her tools, bows and exits the room, leaving me in my solitude where I throw myself onto my bed and weep into my pillow, feeling lost, helpless and alone.

I don't remember falling asleep, only waking to the sound of birds chirping and snoring. *But how can I be snoring if I'm awake?* I bolt upright in the bed. My face flushes with anger and my heart races when I see Claudius's massive form lying in the bed beside me.

I leap out of the bed and wrap a robe around myself.

"What are you doing in my bed?" I smack Claudius on his enormous behind with a shoe.

Claudius jumps and opens his eyes, breathing hard. "What's going on? What happened?"

"What are you doing in my bed?"

"I was sleeping until I was so rudely awakened. What else would I be doing?" Claudius hoists his immense mass into a sitting position.

"But why are you sleeping in my bed? That's what I want to know."

"Oh Valessa, I don't know why you are so angry. We will be man and wife soon. I simply could not wait to know what it's like to sleep with you." Claudius smiles.

A shiver runs down my spine at the thought.

"You don't seem pleased," says Claudius as he rises to his feet.

"Why would I be? I have no desire to marry you, so why would I enjoy the thought of sleeping with you?"

Claudius crosses the room to the door. "You have no choice, dear. Do enjoy the rest of your day."

"Just get out of my room, you pig." I slam the door behind him when he leaves.

Thoughts flood my head once I'm alone. *What happened last night? Did Claudius touch me? How did he enter my bed without waking me? Perhaps he drugged me. He could have done anything to me and I would never know unless he told me.* The thoughts make my stomach knot. I pace the floor for the rest of the day and find it hard to sleep that night.

Several days later, I'm startled awake when my door

bursts open. I bolt upright as Claudius enters. He waddles across the room and seats himself on the edge of the bed.

"What do you want?" I ask, annoyed by his presence.

"Don't be so rude, dear."

"What reason do I have to be nice to you? You hold me here against my will and are forcing me to marry you. I wake up one morning to find you in my bed. Plus, I've been locked up so long I don't even know how many days have passed. I've done everything you've asked. What have I done to warrant this treatment?"

"You have done nothing, my dear girl. I just needed you out of the way while we made preparations. That is all." He reaches out and places his hand on my arm.

I snatch my arm away. "So, this has nothing to do with my finding a certain room?"

"Whatever do you mean?"

"I found a room identical to one I've seen before, where innocent people were being sacrificed and eaten."

Claudius sighs. "Oh, that room. That room is solely to entertain certain guests I see occasionally. I, however, do not partake of the feast when they visit."

"Why have them visit at all?"

"For business reasons. Stop prying, girl. I'll answer no more questions regarding this topic."

"Fine. It was unnecessary to lock me away during your preparations. If you had asked, I would have stayed out of the way."

"Oh, I doubt that, Valessa. You most definitely

would have interfered with the wedding arrangements."

"Those are the preparations you were keeping me away from? I would have cooperated in order to keep Ruven safe. You know that. I might have wanted a say in my wedding. What are you hiding from me?"

Claudius laughs. "I'm not hiding anything. There was a lot to do, and I didn't need you in the way while attending to my duties as governor. It's even more important that you stay out of the way now that the guests have arrived."

"You know what you're saying makes no sense, don't you? I haven't been in your way since being here. Also, shouldn't I meet the guests that will attend my wedding?"

"Yes. And you will meet some of them at the pre-wedding dinner I have promised them, but not before. Until that dinner, you will stay in this room and I will hear nothing more about it."

Claudius heaves his massive girth off my bed and exits the room before I can protest. The revelations he afforded me have left me dumbfounded. I take to my feet and pace the room. So much of what Claudius said makes no sense, and I fear he has not told me the whole truth regarding my confinement. He is hiding something and I hope it has nothing to do with Ruven.

A few days later, my door opens again. A maid enters and drops a dress on the bed. It's the same blue satin and black lace gown I wore to my first dinner with Claudius.

"You'll dress, then we will proceed to the dining

hall for dinner. Master Claudius begs that you be on your best behavior in front of his esteemed guests," she says before exiting the room.

I shrug out of my plain brown shift and step into the elaborate blue dress. Once ready, I step into the hall to be greeted by the butler, who helps me lace the back of my dress up before leading me down the corridor to the grand foyer. We descend the stairs, then he leads me to the dining hall where several people have already seated themselves at the long table and are engaging in various private conversations. Some of them stop talking mid-sentence and turn their attention to me. As I cross the room, I hear murmurs of how beautiful I am and how lucky I am to be marrying the governor of Blackwick. I don't know any of the guests except for Zeke and Zayn, seated halfway down the table. I keep my eyes down and remain silent as I take my seat to the left of the head of the table and await Claudius's arrival, aware of all the eyes resting on me.

Minutes later, Claudius enters through the door at the rear of the room. Two men I have seen before follow him. They must be important to enter with the host. One of them is Dodrik Bloodaxe, the angry dwarf who arranges the proceedings at The Onyx Arena. He rounds the table and seats himself to my left. The other man is the large dark-skinned man I saw thrashing helpless dwarves at The Lower Cresford Mine. My blood boils as he takes the seat across from me. Claudius lowers himself into the chair at the head of the table, smiling at the guests, before turning his attention to me.

"You look lovely this evening, dear." Claudius grins. "Are you enjoying the company of my guests?"

"I guess," I say without looking up.

"Well, I know you've already met Dodrik at the arena."

Dodrik smiles at me. "Yes, we know each other pretty well, I'd say. Ain't that right, sweetheart?" He laughs.

"Yes. How are you, Dodrik?" I ask.

"I'm well. Would be better had you died in the arena, but I can't complain now that yer marryin our governor. That brings joy to me heart, that does," he says with a laugh. "You know there are worse things than dyin." Dodrik pokes me in the ribs, laughing.

I wince. "Yes, well, I'm honored you are attending our big day," I say with a hint of sarcasm.

"Dodrik is our guest, Valessa. Don't be rude to our guests. Now this lad here is Maldrak." Claudius points at the dark man to his right. "He oversees The Lower Cresford Mine. He is a dear friend of mine."

I study the man sitting across from me. His dark skin is smooth and ripples over his muscles. The red tattoos I had seen from a distance are more intricate and elaborate than I imagined. They wind their way down his arms and over his bald head. My gaze settles on his face and I see he is studying me with his dark brown eyes, a smile on his face.

"I've seen him before," I say. "As we made our way over The Cresford Range, we passed The Lower Cresford Mine. That's where I first laid eyes on this one." I point at Maldrak. "He was whipping defenseless dwarves for no reason other than they were not producing fast enough for him. He's a monster."

"Oh, I can be," says Maldrak in his deep thunderous voice, "but there at the mine, I was doing my job. We have quotas to make mind you."

I turn to Dodrik. "How can you dine with him after what he's done to your family?"

Dodrik snorts. "Claudius invited me here as a guest, just as he was. Unlike you, I know how to mind me manners."

"How dare you?"

"Valessa, you're embarrassing me, my dear. You will calm down and behave appropriately for polite society or you will return to your room and eat dinner alone," says Claudius.

"You want me to behave sitting here next to these two? I want them to leave, and I don't want them at the wedding." I leap to my feet.

Claudius slams his hand on the table. "That is enough. These are my guests, not yours, and you will respect me and them. As long as they are in my home, you will say nothing more against them. Do I make myself clear?"

"Crystal." I stomp out of the dining hall.

"I apologize for my bride to be's outburst. It seems the stress has gotten to her," says Claudius as I leave.

I return to my room, disrobe and sink into bed. All the emotions I've been holding inside me come to the surface at once. I'm afraid of what the future holds for me with my impending nuptials and for what they mean for Ruven. I'm curious about Quimby's whereabouts and how Alkin has fared after our showdown in the alley. Tears flow down my face as I realize I have failed everything I set out to do since fleeing The Vauxsard Overhang. I have not protected Ruven and now he may never see his homeland again and it's my fault. If I listened, if I hadn't entered the arena, I wouldn't have attracted Claudius Darkmore's attention. He wouldn't be forcing me to marry him on the morrow, and I would return Ruven to his people in Naren Thalore. I weep for all that I've lost as I drift to sleep.

Chapter 22

I wake the next morning to a gentle knock on the door. The seamstress enters carrying a bundle of white silk and lace and lays the bundle on the bed beside me. Only then do I realize this is my wedding dress. I pull myself out of bed, and the seamstress helps me into the dress. It's floor length with a full skirt and long lacy train. The straight neckline covers my bosom and long lacy sleeves flow down my arms and flare at my wrists. The dress fits me well.

"It's beautiful," I say.

"Thank you, milady. I worked hard day and night to complete it in time."

The seamstress bows then exits the room as another servant enters. She approaches the vanity while motioning for me to join her. I have never seen this woman before.

"Who are you?" I ask.

"Why, I'm your new handmaiden, milady," she says

in a singsong voice. "They sent me to see to your hair and makeup. You must look your best for your big day."

I sit at the vanity and allow the woman to brush and style my hair. She piles it atop my head in a series of curls then applies blush, eye shadow and lipstick to my face.

"I've never worn makeup before," I say.

"That's okay. I will make you look beautiful."

As I watch in the mirror, tears cloud my vision.

"No, no," she says, "if you cry, we will have to start all over."

"I'm sorry. I just . . . I can't . . ."

The handmaiden frowns. "It's hard. I know. But we are with you. You have all of our thoughts and prayers. We remember what you did, Savior of The Twisting Desert."

I gasp. I thought nothing would come from rescuing those poor souls from the Gobines, and I expected no one would ever assign me a title.

"How do you know about that? Were you there?" I ask.

"I was not, milady. But my brother was one of those you rescued. You don't know how grateful we are that you returned him to us. We never thought to see him again." She kneels at my feet. "So many of the common folk love and adore you. Know that you have our support, no matter what comes."

"I don't know what to say. I did what I thought was right. There's no need to thank me." I beckon her to rise. "Tell me, what is your name?"

She stands. "Eve. Eve Carrin, if it pleases you, milady."

"I will always remember the kindness you've done me this day, Eve. If ever you or your family require anything, you need only ask."

"We only want to be free, milady." She leaves the room.

Alone once more, I await the time when I will proceed to my wedding. I gaze at myself in the mirror, taking in all the intricate details of the dress and my hair. For the first time in my life, I feel pretty. I notice that small shining gems adorn the bodice and skirt of the dress, and the pattern of the lace is complex and detailed. The amount of work by the seamstress is clear. I seat myself at the vanity once again and study the tight curls of my hair. I pull a few strands of hair out of some curls and let them fall so they frame my face.

The door opens, drawing me out of my anxious thoughts. Joy fills me when I see Ruven standing in the doorway wearing a royal blue suit with a light blue striped shirt underneath. I race across the room and draw him into an embrace.

"I've missed you so much, Ruven." Tears well up in my eyes.

"I've missed you too, Valessa. I thought I would never see you again. Hell, I didn't think I would ever leave that basement. I'm so happy to see you, even if it isn't under the best circumstances."

I push Ruven away from me and hold him at arms-length. "But what are you doing here?"

"The governor has deemed me the one to give you away at the ceremony. I believe he thinks it will break me further."

A single tear slides down Ruven's face. I brush it away and look him in the eye. "It's going to be okay, Ruven. You have to believe that. We have to believe that."

Ruven nods.

"Have you seen Quimby? Where was he that day we were trying to leave? What held him up?"

"I don't know. I never found him that day and I hadn't seen him since until today. He is the entertainment."

"That's great. I would like to talk to him."

Ruven tucks his hand inside his suit jacket Napoleon style and presents me with his elbow. "We should get going. Everyone is waiting for you."

"I don't want to do this."

"I know. Just know I will never leave you. Let that get you through it." Ruven gives me a weak smile.

I return his smile and take his arm, ready to face my fate and meet my destiny.

Ruven leads me to the staircase of the grand foyer, which is decorated in the most extravagant manner. Strings of pearls dangle from the ceiling, cascading over the chandeliers. A red velvet carpet goes down the stairs into the great hall. Decorative candelabras adorn the room and braziers full of colorful fragrant flowers line the carpet. We stop atop the stairs to take in the magnificent decorations.

"I want you to know I think you look beautiful," Ruven says, leaning into my ear.

"Thank you. You look quite handsome yourself."

"Kind of wish I was the one marrying you and not that fat pig, Claudius."

I say nothing in response. I suspected Ruven had grown fond of me, so his statement doesn't surprise me.

Together, Ruven and I make our way down the stairs, following the red carpet until we enter the great hall. The throngs of people inside fall silent. I don't recognize many of the faces among the crowd, only those I saw at dinner the night before. Claudius's sons and Quimby stand along the wall near the door. Quimby smiles when our eyes meet, which makes my blood boil. His grinning angers me, especially knowing he has done nothing to help free me from the prison of Shadowfield Estate and Claudius's clutches.

They decorated the great hall similar to the grand foyer with the red velvet carpet running down the center of the room to where Claudius stands on a raised platform, sweating and grinning in a lavender silk suit. He looks ridiculous, but no one would dare tell him such. An older gentleman in a black robe stands on the dais with him, who I assume is a priest. As Ruven and I approach, I feel all the eyes in the room focused on me, making me nervous.

"Who gives this woman to be wed?" asks the man in the black robe when we reach the end of the carpet.

"I do. Ruven Keldan," says Ruven. "Her friend and confidant, I give this woman to be wed on this day."

"Very well," says the priest, and Ruven places my hand into Claudius's slimy meaty paw.

Ruven melts into the crowd, leaving me there with Claudius. I search the crowd for him, but I only see Quimby slipping out the rear door, and I wonder where he is going.

"Friends, family and loved ones," says the priest, "we come here today to see these two, Claudius Darkmore, Governor of Blackwick and Lady Valessa Thorley, joined in matrimony. We are here to celebrate the binding of their souls into one and rejoice in the happiness they will surely share. They will grow as a single entity and share in each other's triumphs and defeats. What say you, Claudius Darkmore? Do you take this delicate flower under your wing and promise to protect and cherish her until the end of your days?"

Claudius nods. "I do and I shall always."

"What say you, Valessa Thorley? Do you take this powerful warrior under your wing and promise to support and care for him until the end of your days?"

My mind clouds with fog and everything freezes. I know the words to say, but I can't make them come out. Fear I will collapse at any moment overwhelms me, so I look for a reassuring smile from Ruven, but he is nowhere to be seen.

Claudius nudges me. "I do and I shall always."

I take a deep breath. "I, uh . . . I . . ."

"You can do it. Just say the words," says Claudius.

"I do and I—"

The door flies open, startling all in attendance. All

heads turn to gaze at the figure standing in the doorway. A sharp sudden inhalation fills my lungs with air, and I'm filled with heart rate quickens as my eyes take her in. Lavina, in all her glory, has interrupted the ceremony. I'm thankful for her arrival, even if she is the last person I want to see. She may be the key to escaping the horrible fate in store for me.

Lavina laughs and stalks down the aisle toward the dais where I stand with Claudius. Her purposeful steps make her long black cape billow out behind her, and her green eyes shine with excitement.

"You," she says, pointing a long thin finger at me. "You will be coming with me, you little bitch."

"What is the meaning of this?" asks Claudius. "Who are you? How dare you interrupt this grand occasion?"

"You don't need to know who I am. Only that I am here for her." Lavina points at me once again. "That bitch stole from me and now she will pay."

"You will not talk about my bride in that manner. You have no right to be here. The guards will escort you off my property." Claudius raises his hand to command the guards.

"I don't think so," says Lavina. Her green eyes flare as she flashes a devilish smile.

"They've warded the estate against the use of magic, Lavina. You have no power here," I say.

"Oh, but I do. I broke those wards days ago."

Knowing Lavina will attack, I focus all my energy into my core in preparation to defend myself and the others. Everyone watches the guards close in around

Lavina. When they surround her, there's a blinding white flash and the guards fly across the room and crash into the walls as if thrown by a giant. Every one of them crumples to the floor, still and lifeless. Lavina throws her hands forward and releases a ball of blue flame in my direction. I dodge her assault by throwing myself to the floor. As I gather my wits about me, I hear the shrill screams of the priest as flame consumes his robes. The entire room erupts into screams and chaos as the wedding guests attempt to flee the wrath of Lavina.

I leap to my feet while forcing the gathered energy down my arms and lob a fireball of my own at Lavina. Anticipating my counterattack, Lavina throws a shield up in front of her. We lock eyes through the shimmering pale blue shield. The hum of energy fills the room.

"Stop this," says Claudius. "Stop this right now. You're ruining everything." He stomps his foot.

Lavina ignores Claudius's pleas to stop and lobs another fireball in my direction. I dodge this one, too, and return fire once again. Behind me, the curtains catch fire. I toss fireball after fireball at Lavina, but they bounce off the shield she has conjured to protect herself. Lavina's swift hands bat away the few that make it past. As the battle continues, I feel my strength wane and I fear I won't survive this encounter. My only chance is a reprieve, but I have no hope of a rescue.

"Stop this," Claudius says again. "Maldrak, put a stop to this. Now."

I breathe a sigh of relief, hoping Maldrak can help me defeat Lavina. From the corner of my eye, I watch

Maldrak walk past me toward Lavina. *Is that a glimmer of fear in her eye?* She conjures a bolt of lightning, focusing it on Maldrak. He slows but does not stop. When he reaches Lavina, he smashes an enormous fist into the magical barrier in front of her. Fine, hairlike cracks spread across its surface, but it continues to hold. Maldrak raises his fist to strike the barrier another blow as the door slams open, revealing four potential saviors.

Quimby enters the room and tosses my sword at me. "I retrieved this for you. Thought you could use it."

I grab the sword. "Thanks."

Ruven follows Quimby, carrying a large hammer. He sets his eyes on Claudius and stalks down the aisle. The two figures that follow surprise me. One I have never seen before. He's a large, hulking man covered in orange fur with black stripes like a tiger. The gigantic head atop his shoulders looks like a tiger's as well, complete with razor sharp fangs and piercing yellow eyes. He growls and leaps toward Lavina. I never thought to see the man behind this stranger again, and I'm happy he is here.

Alkin enters the room and rushes to me. He kneels beside me and studies me with his golden eyes. "Are you okay?"

I nod. "What are you doing here? I thought I'd never see you again. You said you wanted nothing more to do with me."

Alkin shakes his head. "I couldn't . . ."

"Zayn, defend your father, boy," says Claudius from the dais.

I scan the room. The flaming curtains have set some furnishings ablaze. Maldrak has bashed his way through Lavina's shield and is closing on her as Quimby and the tiger man approach her from the rear. Terror crosses her face as the tiger man grabs her by the wrist. Maldrak takes her other wrist and the two of them lift her off the floor.

"Look what you've done to me," says the tiger. "Undo this curse you have put on me, witch."

Maldrak swings a powerful fist into Lavina's stomach, causing her to wince in pain as the air whooshes out of her lungs.

"Never," Lavina says.

Maldrak brings his fist into her stomach again while Quimby laughs at Lavina's unfortunate situation.

On the dais, Ruven corners Claudius. He stands over him with the hammer, muttering something I cannot hear as Alkin helps me to my feet.

"Zayn, do as your father commands. Defend me. Kill this insolent boy," says Claudius.

I watch in horror as Zayn picks up his sword and struts toward Ruven.

I grab Alkin's shirt. "Help him. Please. He cannot die."

Alkin nods and lunges toward Zayn. I pick up my sword and walk to Maldrak and the tiger, who are still holding Lavina hostage. The sounds of fighting fill the air behind me.

"What do you want from me?" I say once I am face to face with Lavina.

"No one steals from me. No one plays me as a fool. I want you dead. But they want you alive, so I won't kill you. Not yet. I will take you to them first and when the opportunity is right, then I will take my revenge."

"Who wants me alive?"

"The ones they call the oppressors."

"What do they want with me?"

"They believe you are the one promised by the prophecy, and they want to harness your power."

"They're wrong."

Lavina laughs.

"Put her down."

Maldrak does as I say and releases Lavina, who falls to the floor. Lavina rises to her feet in front of me, raising her hands and muttering an incantation as she does so. Her eyes widen in disbelief as I plunge my sword into her stomach, leaning into it to drive it forward. As I draw it out of her midsection, she crumples to the ground once more, clawing at her stomach. I turn toward the dais to check on Ruven and Alkin. Several gashes criss cross Alkin's arms and legs, but he continues to fight with fervor. Claudius clutches Ruven, but he appears unharmed. I take a few steps forward, but my legs turn to stone and I can move no further. Terror spreads through me as the rest of my body locks up and I drop to the floor. I cannot move or speak, only hear, think, and breathe. Lavina laughs behind me between gasps for air. Alkin and Ruven's eyes widen in fear when they see me fall. Alkin lets loose a fearsome roar as he plunges a hand into Zayn's stomach and tears the flesh of his midsection open, causing his intestines to spill out onto the floor. Zayn collapses, eyes wide as he realizes what has happened. He lies in a pool of bright red blood and takes his final breaths.

"Noooo," says Claudius. He releases Ruven and moves to his son's side. "What have you done, you animal? My boy, my son. You killed him. Guards, Maldrak, take him. Take him now."

Maldrak seizes Alkin. "Shall I kill him, my Lord?"

"No. Death is easy. He deserves a fate far worse than death. He will spend the rest of his days in the prison. See that he arrives there in one piece."

Alkin struggles in Maldrak's grasp but cannot free himself. I can only watch as they carry him away, and I fear I will never see him again. Ruven bolts to my side as I am heaved into the air and slung over a shoulder. All I can see is the orange and black fur of the strange tiger man. Quimby picks up my sword and follows us out the door and into the grand foyer, leaving Lavina bleeding on the floor of the great hall and Claudius weeping over Zayn's corpse.

"This way. Follow me," says Zeke.

Zeke leads us through dark corridors, then outside into the sunlight. We pass through a metal gate and the cobblestones of Blackwick's streets appear below. The tiger man slings me over Sky Blossom's rump before mounting her.

"Thank you for your kindness, young Zeke," says Quimby. "Now return to your father. We must be off."

We gallop through the streets of Blackwick and out

the main gate. The cobblestones turn to dirt under Sky Blossom's hooves as I am ferried away from the horrors I endured in the city.

Chapter 23

We spend the rest of the day galloping down the road in silence. As the sun sets, we make camp concealed within the trees well away from the road. No fire is lit for fear of drawing attention to our position. The tiger man removes me from the back of Sky Blossom and lays me in the dirt beside Ruven, then takes a seat on the ground opposite me.

"Who are you?" Ruven asks.

"My name is Lofthor. I'm a friend of Alkin's," says the tiger.

"I don't know him."

"The wolf boy. He knows her." Lofthor points at me.

"Where did you meet him?"

"In Blackwick. He was a mess when we met. Wouldn't say what happened to him?"

"Why did you help us?"

"Like I said, Alkin is my friend. It seemed important

to him."

"I noticed you went straight for the witch," says Quimby. "Why? What business do you have with her?"

Lofthor turns to Quimby. "You think I always looked like this? I crossed that bitch once, and she cursed me. Made me look like this. Did it so no one would come near me. She took everything from me and doomed me to a life of solitude and loneliness, she did. I want revenge and a cure, but I don't think I'll get either of those now. I thought killing the witch would break the curse, but now she's dead and I'm still cursed. And I can't question the witch thanks to this one here." He points at me again.

"What do we do now?" Ruven asks.

"We carry on. We must get you to Naren Thalore."

"That's fine and well," says Lofthor, "but I won't be joining you. Everyone knows there is nothing in Naren Thalore."

"Where will you go?" asks Ruven.

"Alkin was the first person to talk to me in years. I reckon I will go see him freed from his imprisonment."

"Nonsense," says Quimby. "You know you can't go to Alzalforg. No one can. It's best you leave the poor boy to his fate."

"I will not. Once you reach Naren Thalore and see there's nothing there, you can join me if you wish. The wolf boy saved some of you. You owe it to him to free him, or try to, at the very least."

Lofthor stalks off into the darkness. I yearn to join him, but can do nothing but lie on the ground, locked inside my body like an inescapable fortress. Hot tears roll down my face as my heart aches for Alkin, and I vow I will see him freed if it's the last thing I do, but I must free myself first.

Ruven wipes the tears from my face. "Don't cry, Valessa. We'll do what we can to help both you and Alkin. What is this prison they sent Alkin to?" Ruven asks as he turns his attention to Quimby.

"Oh, Alzalforg is the most hellish of places," says Quimby. "I've never heard tell of any poor soul escaping there. It's the most secure prison in all the land. On the Withered Isle far out in The Wasting Deep lies Alzalforg. Someone aptly named the isle and sea for nothing, and I mean nothing, lives or grows there. Many have drowned in the Wasting Deep, a dangerous sea to cross by boat. The relentless beating of the waves on the isle's shore has sculpted its coastline into jagged rock reminiscent of sharp fangs."

"That sounds terrible."

"That's not even the worst of it," says Quimby. "The prison is a tower that stretches into the sky and disappears into the clouds. Atop the tower, sits Alzalforg's mighty guardian, a fearsome eagle. The magic of the world twisted this one, the largest eagle in Sheonaetara. Its keen eyes watch over the entire island and determine the fate of any prisoners that escape the torments within the tower. The eagle is the last thing they see as it swoops down upon them and devours them."

Ruven's eyes widen. "So even if Alkin gets outside the tower, he still won't escape."

"Aye. Tis true."

"And what of Lofthor? What will happen to him if he tries to approach Alzalforg?"

"Chances are he will never reach the isle. The Wasting Deep is the most treacherous sea in Sheonaetara. Only the most skilled sailors would dare to sail its waters. None of those would grant passage to a civilian wishing to reach the isle for fear of what punishment may await them. If he somehow reaches The Writhing Isle, Alzalforg's guardian will dispose of him. If Lofthor sticks with his plan to rescue Alkin, he is doomed."

Ruven sighs. "What about the prisoners inside the tower? What will become of Alkin once he arrives at Alzalforg?"

"That I cannot say. No one ever returns once they enter Alzalforg. None know what torments the prisoners endure. The common folk tell stories of the prison, though."

"What stories do they tell?"

"They tell tales of the Aracha. Beings so vile that chaos would reign if they were to escape Alzalforg. It's said when a person spends too much time in the depths of the prison, he loses the very thing that makes him human, his soul. A man without a soul is a terrible thing. He has no love for his fellow man. Without a conscience, he does what he wants without thought of how it might affect others."

"That sounds terrible. Is there any hope we could save Alkin from this fate?"

"There's not much hope of that, I'm afraid."

The camp falls silent. My fear turns to despair as everything Quimby has said sinks in. It's my fault they sent Alkin to Alzalforg, and according to Quimby, he will rot in that prison for the rest of his days and I have no hope of rescuing him before he becomes an Aracha. If what Quimby says is true, even attempting to save him would end with my demise. There is nothing I can do while under the effects of Lavina's binding spell, so I resign myself to the fact that I have lost Alkin until I escape my prison. I must put my faith in Ruven and his love for me. I know his love will spur him to undo what has been done and return me to my rightful state.

Ruven wipes the tears from my face again. "It will be okay, Valessa. I will break this spell on you. I will make things better for you."

He lowers himself to the ground and curls up against me. Before long, his breathing slows and I know he has fallen asleep. The information I have learned about Alzalforg races through my mind, but I succumb to my fatigue and drift into restless slumber.

I awake the next morning to the sounds of Quimby and Ruven readying the horses for the day's journey. Ruven smiles when he realizes I'm awake. He seats himself on the ground beside me and places some bread in my mouth, and I realize he would do anything for me and I'm grateful for his friendship. After a few more mouthfuls of bread, Quimby lifts me onto Sky Blossom's back before he mounts up. We return to the road to continue onward toward Naren Thalore.

Every day is the same. We ride while there is light and stop at sunset to pass the night in seclusion. A fire is never lit in the dark to further shield our position. The camp is quiet save for the occasional murmurs of Quimby and Ruven or the soft knickers of the horses. We sleep on the cold, hard ground and wake with the sun every morning. Ruven feeds me bread for dinner every night and for breakfast every morning. After breakfast, I'm slung over Sky Blossom's back before we return to the road to make our way ever closer to Naren Thalore.

I lose track of the number of days that pass. If I was able, I would ask Quimby, for I am certain he knows how much time has passed since we fled Blackwick and how much more time must pass before we arrive at our destination. Every day I stare at the road as it passes beneath Sky Blossom's hooves, always alone with my thoughts of Alkin and the fear I will never see him again, and that if I do, he will no longer be the person he was before. My mind runs rampant, dreaming up the torments he must endure at Alzalforg. I pray we reach Naren Thalore and find Ruven's people and that they can undo what Lavina has done to me.

I lose hope until one night at camp when I hear an exchange between Ruven and Quimby.

"Well, young Ruven, we shall reach Naren Thalore on the morrow," says Quimby. "How does it feel to know you will look upon the works of your people?"

"I don't know," says Ruven. "I was very young. I don't even remember what it's like to be with them."

"Understandable."

"Will they be able to fix Valessa?"

"The Elves are more skilled in magic than anyone else. If they cannot correct Valessa's condition, they will know who can."

Joy fills me at the prospect of being freed from the prison of my body.

"That's good," says Ruven. "The sooner we unbind her, the better."

"Yes, yes. But first we must find the Elves."

"What do you mean find?"

"Naren Thalore used to be a grand Elven city. During the Great War, the Elves abandoned it, along with all the other Elven cities spread across Sheonaetara. The common belief is they are extinct or on the verge of extinction. If any survive, they are hiding, but no one knows where to find them."

"Why are we going to Naren Thalore if the Elves aren't there?"

"Naren Thalore was the last stronghold of the Elves during the Great War. If they left clues to their current location, it would be there."

"What if we find nothing there? What will we do then? How will we free Valessa?" Panic rises in Ruven's voice.

"Don't worry, young Ruven. We will figure out how to reunite you and your young paramour with your people. We will find them. This I swear to you."

The camp falls silent as Ruven curls up beside me on the ground. He runs his hand up and down my arm, caressing my bare skin. Sleeps comes to me fast as I think about the potential end of our journey tomorrow and an end to my imprisonment.

The next day passes as the others, but a palpable anticipation rides the air with us. Around midafternoon, I hear Ruven gasp and I know he has caught his first glimpse of Naren Thalore. A tinge of jealousy runs through me as I wish I could see what has taken his breath away.

We come to a halt and Quimby dismounts. "Come help me, Ruven. Help me with Valessa so she can see too. It is truly a sight to behold, is it not?"

Ruven dismounts and joins Quimby beside Sky Blossom. They wrest me from my mount and turn me toward our destination. It really is a sight to behold. Towering ivory buildings comprise the great city of Naren Thalore and, although they have crumbled from their time unattended, it does not tarnish their grandeur and beauty. Interspersed throughout the city are countless patches of green, winding their way through what must have been streets and alleys in the distant past. But the most remarkable thing about Naren Thalore lies outside the city proper. A dome woven from the branches of the trees encircling the city encloses Naren Thalore, as if someone has turned a basket upside down on it. I can only imagine how lively the city must have been in its prime.

"What do you think?" asks Quimby.

"I don't have words to describe how I feel at the moment," says Ruven.

"Let's get Valessa back on her horse. We will reach

the city by nightfall."

They hoist me back onto Sky Blossom before mounting their own horses and striking out down the road once more. We reach the gate of Naren Thalore as the sun sets on the day.

"We'll camp here for the night," says Quimby, "then begin our search for clues in the morning when we have the light."

Quimby and Ruven dismount and secure the horses before lowering me to the ground. I lie in the dirt and watch them set up camp for the night. Before long, Ruven settles into the dirt beside me and we drift to sleep together, both eager for what will come in the morning.

As the sun rises, so do Ruven and Quimby. They search for a passage into the city. A few minutes pass before they return and carry me to a doorway cut into the dome where they lay me in the dirt before leaving to retrieve the horses. Once inside the dome, the branches weave themselves back together as if no one had ever disturbed them. I'm slung back over Sky Blossom before Quimby leads us deeper into the city. I marvel at the ivory buildings that seem to reach into the clouds. It's clear Naren Thalore was once a glorious city full of life, and it saddens me to see it in its current state.

We walk through the city and find ourselves on the steps of what looks like a city hall. The building is large, with a columned entrance and domed emerald roof that is accented with gold.

"This looks like a good place to start our search," says Quimby.

Ruven ties the horses to a column before removing me from Sky Blossom and carrying me inside the building. More columns decorate the inside of the building, looming over the marble floors and carved crown molding. The interior of the building is just as beautiful as the rest of the city, making me wish I could have seen her in her prime. Ruven carries me through a door and into a room that must have served as a records room or a library. Parchment and scrolls litter the floor, looking as if they have lain here untouched for hundreds of years. Dust covers the books on the shelves that line the walls. Their pages have long since yellowed from exposure to the elements, and I fear they will crumble to dust before much longer. I hope Ruven and Quimby find the answers they seek. My heart aches that I can do nothing to help them. I spend the day watching them search the various texts in the room, seeking clues to the whereabouts of the Elves.

As dusk settles over Naren Thalore, Quimby builds a small fire in the building's entryway that we can huddle around for warmth. As with previous evenings, Ruven feeds me, then curls up beside me on the floor. He wraps his arms around me in a heavy embrace.

"Don't worry, Valessa," he says. "We will find the answers we seek and I'm sure my people can undo what Lavina has done to you. I will go to the ends of the world to fix you if they can't."

I'm unsure if I share the feelings Ruven has for me, and I fear I will break his heart someday. Quimby curls up on his bedroll and, before long, the sounds of his

snoring fill the hall. Ruven's breathing slows and I
realize he, too, has drifted off to sleep. I lie alone in the
dark, wishing sleep would come for me.

The next morning comes far too fast. As the light of
dawn fills the building, Quimby and Ruven rise and head
back into the library to begin the day's search for
answers, leaving me alone in the entry hall. Being a
prisoner in my body makes me feel so useless. My only
solace is the thought that Lavina most likely succumbed
to the wound I inflicted on her.

As with the previous day, Quimby and Ruven return
as dusk falls. Their hanging heads and slumped shoulders
tell me they have found no answers today. The evening
passes in silence and before I know it, Ruven and
Quimby are asleep, leaving me alone with my thoughts
once again.

Every day after passes the same. Ruven and Quimby
rise with the sun and spend the day searching for clues to
locate the Elves. Every few days, we move to another
part of Naren Thalore so Quimby and Ruven can search
through the surrounding buildings. We spend most of our
nights in silence. What conversation occurs is always
about where they should focus the next day's search. The
nights end early, with Ruven and Quimby falling asleep
and leaving me alone with my thoughts.

One night, I'm awakened by a strange voice
chanting in a language I don't recognize. Peering into the
darkness, I see Ruven disappear into a nearby building.
There is a dim flash of blue light, then it becomes dark
and silent once more. Ruven does not return, but there is

nothing I can do as long as I'm locked inside the prison my body has become. I'm forced to wait until the sun rises and Quimby wakes before I can learn what has become of Ruven.

At first light, Quimby drags himself out of bed. He looks around the camp and his eyes widen in surprise. I wish I could call out to him and alert him of Ruven's absence.

Quimby looks at me. "Has Ruven gotten busy without me?"

Quimby heads off in search of Ruven. Several hours pass while I lie in the dirt, worrying about Ruven. As I grow more impatient, Ruven struts out of the building he disappeared into the night before. He sits beside me and places a hand on my shoulder, a huge grin lighting up his face. I long to ask him where he's been.

An hour later, Quimby returns. "I've been looking for you. Where have you been?"

"I found the way. I'll show you. Bring Valessa. They say they can help her."

Quimby picks me up and follows Ruven to a glowing blue doorway. Ruven walks through the door and disappears from view. Quimby steps into the pale blue light. The hair on my body stands on end and a faint buzzing sound fills my ears, then the sensations stop and we are standing in a bright white room surrounded by beings that look like Ruven. Two of them take me from Quimby and carry me down a bright corridor and into a room where they lay me on a table, then exit.

A tall beautiful woman enters the room, her long

silver hair flowing behind her as does her sheer sky blue dress. Her silver eyes peer into my golden ones and she smiles.

The woman approaches the table. "It'll be over soon," she says in a silvery voice.

She raises her hands over me and chants some words I cannot hear. My body loosens its hold over me. She continues chanting until I regain control of myself and sit up on the table.

"Better?" she asks.

"Yes, much better. Thank you." My voice sounds strange to me after not using it for so long.

"Very good. Ruven said your name is Valessa. The queen is eager to meet you."

"Might I know your name so I can thank you properly?"

"I am called Vestele Rogella. I am the Grand Priestess here in Thava Serin."

"Thank you Priestess Vestele. It feels like it's been ages since I had control of myself and I appreciate your help in freeing me from my prison."

"It was my pleasure. Now please ready yourself for an audience with the queen. I have provided adequate clothing for you."

"Thank you."

Vestele leaves the room and I change into the dress provided to me, feeling a little uncomfortable with the plunging V-neck that exposes much of my chest. The long white linen skirt drops to the floor and while the sleeves are short, there are long flowing pieces of sheer cloth that drape to the floor like the skirt. Once dressed, I exit the room and find Ruven awaiting me in the hall.

"It's so good to see you up and about, Valessa," Ruven says, a grin on his face.

"You don't know how good it feels to be up and about."

"This dress is lovely on you."

"Thank you."

Ruven extends his arm to me. "Would you like to meet my mother?"

I take his arm. "I would love to, but I'm supposed to meet with the queen."

Ruven laughs and leads me down the corridor, through a large door and into an expansive room. We walk down the center of the room guided by columns that line the emerald carpet running the length of the room. At the far end is an elaborate gold throne sitting on a raised platform. A beautiful elf sits atop the throne wearing an emerald dress adorned with silver thread and a golden crown of twisted leaves rests upon her head. Her silver eyes light up when she sees us and a smile spreads across her face.

Ruven motions toward the woman on the throne. "Valessa, I would like to introduce you to my mother, Queen Riniya Keldan."

I bow. "It's a pleasure to meet you."

"Likewise, my dear child," says Riniya. "It is a pleasure to have you here. I must thank you for returning my son to me. We thought never to see him again."

"Forgive me, your Grace, for I did not believe

Ruven possessed royal blood."

"It is not necessary to be so formal. You've returned Ruven to me. You are as family to us all. Please call me Riniya."

Ruven grins from ear to ear. "Mother, if it please you, I'm sure Valessa has many questions that she seeks the answers to. I wonder might you provide her a private audience so she may ask the questions plaguing her."

"Of course, my son. You shall both join me for dinner tonight. There, you may receive the answers you seek. Until then, explore our great city and make yourselves at home, for you are home now."

"I never believed Quimby when he said you were a prince," I say once we leave the throne room.

"I hardly believed it myself. I hope it does not change our relationship."

"As long as you stay you, it shouldn't change our dynamic at all."

"I'm happy to hear you say that."

"Where has Quimby gone? I haven't seen him since we arrived."

"Quimby said his work was done now that we have arrived and took his leave. He had become my friend, and I am saddened by his absence."

I say nothing. I never trusted Quimby and I still don't. Good riddance, I think to myself.

"We should explore like your mother said. Where should we go first?" I ask.

"It doesn't matter to me. Let's just roam the city and see what we find."

Hand in hand, Ruven and I leave the palace grounds and make our way to the city proper. I can't believe how lively the atmosphere is. Thava Serin feels so different from any other city we have visited during our exodus from the Chatsraine Forest. The people here seem happy. Ruven and I stumble upon a square that serves as a market. Stalls line the streets as craftsmen hock their wares. Baked goods and other foods line many of the stalls, while others offer household goods such as linens and clothing. The goods are of better quality than any we have seen before.

"We'll have to come do some shopping," I say.

Ruven nods in agreement.

I look at the sky and let the bright sunlight warm my face. It feels good to have a modicum of safety and I hope it lasts.

A neigh draws me out of my reverie. "Let's visit the stables, Ruven. I'd love to see what horses a wonderful place like this possesses."

We ask a nearby vendor for directions, then make our way to the stables. I marvel at the large white building that houses the horses as it comes into view. The stables are brick, with large open windows lining the walls. Vibrant green grass fills the enclosed pasture nearby. We enter the structure, and I stop in my tracks upon seeing the creatures inside. These are no ordinary horses. Every one of them is pure white with gold hooves. A single long ivory horn spirals out of the forehead of each animal housed within.

I gasp. "Unicorns. I can't believe it. They're

beautiful."

"They're quite remarkable. I never imagined creatures such as these could exist."

We watch the stable hands care for the unicorns for a few minutes before heading back out into the street. I spot a building topped with a steeple and pull Ruven in the building's direction. This building must serve as a temple, and I hope I might find Vestele inside. White and gold images of the sun adorn the interior. An altar lies opposite the door and pews line the room. Above the altar stands a detailed sculpture of gold depicting a woman with a halo above her head that looks like the sun.

"It's beautiful, is it not?" asks a soft silvery voice behind me.

I turn to see Vestele has approached undetected. "It is. I wanted to thank you again for what you did for me. It was hell being a prisoner in my body. So many times I wanted to help my friends and couldn't. It was a worse punishment than I could have imagined."

"Dear child, it was nothing, a very easy spell to counteract the witch's curse. I'm quite pleased to see you visiting our temple here."

"Is this your deity?" I motion toward the statue above the altar.

"Indeed, it is." Vestele motions toward a nearby pew where we sit. "Ghyara is goddess of the sun and giver of life. She is a symbol of hope and peace. Our people have worshipped her for centuries. She is the reason our greatest refuge, Thava Serin, has remained undiscovered for so long."

"How does she hide such a wonderful city?" asks Ruven.

"Oh, young one, Thava Serin does not lie on the ground. She floats above the world, hidden within the clouds and disguised by the sun, a magnificent gift from the mother herself. Ghyara provides for all her children as long as they remain faithful."

"So the entire city of Thava Serin is in the clouds?" I ask.

"Indeed. The sky is the last place anyone would search for a city."

"That is true," says Ruven.

"The city and especially the temple here are exquisite," I say. "I'm thrilled to see such things after what Ruven and I have been through."

"You may visit anytime, child," says Vestele.

"I have a question I hope you might answer."

"I will do my best."

"The witch mentioned the oppressors believe I am the one the prophecy refers to. What prophecy?"

"Ah. Long ago, during the Great War, Ghyara granted an oracle with a vision of our salvation. The vision showed a child born of two worlds and gifted in the art of magic. This child will free us from our plight and right the wrongs done to the people of our world. Half elf, half human, the elders secreted this child away to a land unknown for safety. It is said that when the time is right, the child will return and deliver us all from perdition." Vestele wipes a single tear from her eye.

"I'm not the one, am I? I can't be."

"I do not know, child. Anything is possible. It's certainly something to think about."

"I don't believe I'm the one that will right the world, but thank you for answering my question all the same. Now, if you will excuse us, we have dinner with the queen to attend."

Ruven and I rise, but Vestele places her hand on my arm. "I wish you good fortune during your stay here with us. I hope you feel welcome both within The Palace of Light and without in Thava Serin proper."

"Thank you."

On the street, dusk has settled over Thava Serin. The people bustle about on their way to engage in whatever evening activities they enjoy. It's great to see people happy after the atrocities we have witnessed during our journey. Ruven and I weave our way through the throngs of people and arrive back at The Palace of Light. We race to our rooms to prepare for our date with Queen Riniya and her family.

After changing, servants lead us to a great dining hall near the kitchens and seat us at a large oak table. I take in the décor of the dining hall and see it matches that of the throne room. Magnificent chandeliers hang from the ceiling, emitting a dazzling bright light that reminds me of the sun and beautiful green and gold stained glass windows line the walls. A door at the back of the room opens and Queen Riniya enters, followed by two women. The three women share the same golden straw colored hair, but whereas Riniya's eyes are silver, her companion's eyes are a pale green. They are all tall and thin with fair skin and dressed in elaborate dresses of varying shades of gold. Riniya takes the seat at the head of the table, while the others seat themselves across from me and Ruven.

Riniya smiles. "Thank you so much for joining us this evening. I am overjoyed to have you here, as are my sister, Faraine, and my niece, Rania." Riniya points at each of the women.

"It is a pleasure to meet you both," Ruven and I say in unison.

"Thank you," says Faraine. "My sister is quite happy to have her son back. We thought he would never return to us."

"I'm glad to have returned," says Ruven. "I didn't know I had family, or that I had royal blood. It will be a change for me."

"Indeed," says Riniya.

"I'm glad to have you back as well, cousin," says Rania.

Ruven nods to her as servers enter carrying platters of meat, vegetables and fruit. They lay them on the table in front of us and exit the room as quickly as they entered.

"Please help yourselves." Riniya motions at the food arranged on the table. "What's mine is yours for as long as you are here."

The four of us fall into silence as we partake of the victuals afforded us. Everything tastes fresh and delicious and I have to stop myself from overeating. It's been some time since I've had a proper meal. As we conclude our feast, the servers return to remove our plates.

"Now that we have filled our bellies, I know you must have burning questions that require answers," says Riniya. "I will do my best to answer what I can."

"I don't remember ever being here," says Ruven. "Are you sure I belong here and that you are indeed my mother?"

"Believe me when I say you are. Can you not see the resemblance you bear to me?"

Ruven nods. "I can, yes."

"I see it too," I say. "You should not doubt it, Ruven. It's clear this is where you belong."

"Then what happened? How did I end up with the witch?" Ruven asks.

"I do not know, my son," says Riniya. "I laid you to bed one night sixteen years ago and when I arose the next morning, you were missing. There were no clues. You were just gone. I had the entire city searched. I instructed every citizen to look for any sign of you, but there were none. There was no sign of who had taken you or where they stowed you. As the years passed, many citizens believed you were dead and the mystery of your whereabouts remained unsolved. All of Thava Serin rejoices at your return."

"Yes, it is grand that you have returned, nephew," says Faraine.

"I don't remember what happened," says Ruven.

"Are you sure you remember nothing?" asks

Faraine.

"Yes. I remember nothing before the witch. I don't know how I came to be in her possession. She always said I was a stray she had found abandoned in the woods."

"Good. It would be best not to dwell on such awful memories. We should rejoice now that you have returned to us."

"Agreed, dear sister. We will celebrate your triumphant return, Ruven," says Riniya. "Preparations will begin at first light. We should all get some rest. Big things will happen soon. And you, dear girl," she turns in my direction, "you shall receive proper instruction in using magic and how best to control your power."

"That would be wonderful. Thank you," I say.

"Do you have questions for me, child?" Riniya asks me.

"Only a few. I visited the temple today and spoke with Vestele. She told me of the prophecy. Am I the child mentioned in the prophecy?"

"Ruven has told me your story, of how you came to our world through a magic portal. It is likely that you are indeed the child of the prophecy. You are not quite human. You have many elvish characteristics. I will consult the scholars and see what they say regarding this matter."

"Thank you. I would appreciate that. Also, Claudius Darkmore sent a very dear friend of mine to Alzalforg. Would it be possible to free him?"

"I'm sorry, child. That is something we must not

attempt. It would be unwise for us to show ourselves to the world before the proper time. However, should the opportunity present itself, I will make sure you have the manpower to accomplish such a task."

"That was the answer I thought I might get, but I had to ask none the less. Thank you for the wonderful meal, Queen Riniya. Also, it was very nice to meet you, Faraine and Rania."

The three elves nod before rising and exiting the room.

"We should get to bed, Ruven. It sounds like they have grand plans."

Ruven agrees, and the two of us retire to our rooms for the night.

Chapter 24

I can't sleep. I toss and turn, but comfort and dreams do not come to me, so I leave my bed and pace the room. Perhaps some fresh air will do me good. I wrap a cloak around myself and step into the hall. I creep down the corridor, wishing Ruven could join me, but not wanting to wake him. Ahead of me in the dark, a dim light escapes a cracked door. Muffled voices are having a heated discussion within. Curiosity gets the better of me, and I stop outside the door to listen.

"Mother, what will we do now?" Rania asks.

"Quiet, child. Let me think," says Faraine.

"You said giving him to the witch was the best way to keep him hidden. You said he would never return. Now that he has, how do you propose to succeed Aunt Riniya?"

"Half the citizens of Thava Serin support my ascension. We have never had a king. Our ruler should be a woman like our goddess, Ghyara. Riniya had no right to appoint that insufferable brat as her successor. The throne will pass to me and you will reign after my time has passed. We will devise a plan to rid ourselves of Riniya, Ruven, and that little bitch he brought back with him. Once we deal with them, the citizens that support Riniya's progressive decision will bow to me or we will deal with them accordingly."

"You would risk civil war to take the throne?" Rania asks.

"No. I would risk civil war to uphold our honorable traditions."

"Then how will you deal with Aunt Riniya?"

"Poison would be a subtle solution, I think."

"And the other two? How will we deal with them?"

Faraine sighs. "They are mere children. Children have accidents all the time. Just wait. You will see. Everything will go according to plan and soon we shall hold the throne and rule our people as fate deemed before the bastard was born."

"When will we begin, mother?"

"I will set our plan in motion in the morning. It should not take long after that."

I can't believe the discussion I'm hearing and inside the palace walls as well. Faraine and Rania believe they can wrest control of the city from its rightful ruler. I know what I must do. As soon as I can, I must inform Riniya of her sister's plans. I decide to pay a visit to the queen in the morning, then return to my room to prepare myself for what will come.

I rise with the sun the next morning, dress, then race

down the hall to Ruven's room.

"I must speak with your mother immediately," I say when Ruven opens the door.

"What's going on, Valessa?" Ruven asks.

"I overheard something last night and I need to alert the queen or something terrible will happen. I'm asking you to trust me, Ruven."

"Of course, Valessa. You know I trust you. Come, we will speak to mother directly."

Ruven dresses. Then the two of us race through the palace to seek an audience with Queen Riniya. I hope we aren't too late to warn her of the treacherous plot her sister and niece hatched in the dark the night before.

We find Riniya in the dining hall taking breakfast with her sister. Am I too late? Has Faraine already poisoned her sister and thus enacted her grand scheme?

"Ah, good morning, Valessa. Ruven," Riniya says.

"Good morning, mother," says Ruven. "Valessa would like a word."

"Of course. What is it, dear?"

"Could I have a private word?" I ask.

"Yes. But you can say anything you need to say in front of Faraine. She is my trusted advisor."

"Are you sure?"

"Of course, my dear Valessa. We may speak in Faraine's presence."

"She is plotting to kill you, me and Ruven." I point at Faraine. "I heard her planning it with Rania last night."

Both Riniya and her sister laugh. "That is

ridiculous," says Faraine. "Why in the world would I wish my flesh and blood dead?"

"Because you want to rule and you will do anything to accomplish that. You are unhappy that Riniya named Ruven her heir after centuries of being ruled by women. Because the throne should pass to you and then to your daughter upon the queen's demise, you feel as though Riniya has stolen your birthright from you and you want it returned."

"Why, the girl speaks nonsense, dear sister," says Faraine. "I would never turn against my family."

"Faraine is also the one responsible for Ruven's disappearance all those years ago. She stole him from his crib and sent him away to the witch, hoping he would never return. Now that he has and can rule after his mother, Faraine plans to poison you and take the throne from Ruven. She said Ruven and I could have an unfortunate accident."

"Lies," says Faraine. "These are lies, sister. The child is trying to manipulate us. Perhaps she wishes to take control herself."

"Valessa would never do that, mother," Ruven says. "I have gotten to know her well since we met, and I know she would never dare attempt such a thing."

"Ruven vouches for her. I have no choice but to believe what Valessa says is true," says Riniya.

"You can't believe them. I would never do what they claim," Faraine says.

"Why would I not trust what my son says?"

"How could you trust what this boy says, son or not?

You did not raise him. He knows nothing of our people. It would have been best if he had not returned."

"What? How could you say that?"

"I only meant—"

I step forward. "I have an idea that may help shed light on the situation. Have her drink your juice, your Grace. She will refuse if I am telling the truth."

"This is ridiculous, and I refuse to take part in any more of these shenanigans." Faraine rises to her feet. "If you will excuse me sister—"

"You will go nowhere," says Riniya. "Valessa is right. If you have nothing to hide, then you will sample my beverage. I'm sure it is delightful."

Riniya holds her glass out toward her sister.

"I couldn't." Faraine's eyes widen.

"You will."

Faraine reaches out as if to take the glass from her sister, but smacks it to the ground where it shatters, spilling its contents across the floor.

"So it is true then?"

"Sister, please. I . . ."

"What is the meaning of this, Faraine? Why would you take my son from me? Why plot to kill your own sister, the reigning queen of the Elven people?"

"Yes, why Aunt Faraine? I was a baby. What could I have done that was so terrible I deserved exile from my family and people?" Ruven advances on Faraine.

Faraine sneers. "I had to get rid of you, you petulant brat. Women have always ruled our people, but when you came along, Riniya saw fit to change our age-old tradition. She named you her heir, stealing the throne from me, who would have ruled after her, and my daughter, who would have taken the throne after me. I had to make you disappear, so I could take my rightful place as queen after your mother. A man will not rule our people. I will do anything to prevent that from happening. Do you understand me, Riniya? I will stop at nothing to depose you."

With that, Faraine launches a bolt of lightning at me. My muscles tense, ready to spring into action, but before I can act, Riniya waves a hand in front of herself, brushing the lightning bolt aside.

"How dare you attack my guest within the walls of my home," says Riniya. "The people will never side with you once they learn of your treachery, Faraine."

Riniya raises her hand in front of her face and twirls one finger around in a circle. Faraine's body stiffens, and she falls to the floor. I recognize the binding spell that held me prisoner during our journey to Naren Thalore, and I note a look of terror cross Faraine's face.

Riniya calls for the guards. "Take Faraine to the lower dungeon to await her fate, then bring Rania to me in the throne room."

The guards lift Faraine off the floor and carry her out of the room.

Riniya turns toward me. "You have done me a great service, Valessa. You shall forever more be as a daughter to me. Anything your heart desires will be yours. Just name it."

"It was no trouble at all. I was doing what I thought

was right and require no reward."

"As you wish. The two of you shall join me in the throne room."

The three of us leave the dining hall and make our way to the throne room, finding it empty upon entering. Riniya takes her place on the throne and motions for me and Ruven to stand on either side of her. We await Rania's arrival in silence.

Several minutes pass before the large door opens. Two guards enter, dragging Rania as she struggles to escape their grasp. They approach the throne and drop their cargo on the floor at Riniya's feet.

Rania stands. "What is the meaning of this?" She brushes the dirt from her dress. "Where is my mother?"

"The dungeon," says Riniya.

"What do you mean, the dungeon? Why? What has she done?"

"She, along with you, conspired to commit murder and treason. Do you deny it?"

"I don't know what you're talking about. Mother only ever says kind things about you."

"So you did not know of your mother's plans?"

"I did not."

"Were you aware that Faraine is responsible for Prince Ruven's disappearance when he was but a babe?"

"I was not."

"Very well. Leave us." Riniya waves her hand in dismissal.

"What will happen to my mother?" Tears flood Rania's eyes.

"She will suffer the worst punishment given to our people. Tomorrow at noon she will be exiled."

This news sends Rania into tears. She runs from the room, weeping into her hands.

"She lied," I say.

"I know," says Riniya.

"So you're letting her go? She plotted with Faraine and she's not being punished?"

"She will. Guards will escort her from the palace grounds and I will forbid her to return. Faraine was the mastermind of this plot. I cannot exact a harsh punishment on a child for the sins of the parent. What kind of ruler would that make me?"

"What if she rallies the people to her side? What happens if she turns the citizenry against you?"

"I am confident most of the people support my claim to the throne and will support my son's claim as well. Rania can try to rally the people to her side. Should she succeed, I will deal with the threat. As long as the goddess supports my claim, I shall not fall."

Ruven takes my hand and leads me from the throne room. He escorts me to my room and suggests I get some rest. I agree and snuggle into my bed as he leaves the room, shutting the door behind him. It doesn't take long for sleep to arrive, a long sleep that lasts until morning.

I wake early the next day and spend some time in my room reflecting on the previous day and the activity of today. I pass a few hours in solitude before Ruven retrieves me and leads me to the dining hall for brunch. Riniya sits at the head of the table, looking radiant. She greets me as I seat myself, then an uncomfortable silence falls on the room as we eat.

Once finished, Riniya rises, followed by Ruven, who offers me his arm as we leave the room. We descend the palace steps and enter a small carriage for our trip to the forum where Riniya will carry out Faraine's sentence. News of the day's event has spread throughout Thava Serin, and citizens have crowded the streets to witness the passage of their queen. Cheers and accolades for Queen Riniya fill the air as we traverse the city on our way to the Grand Forum. People have already filled the forum, eager to see their queen exact punishment on her treasonous sister. Cheers abound as we exit the carriage and climb the steps to the platform in the center of the forum. We await Faraine in silence.

Before long, the sea of people parts, allowing soldiers to carry Faraine to the platform where we stand. They carry her up the stairs and I see they have relieved her of her elaborate gown and granted her a meager brown shift to wear, stripping her of her regal air. The guards throw her to the ground in front of us and the crowd grows silent as Riniya raises her hands and releases Faraine from the binding spell.

"Citizens of Thava Serin," she says, "we gather here today to exact punishment on my sister, Faraine Keldan, for acts of treason. Faraine conspired to poison your queen in order to wrest the throne from my power and is responsible for the disappearance and exile of your prince, Ruven Keldan. She has confessed her crimes to me in the presence of Prince Ruven and Lady Valessa.

She is a traitor to her family and her people. I come before you to show you how we deal with traitors, be they family or not. Do you deny the charges against you, Faraine Keldan?" Riniya turns her attention to her sister.

Faraine says nothing. She stares at the ground and does not move. I scan the crowd looking for any sign of Faraine's supporters, but see no suggestion of help on the faces stretching before me.

"For your crimes, Faraine Keldan," says Riniya, "I, Riniya Keldan, Queen of Thava Serin and rightful ruler of the Elven people, sentence you to exile. I shall fling you from Thava Serin, never to return. Do you have any last words?"

Faraine looks up at her sister with malice. "You will regret your actions here today. By my hand, yours or forces elsewhere, you will lose the throne. Mark my words."

"Very well."

Riniya raises her hand in front of her and clenches her fist. As she does this, Faraine jerks forward, as if pulled by an invisible force. Riniya raises her hand higher and Faraine rises from the ground. The crowd watches in awe as Faraine floats ever higher into the sky. Riniya swings her arm in a wide arc with immense speed, and Faraine flies through the air and disappears out of sight. Members of the crowd applaud, while others gasp. Far away, amidst the noise, a scream of sadness and rage rings out. I scan the surrounding faces and see Rania crying as she grieves the loss of her mother.

"What will happen to Faraine?" I ask.

"I have cast her out of Thava Serin. She will fall to the ground and must make her way in the world without friends or family to support her," says Riniya.

"The fall won't kill her?"

"It is not so easy to kill a member of a race as ancient as the Elves. She will be bruised and battered, but will heal and recover."

"And this is the worst punishment?"

"Yes. To be exiled and cut off from your people, friends, and loved ones is the worst punishment one could ever endure. Sheonaetara is a dangerous world. It is difficult to be alone in such a place."

This is a fact I know all too well. Had it not been for the help granted me since arriving, I would have perished long before now, and this gives me the understanding of how cruel Faraine's punishment truly is.

Chapter 25

The following weeks pass as I try to grow accustomed to my new surroundings. The beauty of Thava Serin makes me forget the horrible condition of the people who live on the ground below. It's easy to forget the plight of others, and this causes me many sleepless nights as I am filled with guilt at having things so great.

The various lessons Riniya deemed I learn fill my days. I rotate between swordsmanship, archery, riding, magic, and lore. I learn lore in the Temple of the Sun, the beautiful temple devoted to the sun goddess Ghyara. Vestele, who I enjoy spending time with, teaches these lessons. I learn how Ghyara gave birth to the world and its people and how she raised the Elven people up and gifted them with the use of magic.

I take my riding lessons at my favorite place in the city, the stables. The majestic unicorns are the most beautiful animals I have ever seen. Along with basic horsemanship, I learn about the proper care and use of tack and how to care for the animals. The stable master allows me to spend my free time there as well, so I spend my free days tending to the unicorns and their needs. The Elves even allowed Dava and Sky Blossom to cross into Thava Serin through the portal, so I can spend time with my faithful companion, who carried me toward a destiny I did not know existed.

Riniya teaches my magic lessons herself. She is the most powerful in twisting the world's energies in ways that are useful and fills my lessons with various incantations and conjurations she believes will prove the most helpful to me. I have grown proficient in using my power, and Riniya says I show even more promise. Given my aptitude for magic, Riniya believes I am the child mentioned in the prophecy, and she continues to look for news of my birth parents.

Ruven has his own lessons his mother suggested he attend, but we spend our free time together. He has become my dearest friend and often accompanies me to the stables and the market. We see each other at breakfast and dinner, which we take in the grand dining hall with Riniya. After dinner, we retire to my room, where we spend time together before Ruven returns to his own room for the night.

The days pass into weeks, which run into months. The Elves have honed me into a warrior. I am now efficient in all aspects of the training I have received. Ruven, too, has transformed from the meek boy I have known into a capable young man. He often attends the portal room, awaiting Quimby's return, although I have told him he should not.

One afternoon, I receive a frantic summons from Ruven to come to the portal room. I race through the corridors and enter the room to find Ruven grinning from ear to ear. He's ecstatic about something.

"I told you, Valessa," Ruven says. "I told you, did I not? You said I shouldn't wait, but I knew you were wrong."

"What are you talking about, Ruven?" I ask, although I'm sure I already know the answer.

"Quimby. He came back. They're opening the portal for him now."

"But why would he come back, Ruven? His goal the entire time we knew him was to get you here. Why would he come back?"

"I don't know, Valessa. Perhaps he missed us and wanted to see us again."

I doubt that, but don't have the heart to tell Ruven. I have never had much love for Quimby Carver, nor have I ever trusted him, and now that he has reappeared, I grow ever more suspicious of him and his motives. Ruven's face lights up as Quimby passes through the portal. He shakes Quimby's hand before pulling him into a light embrace.

"It's so good to see you again, Quimby," says Ruven.

"Yes, it's great that you have returned after leaving us," I say.

Quimby shakes his head. "Now, now, Valessa, there's no need to be that way. I returned Ruven to his people, then left to attend to my own matters. Once I sorted that out, I returned to check on the both of you. How have you fared since I left?"

"Everything has been great," says Ruven. "We've both learned so much. You should see what Valessa is capable of."

"Oh, I'm sure I shall see that in time," says Quimby. "Might you show me to a room, young Ruven? I fancy the opportunity to rest after my long journey."

"Of course. If you will follow me." Ruven leads Quimby from the room.

I follow behind, intending to speak with Ruven once we have installed Quimby in his room.

"What are you doing?" I ask Ruven once he exits Quimby's room.

"Why are you so angry? He's our friend."

"I don't trust him."

"You never have, but he's only ever helped us."

"Helped us? He failed to warn us about the Twisting Desert and disappeared when we needed him the most in Blackwick. I hardly call that help." I storm off down the hall.

Later that evening, I meet Riniya, Ruven and Quimby in the dining hall for dinner. The others are already seated when I enter the room and take the seat opposite Quimby. I meet his grin with a scowl.

"You should be kind to our guest, Valessa," says Riniya.

"I'm sorry. I just don't trust him."

"Don't worry about it, your Grace," says Quimby.

"Valessa's attitude will not affect my gracious mood. In fact, I've prepared a song for this most joyous occasion."

"Have you?" Riniya asks.

"Aye, I have. It's an original. I wrote it just this afternoon while in my room preparing for the evening. I shall perform it for you all as soon as we have concluded our dinner."

Riniya claps her hands and the servers enter carrying platters laden with meat and vegetables. They lay them on the table before us, then exit as fast as they came. We eat in anticipation of Quimby's new song. When our bellies are full, Quimby stands and walks to the end of the table so we can see him. He takes a deep breath and begins singing in his confident air.

Been a bard me whole cursed life
Riddled with misfortune and nothing but strife
Found meself in some trouble I could not escape
Presented an opportunity for my fate to reshape
Met a stranger with an offer and a grisly face
Bid that I find the entrance to a hidden place
Fortune saw fit to unite me with a long-lost prince
His friend was much less easy to convince
Promised to see him returned to his people
The journey turned out to be quite a steep hill
The way to their gate was hard to find
But I saw that he safely made it to his kind
I left in a hurry some travel to make
Returned with some friends that will make you all quake
The ones that you have reason to fear

Will very soon arrive and find you here

Quimby stops singing and takes a bow. Ruven looks just as confused as I am. I lock eyes with Riniya and see fear. Uncertain what she has to fear, I turn back to Quimby and see him fleeing the room.

"Guards, stop him," says Riniya. "Ruven, Valessa, retrieve your weapons posthaste! He has led them here. We must prepare."

"Where is he going?" asks Ruven.

"He's gone to the portal room. We must stop him." Riniya flies from the room in pursuit of Quimby.

"What is happening?"

I shake my head. "I don't know, but I told you not to trust him."

Ruven and I race to our rooms and gather our weapons, then tear through the corridors to the portal room. We arrive to find the portal keepers lying in the hall, barely clinging to life, blood pooling around them. Riniya approaches, followed by Vestele, who begins tending to the wounded.

"Come," says Riniya, "we must put a stop to this if we hope to survive."

We enter the portal room and find Quimby at the controls, laughing. "You're too late." He flashes us a devilish grin. "They're already here. You will fall with the city and her people. The Elves' time has ended."

I step forward. "Stop, Quimby, or I will stop you."

"Quimby, how could you do this?" Ruven asks. "I thought we were friends."

Quimby laughs. "We never were, dear boy. You

were nothing more than a means to an end. My goal was never to return you to your people. It was only to find where your people were hiding. Once I did that, I returned to the Oppressors and shared their location, then led their forces here, right to the doorstep. And now I will do what they have desired all these centuries. I will let them in."

"Stop this now," says Riniya.

I take matters into my own hands and pull the surrounding energy into my core while raising my sword above my head with one hand and release a gout of flame from my other, directing it in Quimby's direction as a monstrous scream escapes my lips. Quimby screams and Ruven gasps behind me.

Riniya steps between me and Quimby. "Stop. Valessa, you cannot do this."

I lower my hands to my sides. "What do you mean? You said to stop him. That's what I intend to do."

"I cannot let you kill him. Yes, he deserves to die for what he has done, but he could be valuable in the grand scheme of things to come." Riniya raises a finger and casts the binding spell on Quimby. "The guards will take him to the dungeon where he will suffer unimaginable torments as he awaits his final judgment."

Two guards step forward and pick Quimby up for his trip to the lower reaches of the palace. Terror fills his eyes as he disappears from view.

"Seal the portal. Come, we must see how bad it is." Riniya leaves the room, Ruven and I following behind.

"Where are we going?" I ask.

"To the viewing room. There we can look down on the world below and see what Quimby has brought to our doorstep. We must know what we are dealing with in order to mount a proper defense of the city and her people."

We enter a room I've never seen before. In the center lies a large marble basin, a pale blue mist swirls and twists within. Riniya approaches the basin and waves her hand over it. The mist pulses, then recedes to the edges of the basin, revealing the ruins of Naren Thalore below. Riniya gasps. I approach the basin and gaze at the scene laid out within. Spread out before my eyes, a great army has amassed below. The soldiers are large, many of them sitting astride fearsome beasts. There are so many that they appear small, making it difficult to discern the true numbers of the army. At the head of the forces arrayed before the gate to Thava Serin are two tall, thin beings dressed in long black robes, their faces hidden within the large hoods covering their heads. It's impossible to make out the features of these two beasts.

"What do we do?" I ask.

"We muster our forces and ready our defense. We must not allow this city to fall." Riniya turns her attention to me. "Ready yourself, Valessa, your time has come." She turns to a guard. "Send word to the generals. Tell them our enemy has come, and the time is upon us. Tell them the war has begun."

Made in the USA
Middletown, DE
01 June 2022

66476503R00176